# SOLDIERS OF LOVE

## BEAUTIFUL SCARS

# N'TYSE
# & UNTAMED

## INSPIRED BY TRUE EVENTS

BLACK
ODYSSEY
MEDIA

WWW.BLACKODYSSEY.NET

Published by
BLACK ODYSSEY MEDIA

www.blackodyssey.net
Email: info@blackodyssey.net

SOLDIERS OF LOVE: *BEAUTIFUL SCARS*. Copyright © 2023 by N'TYSE

Library of Congress Control Number: 2020915107

First Trade Paperback Printing: July 2023
ISBN: 978-1-957950-07-5
ISBN: 978-1-7354431-1-9 (e-book)

Cover Design by Navi' Robins

10 9 8 7 6 5 4 3 2

Manufactured in the United States of America

Distributed by Kensington Publishing Corp.

Dear Reader,

I want to thank you immensely for supporting Black Odyssey Media authors, and our ongoing efforts to spotlight more minority storytellers. The scariest and most challenging task for many writers is getting the story, or characters, out of our heads and onto the page. Having admitted that, with every manuscript that Kreceda and I acquire, we believe that it took talent, discipline, and remarkable courage to construct that story, flesh out those characters, and prepare it for the world. Debut or seasoned, our authors are the real heroes and heroines in *OUR* story. And for them, we are eternally grateful.

Whether you are new to N'Tyse, Untamed, or Black Odyssey Media, we hope that you are here to stay. We also welcome your feedback and kindly ask that you leave a review. For upcoming releases, announcements, submission guidelines, etc., please be sure to visit our website at www.blackodyssey.net or scan the QR code below. We can also be found on social media using @iamblackodyssey. Until next time, take care and enjoy the journey!

Joyfully,

Shawanda Williams

Shawanda "N'Tyse" Williams
Founder/Publisher

*"Your story is what you have, what you will always have. It is something to own."*
—**MICHELLE OBAMA**

*An ode to love . . . and a couple of forevers.*

# TRIGGER NOTICE

This book contains sensitive material, including some profanity, violence, and the mention of sexual assault. Reader discretion is advised, and please remember to practice self-care before, during, and after you read.

# PROLOGUE

QUINCY'S HEAD FELL back as he brought his hands upward and dragged them down his face before looking back at me. "Liberty," he breathed out.

Instantly, my chest heaved up and down and my skin felt flush. It was the way he'd said my name that made every nerve ending in my body stand at attention. Although I was suddenly fearful of the next words that seemed to dance on his lips, I had to hear this. I had to know if I had some merit to cuss this woman out. Surely, if he admitted some wrongdoing, Eva's tongue-lashing wouldn't even scratch the surface of what I'd implode onto Quincy.

"Don't you 'Liberty' me. Who is Eva, and why the hell is she calling your phone—rather comfortably—in the wee hours of the morning, looking for some quote unquote, friendly advice?"

Quincy exhaled nervously. Still, his voice must have been stolen because all he could do was stare at me, not fully awake. Leaning back, my face turned into a deep scowl. I crossed my legs and unlocked my phone. "Since you're on mute, let me help you out." In a matter of minutes, I had everything I needed in the palms of my hands.

Eva Marie Campbell, thirty-six years old, no kids, no husband, nurse, lived in Dallas, Texas then moved to New York City, and is now back in Dallas, Texas, formerly a member of Mount Olive Baptist Church—*your childhood church*, mother's name is Vanessa Benedict-Campbell, father is Everett Ignacio Campbell, one sister, Victoria Inez Campbell-Wright, no criminal background, drives a

1

smoke-gray Acura, lives in Cedar Hill, and works out at Z Fitness. Should we take a drive over to ask her in person what you obviously can't seem to answer?" With a hair toss, I placed my phone on the TV stand after displaying my investigative journalistic skills, then folded my arms with my legs crossed, awaiting his response.

Quincy brought his steepled hands to his face. "It's not what you think, Liberty." He rested his hands on his waist, eyeing me momentarily. When he seemed to resolve within himself that I wasn't going to let this go, he tossed his hands in the air and slowly took a seat on the edge of our bed. "She's an old friend. We did grow up in the same church together, and yes, she used to work at Bainstone years ago."

"Tell me something I don't already know, Quincy! Like why the hell she's calling you at two in the morning!"

"Babe, please calm down," he said, and quickly shifted gears when he saw the steam that seemed to be visibly floating from me. "She has cancer."

"But you're no doctor!" I didn't mean to sound so insensitive, but this woman had infiltrated my marriage.

His forehead crinkled with his face turned up, visibly touched by my words before he could catch himself. Enraged, I threw on my lounge pants and a tank top that lay across the chaise as if I were preparing to go to war. Because I was.

Quincy ran over to me, gently grabbing my arm. "I'm sorry, baby. It's not like that—"

"Are you fucking her, Quincy?" My words sprayed like bullets and seared into him.

"What? No. No!" he declared, trying his best to keep me pinned in place.

"Liar!" I seethed with vibrato as my lips quivered. Emotion consumed me as the possibility that my husband had been unfaithful hit me like a ton of bricks. "Let me go, Quincy. I'm not stupid. Let me go!"

"No, baby, not until you calm down," he said sternly. He lightly gripped my chin with the cup of his thumb and index finger, forcing me to look up at him. "I'm not cheating on you. I've never cheated on you. And I never will cheat on you. Come on… I'm not that kind of man, Liberty. I love you."

"Does Ms. Body Party know that you don't cheat on your wife?" My eyes zeroed in on him for answers. I folded my arms, giving up my momentary efforts to flee since he wouldn't move out of my way.

Quincy's head fell forward as he placed his hands on my arms. "I will tell you everything if you promise to calm down and allow me the opportunity to explain."

Momentarily, I considered his request and against my better judgment, I sat down on the chaise and nodded for him to continue. "I'm listening."

"Okay, Eva is a woman I've known since childhood. We did go to the same church. She did used to work at Bainstone. When Carlos had his cookout, she was there. We caught up on old times, she confided in me about the cancer, and we exchanged numbers so she could keep me up to date on what was going on with her health. I didn't really believe she would call, but she did. Somewhere along the way, it became two friends talking and keeping each other lifted. I swear that's all it was."

"If that is all it was then why is she calling you only while she believes you're at work? Why does it sound like these 'talks' are a lot more intimate than they should be? Why don't I know anything about her, or this? And why was she at your friend's Carlos's cookout?" I pressed.

Quincy slid his hands down his face. "She knows somebody Carlos knows. I'm not a hundred percent sure. I didn't invite her, and it wasn't my business why she was there. All I know is that she was there."

I took a beat.

Allowed him to gather his truths.

Rearrange his lies.

Quincy groaned before exhaling deeply. "Deep down, baby, I knew you might have an issue with Eva calling me. And please believe me, I didn't want to disrupt my household, and at the same time, I wanted to be there for her as a friend."

"If you knew I'd have an issue with it, then why didn't you come to me yourself, instead of waiting for me to find out like this? Because then it looks like you're hiding something." He cast his eyes downward. That's when it dawned on me. "Wait. You knew she had a thing for you, didn't you?"

He cupped his mouth with his hand and shook his head, his eyes filled with regret.

"Quincy!"

"Okay! Yes! I knew she did, but *I* knew I wasn't going to let it go any further than friendship, and I knew you'd see right through her if I told you. We've been friends since kids, and I wanted to be there for her during her time of need. I thought as long as I kept the other stuff at bay that I could handle it. But I swear to you, I don't have feelings for her. Eva is nothing more than a friend."

So many thoughts swirled through my mind as I stood there engulfed in Quincy's arms. Although there had been no physical betrayal—if I took his word for it—there was still the emotional betrayal. It wasn't the fact that he didn't allow it to go further or even the possibility that he was feeling her in a way that he felt for me, but there was still a tie, a bond, that I wasn't privy to. There was some type of pull that this woman, whom I didn't even know, had over my husband that had forced him to hide their relationship from me. That in itself was still a betrayal.

"But you let her in. You gave her access. She has had a part of your time and attention that I did not have, and it's gotta be more than cancer. Don't insult my intelligence, Quincy!"

He turned away before facing me again. "Baby. We dated briefly. I'm talking freshmen year in high school, and it didn't even last a month. We just weren't a good fit and were better off as friends. And when she told me about the diagnosis, I only wanted to be there for moral support. Nothing more. I swear."

And there it was.

The truth.

It hurt to hear, but it hurt worse not knowing. As odd as it was, his admission gave me a bit of relief because it meant that he was being truthful. If he'd hidden it, then I would've known that he felt more than what he'd let on. Still, it did something to my soul to know that he had carved out time for his ex.

Not just any old ex.

An ex who was battling cancer.

"Liberty," he said, eying me lovingly. "I love you. I'm sorry, and I was wrong." He pulled me in close to him. "Please say you forgive me."

I swiped at the tears that flowed down my face. "I need time to think about this."

"I love—"

I put my hand up. "Don't," I warned. "Not right now. I need to rest."

He gave me a slight bob of his head. "Okay, baby."

I walked to our bed and instead of sliding inside, I lifted both of his pillows and handed them to him. "Guest room."

"You're kicking me out of our bedroom?"

"Do you prefer the house?"

He grabbed the pillows willingly. "Liberty, I swear nothing happened."

I walked past him to our bedroom door and opened it. "Oh

no, something happened. My husband kept a secret friendship with an ex-girlfriend behind my back. Now I need you to go while I rest and consider what I want to do next. You owe me that much."

Conceding, Quincy threw the pillows under his arms and walked through the door. He stopped when he was next to me and leaned over. "I'm sorry. I'll do whatever it takes to make this right."

His kiss landed on my cheek, and he walked out toward the guest bedroom as I shut and locked our bedroom door.

That was typically how all affairs began.

Innocent intentions.

An emotional connection.

A convenient truth.

Then enter the lies.

My soul felt betrayed.

# CHAPTER 1

*September 28, 2014*

"MOMMY, CAN I have those pleeeasssseeeeee... Mommy!"

Milk, eggs, spaghetti, tissue—

"MOMMY, ARE YOU LISTENING? I SAID I WANT THOSE CHIPPPSSS!"

The sudden yank of my blouse startled the hell out of me. I immediately stopped checking off the grocery list in my head and brought the shopping cart to a halt, dead in the middle of aisle seven. The miniature bright-eyed look-alike that strolled alongside me was *not* the child I'd spent twelve hours, thirty-two minutes, and forty-seven seconds—waiting on my doctor—to bring into this world via our scheduled C-section. Couldn't have been. I coolly looked around to see if anyone had witnessed the tantrum. For her sake, apparently, no one had.

"Queenie Chenell Bridges," I began as I leaned into her, "why on earth are you catching that tone with me, little girl?" Her radiant cocoa complexion glistened from a shea butter cocktail while her naturally smiling eyes sparkled like chocolate pearls under the bright shopping lights. There was no denying it. Queenie had eyes like mine. Eyes that spoke in free verse with a little rhythm and a whole lot of soul. That was our secret weapon. And since birth, Queenie knew precisely how to use them.

On me.

On her father.

On everyone.

Her bottom lip curled into a pout. "I'm sorry, Mommy."

7

"I'll accept your apology, Queenie, but you have to understand that in life, crying won't get you—"

"There y'all go!"

"Daddy!"

Queenie jetted down the aisle. Her long cornrows danced and the pink and white beads on the ends clanked harmoniously against one another. I knew what was next. Still, I watched on as she outstretched her right arm and her favorite index finger pointed to the glorious tower of Doritos on the endcap. As if on cue, my husband, Quincy, grabbed two bags before scooping her up in his muscular arms. As they walked my way, I instantly shot him *the look.*

"Uh-oh. What I do, babe?"

My eyes darted to our number one household vice—*chips.*

"It's my cheat day." A sheepish grin spread across Quincy's face as he placed the snacks in the cart.

Queenie gushed and batted her eyes. "Mine, too."

"You see that?" I directed toward Quincy. "You're mollycoddling again."

"Anything for my princess." He leaned in and stole a kiss. "And my beautiful queen," he finished before cuffing my derriere with one hand and giving it an energetic squeeze.

This time I gushed.

"You 'bout ready to go so we can wind down before the game?" he asked.

"I am. But I feel like I'm forgetting something." I scanned everything in the cart a fourth time.

"Don't worry about it. I can get back out later if you need me to."

I smiled. "Okay."

"Mommy, I have to potty."

Before Queenie could get the last word out, Quincy quickly placed her back on her feet.

"I'll take care of this and meet y'all in the car," he said.

"All right." I grabbed Queenie's hand, and we trotted down the aisle. We zigzagged past several shoppers and made a beeline straight for the ladies' room.

———

"Well, I'll be damned! Liberty Banks. Is that really you, gurl?"

I cautiously turned around from drying my hands at the reference to my entire maiden name. Wasn't long before Queenie found her position next to me. I strained my eyes to make out the individual, but it was impossible through the blue and white face paint. Their hair was trimmed low with a white star plastered on the left side. It was obvious they were a Dallas Cowboys fan sporting a Dez Bryant football jersey—modeling the spirit Quincy and I were in for that night's football game.

"Libby B, don't stand there and act brand new!"

"Terica!" I shrieked. I rushed over to my childhood best friend and swaddled her in a teddy bear hug. "Oh my God! It's been what… fourteen years. Look at you!" I was caught between disbelief and amazement. Had it not been for the face paint, the bald fade, the slightly deeper voice, and the peach fuzz that covered her chin, I would have recognized Terica in a heartbeat.

"You haven't changed one bit," Terica said, looking me up and down with the same shock. Her eyes bounced from me to Queenie. "I can see this here is your little twin." She smiled as she reached out to shake Queenie's hand. "I'm T. An old friend of your mom's."

"Hi. My name is Queenie."

"Beautiful name. How old are you, Queenie?"

"Four."

"Wow! Sounds like I have some belated birthday gifting to do."

Queenie and I both smiled at the gesture.

"Wait, is that a wedding ring?" Terica lifted my left hand to inspect the ring more closely. An approving smile crossed her lips.

"I see bro finally came to his senses and put a ring on it."

My brows furrowed in confusion. "Oh no, not Zi—" I tried to correct her before her cell phone started ringing.

"Hold that thought. This my wife."

I nodded with a smile.

"What's up, baby? All right. I'll swing by and pick him up before the game. Love you, too." Terica ended the call. "Yo, this is wild! Never in a million years would I have thought I'd get a chance to see my best friend again. Like maybe on television or something, but not in *Tarjay* of all places," she said, manufacturing her best faux French accent to pronounce the supercenter's nickname.

"Well, let's not leave out this scenic backdrop," I added at the sound of a toilet flushing.

"Definitely one for the Gram!"

We collapsed into giggles. Back in the day, we used to refer to one another as being "goofy" whenever we found the same thing funny—even when others weren't dialed into our comicality.

"Nah, but on a serious note, I thought for sure you'd be living it up somewhere in New York or California, enjoying the high life and those fancy donuts you love every morning. Man, what were they called again?" I parted my lips to speak. "Nah, don't tell me... ummm... beignets. Yeah, that's them. I imagined you in your executive C-suite with lavish furniture, a few assistants, sipping on a latte, eating beignets, and taking over the music industry."

"Wow, I can't believe you remember all that."

"How could I not? It was all you ever talked about when we were kids; getting the heck up out of the hood, starting an all-female hip-hop label, getting married, and having babies." She paused. "You had a dream, Liberty. And I always knew your gifts and your passion for music would take you as far as you wanted to go."

Our childhood conversations and that entire 90s era swirled like a cyclone in my mind, and before I knew it, I was back on that roller coaster of sweet teenage fantasies, wrapped in tall tales, smoking on pipe dreams laced with trap beats, and chasing an American dream cloaked in designer fashions that never came in my size.

"Well, let's just say I had to remix that plan," I admitted.

Terica nodded. "I feel where you're coming from."

I began to wonder if she'd suppressed her childhood pain like I had. Or if she was constantly reliving the trauma. I was too afraid to inquire. Besides, some things were better left unsaid.

There was an awkward drift between us.

"When I joined the military, sis, hell, I didn't bother looking back. Couldn't face those demons then."

Terica had read my mind. I wanted to hug my friend because I knew the demons she spoke of. She hung her head briefly before clearing her throat and looking me dead in the eye.

"It's all good, though. Our past doesn't define us."

Another moment of silence hung between us.

"Now let's talk about how you definitely seem to have a better grip on these thirties than I do," Terica said, switching the subject.

"I don't know about all that, T." I now addressed her by the nickname she'd given Queenie. "Despite this twelve-pound struggle, I try. And I don't know what you're talking about. You don't look too shabby yourself."

"This here, my friend, is called an illusion."

We broke into a fit of laughter. Queenie, however, didn't mask her boredom.

"I remember a time when my metabolism and knee joints were the last thing I had to worry about going to the doctor for," she continued, motioning for us to take the conversation outside of the restroom. Queenie and I followed.

I quickly covered Queenie's ears and packaged my greatest confession in a hushed tone.

"Well, imagine the reality check I was served once I discovered platinum-colored hairs in places that I can't apply a flat iron or jet-black hair dye."

I pulled my hands back. Queenie looked up at me in sheer confusion with her face wrinkled up.

Terica's mouth hung open. "You playing, right?"

I pursed my lips and shook my head slowly.

"Awwww mannnnn, I sooooo thought that would skip our generation."

"My friend, I'm here to warn you that it didn't."

We fell into another round of laughter, this time at my vagina's expense.

"The privileges of youth," Terica conceded.

"I share the sentiment."

My smile widened. It felt like old times.

"We gotta catch up!"

"You took the words right out of my mouth," I said. I reached into my purse and fished out my cell phone. We exchanged numbers.

"We can never lose contact again."

"Definitely not happening," I added. I leaned in, and we hugged each other tightly before saying our goodbyes and parting ways. However, before Queenie and I could make it ten steps, Terica hollered out my name once more.

"Be sure to tell my boy, Zion, I said 'what's up'!" she said before turning her Chuck Taylor's in the opposite direction.

"Mommy, who's Zion?"

My heart skipped a few beats and my chest tightened. I pretended not to hear Queenie, but that didn't stop his name from ringing like fire horns in both of my ears. I knew the feeling rushing me all too well.

I couldn't hide.

Zion had found me.

Just like he'd said he would.

# CHAPTER 2

Running into Terica was like being transported in time. It placed me in an awkward balance in the time continuum of the past and the present. How could it be that someone who'd impacted my life for years, underwent a life changing transition and returned as someone I barely even recognized? It was difficult to accept the truth, which was that we all seemed to abandon each other as time went on. I used to believe it was out of selfishness, when truthfully, it was really out of self-survival. It was as though, despite the love our old crew had for one another, that bond was steeped in the realities of our struggles and shortcomings. As the nostalgia of those times engulfed me, I couldn't help but think back to the moment our entire crew came together my fourth-grade year. The day I met the one and only—Zion Malik Mitchell.

*December 2, 1991*

"Attention class!" our homeroom teacher, Mrs. Dexter, announced. "We have a new student joining us today," she informed before stepping outside of the classroom to usher them into the room. We sat forward in anticipation. Some of us groaned because Mrs. Dexter always tried to force someone to be the new person's friend. I was one of the groaners. It wasn't hard for me to make friends at all because once we clicked, we clicked. I only detested Mrs. Dexter's approach. She seemingly didn't understand that, like with nature, there was an organic process to a real friendship connection.

Mrs. Dexter walked back inside with the new student trailing behind her with his head down. Yes! A boy. That meant one of the other knuckleheaded boys could be his *fake* new friend until he went through the process and made some of his own.

"Class, this is Zion Mitchell," Mrs. Dexter introduced. "Say hello, everyone."

"Hello *everyone!*" Pac-Man blurted. The entire class burst into laughter.

Mrs. Dexter gave him the warning eye. "All right, Mr. Johnson. Keep it up, and you'll be working on a trip to the principal's office." With her focus back on the class, she started up again. "Now everyone say hello to *Zion*." Her words accompanied a daring raised eye in Pac-Man's direction.

Zion slowly raised his head, and I thought I'd died and gone to Heaven the second we made eye contact. He was tall and slim with golden brown skin, and his dreamy honey-hazel eyes were like magnets. He was so fresh to death rocking a black Run-D.M.C. T-shirt, acid-wash jeans, and black Chucks with a black Members Only jacket. He looked as if he had stepped off the set of *Yo! MTV Raps.*

"Hello, *Zion!*" the rest of the class forcefully greeted at once.

"Heyyy, Zion," I dragged out.

He looked dead at me. "What's up," he replied with a single head bounce. I blushed so hard my cheeks hurt.

"So, guess what class?" Mrs. Dexter interceded. "This is a very special moment for Zion because today is December 2nd, the first Monday of the month, and you all know what we do for the first Monday, right?"

"Birthday shoutouts!" the class roared.

"That's right, birthday shoutouts!" Mrs. Dexter repeated with excitement, then turned to Zion. "And Zion gets to be celebrated because his birthday is this month, too." She turned to face the class and looked directly at me. "Come on up, Liberty!" She waved me over.

Normally, I would've loved to prance to the front of the class to get my birthday recognition, but not that day. Not in the presence of the finest boy at Truett Elementary. Suddenly, butterflies swarmed my stomach. I second-guessed my outfit, my hair, and my hygiene—which on an ordinary day, was always on point.

The entire class shifted their attention to me. I moved slower than a turtle, my nerves getting the best of me. And it didn't help that Zion was staring at me like I had a third eye. Once I reached the front of the class, Mrs. Dexter placed me right beside Zion and directed everyone to sing the "Happy Birthday" song to us. When they were finished, I almost grew wings and flew back to my desk, but as my luck would have it, Mrs. Dexter extended my torture.

"Zion, since you two are birthday buds, why don't you go on and take your seat next to Ms. Banks."

"Yes, ma'am," Zion replied.

"And Liberty, please share your textbook with Zion until we can get him one assigned."

"Yes, ma'am," I said.

Zion pulled one of the empty desks closer to mine and sat down. As if it weren't close enough, he scooted it over some more until they touched. I placed my Liberty-designed paper sack-wrapped textbook onto his desk.

"Here. You can use it to follow along. I've already read this chapter and know the answers to the discussion questions."

He laughed. "Ok, smart-tart."

I grinned at the nickname. "So, what day is your birthday?" I asked once Mrs. Dexter retreated to her desk and started reviewing our Bell Ringers. Zion swept his palm over his deep Caesar waves. That's when I noticed the square-cut diamond stud in his left ear.

"It's the fifteenth."

"No way! Mine is on the fifteenth."

"Quit lying."

"My mama said I'm supposed to say *fib*. *Lie* is a curse word."

"*Lie* is a word, just like *cuss* is a word."

A deep sigh escaped my lips as I rolled my eyes and huffed. "The point is, it's a bad word."

"What makes it so bad then?" he challenged.

"And what makes it so good then?" I threw back with a neck roll.

"You got me with that one," he admitted.

Mrs. Dexter cleared her throat. "I sat you two next to each other to finish the lesson, not to disturb the others who are still reading. Lead by example, Liberty."

"Yes, ma'am."

Zion and I giggled quietly amongst ourselves. He placed the book in the center of our desks. "Let's read it together, smart-tart," he said, flashing that handsome smile my way.

"Okay, birthday twin."

# CHAPTER 3

*December 15, 1991*

THAT DAY, I had woken up well before my alarm went off and before my seven-year-old brother, Justice, could hog the shower. I'd even beat Mama's morning shouting drill that I'm sure the neighbors had grown sick of. She would holler from downstairs, *"Liberty, I hope you're up and getting dressed for school! You better not miss your bus again!"* I had missed the bus one time, but Mama acted as though I was always late, hence the daily reminders. Like most girls and women, I took great care of my appearance and how I presented myself to the world. Grandma Sadie Pearle had taught me that. And that was exactly why I wanted to look extra fly on my special day. So late or not, the birthday girl deserved to have it her way.

As I began to lace up my new white-on-white Reebok's, I could sense someone in my room. I turned around to find Mama standing in the doorway sporting those jumbo pink rollers she'd gotten from H.L. Green's and her burgundy silk kimono robe she'd bought last Christmas from Avon. Even in her morning getup, Mama was beautiful as ever. And as the Creator would have it, I was blessed to have pulled most of my looks from her gene pool, including our sun-kissed butterscotch complexion, long black mane, and high cheekbones. The only distinctive feature that separated us was my eyes. Anyone who could see straight knew I didn't get them from Mama.

"I can't believe my firstborn is nine years old today." Mama smiled softly. She moved in closer. "Give me a hug, baby."

I got up from my bed and wrapped my arms around her. She smothered me with her motherly embrace and kisses to my cheeks.

"Happy birthday, Liberty."

"Thank you, Mama."

"You want Eugene to drop you off after he takes Justice to school?"

I cringed at the first syllable of my stepdad's name. Those rollers had to be wrapped too tight for Mama to ask me a question like that.

"No, I'll catch the bus."

"Happy birthday, Liberty!" Justice snaggletooth self came rushing into my room. He gave me a big hug.

"I made this for you," he said. In his outstretched hand was a beautifully colored page from his coloring book.

"I love it! Thanks, Justice."

"You're welcome! Gotta go finish my breakfast," he said, making a dash back downstairs.

I quickened my pace before Mama's attempt to talk me out of catching the bus. I shoved both feet into my new kicks, snatched my bubblegum-pink windbreaker off the bed, and made every effort to vanish before Eugene's Jheri curl juiced head lifted from that pillow.

"Well, when you get home, Liberty, I have a birthday surprise for you."

"Okay, Mama." I took one last look in the mirror, slung my backpack over my shoulder, and scrambled.

When I walked into the rowdy classroom, I was met by my friends Unique and Shaneria.

"Happy birthday, Liberty!" they shouted together, exchanging hugs with me.

"You looking too cute, friend!" Unique complimented.

"Aww, thanks you guys."

I turned around once I heard someone beatboxing. It was my best friend, Terica. She walked toward us, clad in an identical windbreaker jacket, Tweety Bird *Looney Tunes* shirt, semi-ripped blue jeans with blue tights underneath, and her drill-team-loving Keds. We had stayed up a little longer than usual the night before planning our twin outfits for my birthday, right down to our poofy side ponytails. We began jigging from side to side, bobbing our heads and using our fists as pretend microphones.

"I said uh mic check, one two, one two. It's ya girl Te-ri-ca and I'm coming through. Shouting out that it's a special day cause it's my girl Liberty Banks—"

"BIRTHDAY!" I shouted after Terica pointed to me.

All of us high-fived each other and carried on the birthday banter until Zion, Lonnie, and Pac-Man entered the room. They headed toward our circle.

"So y'all think you got some skills, huh?" Lonnie contested.

"*Think*? Pshh, you better give us our props, 'cause we got mad bars from Mars, spitfire flows, and rich-girl goals . . ."

Terica checked Lonnie so fast that he didn't even see it coming. Neither of us did. She was spitting lyrical flames as he stood there stone-faced and obviously embarrassed.

"Ahhhhh dayummmm! Don't hurt the kid! I got five dollars on Terica, right here, right now," Pac-Man laughed, waving his lunch money for the week and egging them on.

Zion walked forward and stood directly in front of me while Terica and Lonnie continued swapping verses.

"I'd love to see you rock the mic," Zion said.

I held back what I really wanted to say, though my eyes betrayed me every time. Truth was, I would sing, rap, and even tap-dance if he was worth entertaining.

"I was only clowning around with Terica."

Shaneria nudged me with her elbow. "She lying! This here is Liberty 'Jam Master' Banks. Her flow is sick. Don't let her play you like that."

I shot Shaneria a hard glare. It was one thing to cut up with my girls, but I had never freestyled in front of the guys before. She caught my side eye and the hint.

"It's all good. Ima get you to flow for me one day, smart-tart."

"Humph. Guess we'll just have to see how that goes."

Our eyes were glued on one another as we sat in the moment. It was as if I could read his mind because those big lips weren't moving at all anymore, yet we were having a conversation—telepathically.

The school bell rang, and our principal's voice boomed through the speaker. Several of our classmates rushed into the room before Mrs. Dexter could close the door. Otherwise, they would have been marked as tardy. And if you had three or more tardy marks in a week, that was a guaranteed trip to Mr. Dupree's office to be paddled.

Zion and I took our seats beside each other. I opened my bag and pulled out my Trapper Keeper to begin that morning's Bell Ringer. It was a writing prompt exercise. My favorite way to warm up. I looked over and saw that Zion didn't have his binder out.

"Here." I slid him a few blank sheets of notebook paper and one of my cute pencils with the scented eraser that I'd bought from the Scholastic Book Fair.

"Really? *Tweety Bird?*"

"Yep! And you better not lose it."

He laughed, but I was as serious as a heart attack.

━━━━━━━━━

After lunch, Mrs. Dexter threw her traditional birthday party for the month. Since Zion and I had the same date, we were able to celebrate together, which made it even more special. He and I sat at the round table while the entire class sang "Happy Birthday" once again. Afterwards, Mrs. Dexter served us all one of those delicious buttercream cupcakes and some fruit punch to wash it down.

"Happy birthday, Liberty," Zion whispered in between bites.

"Happy birthday to you, too." I scoped him out from head to toe and watched him devour that cupcake in seconds. *Wait, is that a mustache?* "So, how does it feel to hit puberty—I mean to be nine?"

"I guess it feels no different than ten." I gave him a questioning stare. "I turned ten today," he clarified.

"Ten! Oh, you started school late."

"Nah, *you* started school early," he countered with a light chuckle.

Zion loved a friendly debate and teasing me. It seemed to be the highlight of his day. And whether he knew it or not, I loved the special attention and his friendship. We clicked, organically.

"Oh, and I got something for you. But you gotta close your eyes first," he said.

I tossed the last morsel of cupcake into my mouth and squeezed my eyes shut.

"Can I open them yet?" I was so anxious to see what it was.

"Hang on, smart-tart."

The suspense was killing me.

"Ooookay, now open them."

I popped my eyes open, and he handed me a cassette tape.

"One of my homeboys gave it to me, but I want you to have it."

I accepted the tape and brought my eyes to his. "Wow! But this is Run-D.M.C. They're like your favorite rap group, Zion."

"I know. But I wanted to be able to give you a gift for your birthday. You've been really nice to me since I got here. And…" He shrugged. "You're my best friend, Liberty."

My hands grew clammy, and my armpits started to tingle. There was a special glow in his eyes, and I might have been the only one who could see it.

"Thank you." Those two words floated out of my mouth. "I'll cherish it forever."

"Shiiddd, you better!"

My body stiffened. I coolly looked around to see if anyone had been eavesdropping on our conversation, especially Mrs. Dexter with her supersonic hearing. Good thing she was busy writing our homework assignment on the chalkboard. Instead of reprimanding Zion for swearing, I let it go. Besides, I was his best friend. And if you couldn't be the realest version of yourself with your best friend, then who could you be real with?

# CHAPTER 4

"SHE TOLD ME to walk this waaaay... Talk this waaaay... School girl sweetie with the classy kinda sassy—"

"Aye, smart-tart! Hold up. Smart-tart!"

With my Walkman headphones bonded to my ears, I cruised down the sidewalk along Buckner Blvd. and Grove Side Street, spitting the lyrics to Run-D.M.C.'s "Walk This Way." I paused the cassette and turned around when I heard hollering. It was Zion practically power walking. I slowed up so he could catch up to me.

"What you doing walking? I thought you rode the bus?" he asked.

"I do. I missed it, playing around with Unique and Shaneria. What are you doing? Shouldn't you be going home?"

"I am. I live this way," he answered. "Before you ask, because I know you're going to, I don't live far from you. I just choose to walk home. Now give me your book bag."

"You don't have to carry it. I got it."

He blew out in frustration. "I know you got it, but can I be a gentleman? Dang."

I held my hands up in surrender and handed him my bag. He placed it on his shoulders with the bagged part in front of him. We walked in silence for a few minutes.

"Aren't you gonna ask me why I walk home instead of riding the bus?"

I shrugged my shoulders. "Nope, because I get it. It's peaceful." Zion stopped in his tracks, and I turned to look back at him.

23

"Wow. That is why. How'd you know that?"

"It's why I like the outside, too." After a few more minutes of walking in silence, I pulled a slip of paper out of my back pocket and held it out to him. "I didn't give you this earlier. Happy birthday."

Zion laughed. "You didn't have to give me anything just because I gave you something."

"I know," I smiled. "And I didn't. I had already written it." He looked at me skeptically. "I swear!"

"A'ight, a'ight." He unfolded the piece of paper. "Let me see what you got here." He read in silence for a few minutes and then stopped walking. "You wrote this?"

*Great! He hates it.* I knew I should have gone with regifting one of Justice's old footballs and giving it to him. "Yeah," I answered shyly and full of embarrassment.

"This is tight, yo!"

I looked up in shock at his reaction. "You like it, for real?"

"Looks like I gave you the right gift. You've got skills, girl."

His compliments were shooting arrows straight to my heart.

"For real." He smiled at me, and it was something about the gaze in his eyes. I was a complete and total goner. Zion had me hook, line, and sinker and didn't even know it.

"Ain't nothing but a few words." I waved it off.

"Nah, 'happy birthday' is a few words. *This* is poetry."

Writing had always been my way to express myself. It was my outlet, and up until that moment, it was simply a remedy to pass time. With Zion's cosign, I suddenly felt like I was Maya Angelou.

"This is my house," I said as we stopped. He handed me my book bag. "Thanks again for the gift and the walk home." Before I knew what was happening, he reached out and hugged me.

"Happy birthday, Liberty."

Zion being that close to me made my heart do flip-flops. The universe could've blown up at that moment, and all would've been right in my world.

"Bye, Zion." I had to control myself from skipping inside the house because I was floating on cloud nine. I retrieved my house key from my bag, unlocked the front door, and walked inside.

*SLAP!*

The force of the blow slammed into me so hard that I fell back. I didn't know what had struck me. I shook my head to clear my vision. Eugene's snarl was first in my hazy eyesight. If there was such a malevolent evil called a devil, my stepdad, Eugene, was it in the flesh.

"Your little fast ass ain't got no business walking home and hugging on no boys! Where you been, huh?" Eugene's baritone voice sent chills up my spine. "Probably out doing God knows what with that manish-ass boy—"

"I didn't do nothing!" I yelled back, hot tears streaming down my face. He jumped in my face so quickly that it caused me to recoil.

"What did you say to me?" he seethed with so much venom that spittle landed on my nose and cheeks.

"EUGENE!" Mama hollered. "I'll talk to her. Stop, Eugene, please!"

He turned to Mama and pushed his finger into her forehead. "That's your problem, Lucille. You never want me to discipline this fast-ass girl. She gon' end up being a good-for-nothing little whore." He mushed her face.

Mama's lips trembled as she struggled to hold back her tears. "Please, Eugene," she begged. "Let me deal with her." She placed her hands on his chest as if to calm him. "It's her birthday, please."

He looked down at me in disgust. "Bad company ruins good morals," he said, spouting one of several Bible verses that seemed to be etched in his memory. "You're lucky it's your birthday." With that, he walked off.

Mama kneeled to help me. "Hey, sweet girl—"

I shrugged her off and managed to get back on my feet. "Leave me alone. I hate him!"

"Liberty Mae Banks!"

I ran up the stairs to my room and slammed the door. In a fit of anger, I slung my bag across the room just before I collapsed onto my bed, crying my dear heart out.

# CHAPTER 5

THE STENCH OF alcohol and stale cigarettes permeated through the air. It met my nostrils before the door could swing fully open. Mama was in her usual lounging spot watching *Matlock* and braiding my sister's hair. I tried my best to make it to my room unnoticed.

"Zion! Where the hell you been?" Mama drilled. Janet was propped on one of our raggedy sofa cushions chomping on a pickle with a peppermint stick stuffed in the middle. She mean-mugged me with those beady eyes and I knew she was ready to flip her lips.

"He was probably with that girl he keeps pretending he don't like," Janet laughed.

My eyes bucked. "Mind yo' business, Janet!" I jumped at her.

"It is my business," she mocked.

"You get on my nerves." While Janet may have been the oldest, she was immature as hell.

"Don't talk to your sister like that boy! If you do like some little girl, you better leave her ass alone and focus on keeping those grades straight. I ain't got time to be going up to no damn school behind your ass."

"Man, y'all buggin'," I mumbled, taking off for my room.

"Oh, and your Uncle Ronnie coming to stay with us for a little while 'til he get back on his feet after that divorce. I told him he can use your room."

"Then where am I supposed to sleep?"

"Hit the couch. It's only for the time being."

I glared at her. Was she being for real?

"Problem?"

"No, ma'am," I managed through a clenched jaw.

I gripped the strap of my backpack mad as hell and beelined to the kitchen. Wasn't no sense in fighting her on it because I wasn't going to win. Never did.

"Mama, we need milk!" I hollered after discovering that the refrigerator was on E, including no milk.

Silence.

I walked back into the living room. My eyes bounced from Mama to Janet and then back to Mama. She lifted her cigarette to her mouth and took a puff.

"My stamps ain't came in yet, Zion. It might be some noodles and tuna fish in there."

I stood there for a minute. "So, I guess y'all don't even care that it's my birthday and ain't no food in this house. I'm hungry."

"Here!" Janet said, tossing me a preserved Twinkie that had been buried in her purse. It was all mashed up. "Happy birthday, knucklehead."

"I'll make it up to you, son."

I wasn't going to hold my breath because when it came down to Mama's cigarettes, weed and alcohol, nothing came before that.

"Hell, if that tired-ass daddy of yours paid his child support on time, we wouldn't be going through this."

I wasn't convinced. And the way I saw it, that sperm donor of mine was nonexistent anyway. He didn't pay child support. He didn't visit. He just didn't give a damn. At least Janet's daddy sent money, bought her gifts, picked her up on the weekends, and participated in her school activities. My deadbeat was just that… *dead*!

"I'll buy you something off the ice cream truck when he come through."

"Thanks, Janet," I managed. Mama slid the comb down Janet's long hair and sectioned it off with a rubber band. As I turned to walk away, the doorbell rang. I wondered if it was Uncle Ronnie. I eased the door open and was happy to see my homeboy Freddie from around the way. He was only one year older than me, but Freddie was living the good life. He always had the flyest clothes and the flyest shoes.

"Sup, bro! Your T-Jones home?" Freddie asked.

I nodded. "Aye, Mama! Can I go outside?"

"Don't you have homework?"

"No."

"Well, you better have your behind back here before dark."

"Okay."

I eased the door closed, and Freddie and I took off down the street.

"You wanna go to my crib and play video games?"

"Yeah, that's cool."

When we made it to Freddie's street, his dad's pimped-out Cutlass with the gold rims was pulling into the driveway. Rap music blasted from the shakers in his trunk. A smile cut across my lips.

"Boys, y'all come help me with these bags!" his dad called out, waving us over. Freddie and I raced each other, anxious to help out. His dad opened the trunk, and it was filled with groceries. Freddie grabbed two arms full, and I followed his lead.

"Y'all down for some pizza and hot wings?"

"Yes!" Freddie and I said in unison as we filed into the house. The instant we walked in and placed the bags on the dining room table, Freddie's mom rounded the kitchen corner with a cake in her hands and lit candles atop it. With a wide smile showing her one gold tooth, she walked straight toward me. My eyes lit up in surprise.

"Happy birthday to you..." she started out.

I couldn't believe it. Freddie joined in, and then his dad.

"… happy birthday, dear Zion, happy birthday to you!"

Words could not express how happy I suddenly felt.

"I bet you thought I forgot, huh?" Freddie asked.

"Time to make a wish," Mrs. Williams said.

I closed my eyes, and my jaw flexed. Yeah, I was thankful for my friend and his family, but it also reminded me of what I didn't have in my own home. Instead of speaking on it, I blew all ten of my candles out and swore to myself on everything I loved, that when I got older, I was never going to be broke.

# CHAPTER 6

*April 5, 2015*

"HEY, BABE!" I greeted my husband, Quincy, with a bit of shock etched in my tone as I paused from typing on my laptop.

Usually, he worked the third shift at Bainstone Tires which explained my surprise at seeing him enter the family room a little after midnight. Throwing his keys in the key dish, he sauntered over to me and gave me a quick peck on the lips, his body wracked with exhaustion.

"Troy decided to stay tonight since I've been pulling doubles to make sure the new equipment was fully functioning for the machine operators."

"That's good. And Daddy finally gets a break."

He'd been working extended hours far beyond the graveyard shift as of late, as the company had purchased newly updated, state-of-the-art equipment. Of course, like with every new piece of technology, the promises of ease and efficiency were absent at the implementation stages. One thing about tech, it made your life a hundred times worse before it began to make it only ten times better. Ever since his company had launched the new phase of machinery, Quincy had seemed to be a figment of our imagination because he was always working, and understandably so. As one of Bainstone's managers, it was his duty to ensure the transition went as flawlessly as possible. Therefore, I'd gotten used to him working both the second and third shift, hence why his current presence caught me by surprise.

"You working?" he asked, eyebrows knitted as he scrubbed his beard.

Nodding, I shrugged my shoulders. "I have a deadline. I only have a few minor touches, but I must have this turned in before 5 a.m." I stood and draped my arms around his shoulders. "I promise I won't be up much longer." He bit his lip and leaned his head down. Our foreheads touched tenderly.

"Don't burn yourself out, baby. I love your drive, but you need your rest too." He pulled me closer to him about my waist. "Can I help?"

Peering up into his eyes, I could see the redness in them. Tiredness consumed his gorgeous face. His disposition made him appear as if he hadn't rested in years. Still, here he was offering to take care of me.

"I'm good, babe. Go take a shower and get some rest. You've been working tirelessly, and you look exhausted. Queenie is asleep, and I don't have much left to do on this write-up for *Love & Lifestyle* before I submit it to the editing department." I rubbed my hands down his face and cuffed his beard in my hand, bringing his lips back to mine and kissing him again. "I'm good."

Sucking his bottom lip between his teeth, the glint in his tired eyes spoke to the yearning within my loins. "I'd much rather be put to sleep. I'd rest like a baby then."

"You do know that newborn babies scream and cry instead of resting, right?" I joked, while dancing seductively in front of him.

A guttural moan rumbled deep from his belly as he let out a harrowing bellow. "That's what I plan to do, scream your name, cry when I release, and fall sound asleep."

The howl that escaped my mouth could've awakened the entire neighborhood. He held me close to his chest to bury my boisterous bouts of laughter.

"You're gonna wake up Queenie," he chuckled, trying to calm me down.

I lightly tapped his arm. "It's your fault with that foolishness."

"Nah, you walked right into that one, baby. You know it."

Hands on my hips, eyes rolling, and lips pursed, I quipped, "If you don't let me finish up my work, I won't be walking into nothing else."

Immediately, his hands flew up in the air in surrender as he slowly stepped backward. "Say no more. I'm gonna go shower. If I'm asleep, you know how to wake me up." He winked as I stifled a giggle, then turned to sit back down at my laptop.

Before I could sit, he playfully grabbed a sizeable chunk of my butt cheek and love-tapped it. Amused, I turned and wagged my finger at him. "Shower, sir!" I ordered lightheartedly while pointing my finger in the opposite direction. He nodded, then turned and jogged upstairs.

I sat at my computer to finish up my work, but I had every intention of waking him up, only to put him right back to sleep. The vampire hours that we'd been working had put a serious monkey wrench in our intimacy lately, and it was beyond time to drench the drought. I flew through the last-minute touches with ignited vigor, not because I was overly excited about the editing process, but because I was eager to climb those stairs and climb my husband.

An hour later, when I finally reached upstairs, I checked on our baby girl. Queenie was kicking it into a cruise-controlled slumber, and for that, I was grateful. We could possibly get those desired screams and cries in even if they had to be muted by kisses and pillow bites.

When I entered our bedroom, I found my husband sprawled on his back, fast asleep. He'd donned lounge pants and no shirt. It was an indicator that he was prepared to shed the only layer of clothing he wore. Following suit, I showered, oiled my body down, and pulled the silk robe around my naked body as I made my way over to our bed. Peeling back the duvet, I eased into the bed and carefully straddled him. I leaned down and lightly kissed his forehead, and then his lips.

"Liberty," he moaned lightly in a lazy haze.

I smoothed the layers of his freshly cut Caesar with my hands and slid my manicured nail down the side of his face.

"Wake up, babe," I whispered seductively, "so I can put you back to bed."

A flirtatious smile graced his face before his eyes opened. Lust danced in his dark brown orbs as his hands gripped my butt in place. He rubbed his nature between the apex of my thighs, showing me in no uncertain terms that he was prepared for me, despite his recent comatose state. I'd awakened the beast.

My eyes fluttered under the feel of him teasing my liquefying love button. The sensation radiated through my body so intensely that I could've succumbed to his touch alone. No penetration needed. But it was damn sure wanted. As much as I wanted to let go, I needed him inside of me as much as he needed to be inside of me. Quincy's deep groans brought my attention back to him, and when he tapped me to rise, I lifted so that he could remove his lounge pants. How he managed to slip them off and kick out of them in one motion was unbeknownst to me. It didn't matter either because the next thing I felt was him entering me. We paused for a moment, basking in the missed connection between us. It was as if it was our first time reuniting, and we needed a minute to re-familiarize ourselves with each other.

A collective gasp respired through our lips as we gazed into each other's longing eyes. When Quincy moved, I fell in line with his rhythm. Our movements were slow and measured, as we took the time to enjoy the feel of one another. Our lovemaking felt like the sweetest love song as my hips rode melodically to the beat of his stroke.

"Damn, Liberty, baby. I've missed this shit," Quincy groaned, gripping my hips as our strokes increased.

Unable to speak, I leaned forward and delivered a passionate kiss on his lips to exemplify all the emotions that welled inside of me. He was right. Our schedules had severely impeded our intimacy, more so than we'd thought, and this feel-good lovemaking session was proof positive that we needed to get back to taking care of ourselves. We loved each other immensely but loving *on* each other was equally as important.

Once the sweet moments were consumed, the freaky moments prevailed as we picked up our pace. Our excitement for each other was in overdrive as we sensually moved from position to position, unable to get our fill of one another. With our bodies drenched in sweat, sheets wet, and my edges be damned, we marathoned our way into those screams and cries we'd teased each other about hours ago. We were in show-and-prove mode as I gripped the headboard with my eyes squeezed shut, taking all of what my man had to deliver.

"Shit, Liberty!" he huffed, long-stroking me to another countless completion.

"Quincy," I moaned out, crumpling forward on the sheets the moment he found his release.

He collapsed beside me. His eyes found mine as he swiped the stray hairs from in front of my face. We were all smiles as our raspy breathing worked to return to a slowed pace. He licked his lips and nodded.

"That's how you wake your man up and put him back to sleep," he joked around a deep yawn.

I stroked my hand down the side of his face. "I love you."

"I love you more," he whispered before pulling me into his chest, where we both fell into an easy deep slumber.

The constant buzz woke me up as I groggily sat up and turned my face, peering at the clock on the nightstand. It read 2:23 a.m. Turning to the side, Quincy was still fast asleep. Both of us were so tired from our late-night rendezvous we were still stark naked. The sound went off again, and I looked to Quincy's side of the bed and noticed his cell phone bouncing around. I got up and wrapped my body in my silk robe, flinging my hair to the side. It had to be his job or his parents. Those were the only phone calls he received at this ungodly hour.

I tapped Quincy's foot to wake him, but he didn't budge. I figured he wouldn't because he was exhausted. In an effort to make sure it wasn't his parents with some sort of emergency, I walked around the bed to check the phone notification. As soon as I picked it up, it buzzed again, signifying another incoming call from the same number. I didn't recognize the number, so I assumed it had to be someone from his job, and if that were the case, it had to be urgent. I pressed the button to answer the call.

"Hey, Quincy," a woman said, her voice floating through the line before I could utter one word.

For a minute, my voice was stolen, stuck in my throat. Instead of machinery and loud noise, I heard soft music. *Is that... Is that "Body Party" by Ciara playing in the background?* My ears honed in and anger plowed through my body. Pulling the phone back and looking at the unsaved number, I knew this didn't have anything to do with his family or Bainstone Tires.

"Who are you?"

"This is Eva. Is this Quincy's phone?"

"It is, and I am Quincy's *wife*. So, unless you can give me a valid reason as to why you're calling my husband's phone at O'dark-thirty in the morning, I suggest you hang up and lose this number.

"Liberty, Quincy and I are *just* friends. I worked at Bainstone with him, and we attended the same church as kids. I've known Q for a long time. I only needed some friendly advice, that's all."

"Well, Eva. Please don't call my husband's phone at two o'clock in the morning seeking some friendly *anything*. That's what a good girlfriend is for. I suggest you find yourself one of those, in Jesus's name." I ended the call as I glanced at Quincy who hadn't moved a muscle through all the commotion. I set his alarm tone to *sound* which I knew would stir him out of his temporary coma. When the shrill sound of the alarm activated, Quincy bounced up and glanced to the nightstand.

"Over here," I said plainly as he caught my voice and turned to face me.

"Liberty? Baby?" he called out, swiping his hands down his face before turning to the nightstand to see that the clock read 2:31 a.m. "What are you doing up?"

I pointed at him. "That's a good question, Quincy. What's going on?" When he looked at me with a confused expression, I huffed, shaking my head, and continued. "Well, I'll tell you what's going on. I was sleeping peacefully, sexed out from my husband when at exactly 2:23 this morning the buzzing of your cell phone awakened me. I tried to wake you thinking it was Bainstone or your parents, but you didn't budge. So, I answered the incessant buzzing, and lo and behold, I answered the phone to a woman on the other end asking for you. Typically, I wouldn't have been bothered. You work multiple shifts, and you have female employees, but last time I checked Bainstone didn't hire Ciara." When he looked confused again, I filled him in *again*. "Some 'woman,' for lack of another term, called your line after two in the morning with "Body Party" by Ciara playing in the background. The way she said your name was extremely disturbing for two reasons: it seemed more than friendly, and it seemed as if she was overly comfortable with talking with you at this time of the night. A time of night that you are typically 'working.'"

Quincy's head fell back as he brought his hands upward and dragged them down his face before looking back at me. "Liberty," he breathed out.

Instantly, my chest heaved up and down and my skin felt flush. It was the way he'd said my name that made every nerve ending in my body stand at attention. Although I was suddenly fearful of the next words that seemed to dance on his lips, I had to hear this. I had to know if I had some merit to cuss this woman out. Surely, if he admitted some wrongdoing, Eva's tongue-lashing wouldn't even scratch the surface of what I'd implode onto Quincy.

"Don't you 'Liberty' me. Who is Eva, and why the hell is she calling your phone—rather comfortably—in the wee hours of the morning, looking for some quote unquote, friendly advice?"

Quincy exhaled nervously. Still, his voice must have been stolen because all he could do was stare at me, not fully awake. Leaning back, my face turned into a deep scowl. I crossed my legs and unlocked my phone. "Since you're on mute, let me help you out. In a matter of minutes, I had everything I needed in the palms of my hands.

Eva Marie Campbell, thirty-six years old, no kids, no husband, nurse, lived in Dallas, Texas then moved to New York City, and is now back in Dallas, Texas, formerly a member of Mount Olive Baptist Church—*your childhood church*, mother's name is Vanessa Benedict-Campbell, father is Everett Ignacio Campbell, one sister, Victoria Inez Campbell-Wright, no criminal background, drives a smoke-gray Acura, lives in Cedar Hill, and works out at Z Fitness. Should we take a drive over to ask her in person what you obviously can't seem to answer?" With a hair toss, I placed my phone on the TV stand after displaying my investigative journalistic skills, then folded my arms with my legs crossed, awaiting his response.

Quincy brought his steepled hands to his face. "It's not what you think, Liberty." He rested his hands on his waist, eyeing me momentarily. When he seemed to resolve within himself that I wasn't going to let this go, he tossed his hands in the air and slowly took a seat on the edge of our bed. "She's an old friend. We did grow up in the same church together, and yes, she used to work at Bainstone years ago."

"Tell me something I don't already know, Quincy! Like why the hell she's calling you at two in the morning!"

"Babe, please calm down," he said, and quickly shifted gears when he saw the steam that seemed to be visibly floating from me. "She has cancer."

"But you're no doctor!" I didn't mean to sound so insensitive, but this woman had infiltrated my marriage.

His forehead crinkled with his face turned up, visibly touched by my words before he could catch himself. Enraged, I threw on my lounge pants and a tank top that lay across the chaise as if I were preparing to go to war. Because I was.

Quincy ran over to me, gently grabbing my arm. "I'm sorry, baby. It's not like that—"

"Are you fucking her, Quincy?" My words sprayed like bullets and seared into him.

"What? No. No!" he declared, trying his best to keep me pinned in place.

"Liar!" I seethed with vibrato as my lips quivered. Emotion consumed me as the possibility that my husband had been unfaithful hit me like a ton of bricks. "Let me go, Quincy. I'm not stupid. Let me go!"

"No, baby, not until you calm down," he said sternly. He lightly gripped my chin with the cup of his thumb and index finger, forcing me to look up at him. "I'm not cheating on you. I've never cheated on you. And I never will cheat on you. Come on…

I'm not that kind of man, Liberty. I love you."

"Does Ms. Body Party know that you don't cheat on your wife?" My eyes zeroed in on him for answers. I folded my arms, giving up my momentary efforts to flee since he wouldn't move out of my way.

Quincy's head fell forward as he placed his hands on my arms. "I will tell you everything if you promise to calm down and allow me the opportunity to explain."

Momentarily, I considered his request and against my better judgment, I sat down on the chaise and nodded for him to continue. "I'm listening."

"Okay, Eva is a woman I've known since childhood. We did go to the same church. She did used to work at Bainstone. When Carlos had his cookout, she was there. We caught up on old times, she confided in me about the cancer, and we exchanged numbers so she could keep me up to date on what was going on with her health. I didn't really believe she would call, but she did. Somewhere along the way, it became two friends talking and keeping each other lifted. I swear that's all it was."

"If that is all it was then why is she calling you only while she believes you're at work? Why does it sound like these 'talks' are a lot more intimate than they should be? Why don't I know anything about her, or this? And why was she at your friend's Carlos's cookout?" I pressed.

Quincy slid his hands down his face. "She knows somebody Carlos knows. I'm not a hundred percent sure. I didn't invite her, and it wasn't my business why she was there. All I know is that she was there."

I took a beat.

Allowed him to gather his truths.

Rearrange his lies.

Quincy groaned before exhaling deeply. "Deep down, baby,

I knew you might have an issue with Eva calling me. And please believe me, I didn't want to disrupt my household, and at the same time, I wanted to be there for her as a friend."

"If you knew I'd have an issue with it, then why didn't you come to me yourself, instead of waiting for me to find out like this? Because then it looks like you're hiding something." He cast his eyes downward. That's when it dawned on me. "Wait. You knew she had a thing for you, didn't you?"

He cupped his mouth with his hand and shook his head, his eyes filled with regret.

"Quincy!"

"Okay! Yes! I knew she did, but *I* knew I wasn't going to let it go any further than friendship, and I knew you'd see right through her if I told you. We've been friends since kids, and I wanted to be there for her during her time of need. I thought as long as I kept the other stuff at bay that I could handle it. But I swear to you, I don't have feelings for her. Eva is nothing more than a friend."

So many thoughts swirled through my mind as I stood there engulfed in Quincy's arms. Although there had been no physical betrayal—if I took his word for it—there was still the emotional betrayal. It wasn't the fact that he didn't allow it to go further or even the possibility that he was feeling her in a way that he felt for me, but there was still a tie, a bond, that I wasn't privy to. There was some type of pull that this woman, whom I didn't even know, had over my husband that had forced him to hide their relationship from me. That in itself was still a betrayal.

"But you let her in. You gave her access. She has had a part of your time and attention that I did not have, and it's gotta be more than cancer. Don't insult my intelligence, Quincy!"

He turned away before facing me again. "Baby. We dated briefly. I'm talking freshmen year in high school, and it didn't even last a month. We just weren't a good fit and were better off as friends. And when she told me about the diagnosis, I only wanted to be there for moral support. Nothing more. I swear."

And there it was.

The truth.

It hurt to hear, but it hurt worse not knowing. As odd as it was, his admission gave me a bit of relief because it meant that he was being truthful. If he'd hidden it, then I would've known that he felt more than what he'd let on. Still, it did something to my soul to know that he had carved out time for his ex.

Not just any old ex.

An ex who was battling cancer.

"Liberty," he said, eying me lovingly. "I love you. I'm sorry, and I was wrong." He pulled me in close to him. "Please say you forgive me."

I swiped at the tears that flowed down my face. "I need time to think about this."

"I love—"

I put my hand up. "Don't," I warned. "Not right now. I need to rest."

He gave me a slight bob of his head. "Okay, baby."

I walked to our bed and instead of sliding inside, I lifted both of his pillows and handed them to him. "Guest room."

"You're kicking me out of our bedroom?"

"Do you prefer the house?"

He grabbed the pillows willingly. "Liberty, I swear nothing happened."

I walked past him to our bedroom door and opened it. "Oh no, something happened. My husband kept a secret friendship with an ex-girlfriend behind my back. Now I need you to go while I rest and consider what I want to do next. You owe me that much."

Conceding, Quincy threw the pillows under his arms and walked through the door. He stopped when he was next to me and leaned over. "I'm sorry. I'll do whatever it takes to make this right."

His kiss landed on my cheek, and he walked out toward the guest bedroom as I shut and locked our bedroom door.

That was typically how all affairs began.

Innocent intentions.

An emotional connection.

A convenient truth.

Then enter the lies.

My soul felt betrayed.

# CHAPTER 7

THE STILLNESS OF the house exuded a feeling of a quiet storm. I'd risen before everyone, which wasn't untypical. With Quincy working nights, it wasn't uncommon for me to be the first to hit the ground running with preparing the household for the start of the day. Yet, on this particular day my grand rising wasn't out of necessity but rather out of restless anxiety. As a dedicated coffee drinker, I'd even decided to forego my usual morning picker-upper because I was on a natural high today. I spun some of that energy into preparing a breakfast platter fit for the royal family: egg white omelets with peppers and cheese, turkey sausage, cinnamon oatmeal, buttered croissants, a fruit medley, and orange juice for Quincy and Queenie... and a mimosa for me. I needed it. Hell, after that fiasco this weekend, I *deserved* it.

Tapping on the door to my daughter's bedroom, I opened it shortly afterward to find her stretching groggily, her pigtails flopping to and fro as she tried to wipe the sleepiness away from her eyes. "Good morning, sweetie. Get up, wash your face and hands, and come downstairs to eat breakfast."

"But Mommy, it's Sunday." She yawned. "Why are we up so early, and why did you cook breakfast on Sunday?"

Walking over to the bed, I lightly brushed my hand across her forehead and then caressed the side of her cute little brown face. "Because you need to have a full stomach. We're going to church this morning."

"Church?" she reiterated, as if both confused and in shock.

I giggled. "Yes, church. You act like it's a foreign concept. You've been to church before. Please don't act like this is something new."

Groaning, she finally stared up at me with questioning eyes. "But it's like usually for a reason."

"Well, there is a reason, Queenie," I said with my hands on my hips as I returned her gaze with a stern one of my own. Placing my hands on my hips, I uttered, "To thank God for this day, for life, and for this family. Now, get up and let's not waste any more time, so we can be there on time," I explained, tapping her little feet as encouragement.

The displeasure shone on her face, but she didn't put up an argument. Rather, she simply nodded her head, although begrudgingly as she submitted to my request. With a smirk on my face at her useless resistance, I exited her room and closed the door behind me.

"And Queenie!" I softly called out to her.

"Yes ma'am?"

"Don't lie back down. Get out of that bed," I stressed, and within seconds I heard bedsheets shuffling and the thud of her feet against the carpeted floor.

*She is her mother's child,* I thought as I sauntered back downstairs to the kitchen. Retying my robe tightly, I made my way over to the sink, rewashed my hands, and began making our plates to place on the dining table in our breakfast area. As I placed the last plate down, I glanced up, startled to see my husband making his way into the kitchen. I hadn't awakened him yet, so it took me by surprise to see him up bright-eyed and bushy-tailed. I paused, briefly taking him in. He slowed his stride when he noticed me watching him.

There was no denying the obvious. My man was fine. Those gray sweatpants and that muscle T-shirt which exposed his rippling physique and slight morning wood sent my libido into a frenzy. Although, I wanted nothing more than to run into his arms, say "forget church" and call Jesus's name in other ways, I forced the thought to the back of mind. Some rectifying was in order before we could even consider the makeup.

"Good morning, baby. It smells good up in here," Quincy said, making his way over to me.

"Your breakfast and OJ is on the table," I replied dryly.

"Baby—"

"And let's hurry and eat because we're going to church this morning," I said, interrupting whatever was about to pour out of his mouth.

His gasp was evidence of the shock effect of my declaration. "Okay." He leaned over and kissed my cheek which I allowed even though I was still quite upset.

A few seconds later, and before I could go into full mommy-tude, Queenie came barreling down the stairs and plopped onto her seat. She and Quincy exchanged morning pleasantries before he playfully picked up our baby girl, tickling and hugging her. Her laughter and their playful exchange caused a smile to spread across my face. Regardless of our issues, these moments would always be precious to me, not only because Quincy was an amazing father, but because we went through so much to bring our baby girl into this world. Tears clouded my eyes as I thought of all the miscarriages we'd endured and the countless gynecological visits before it was determined that I needed surgery to even have the possibility to carry full term. Thankfully we found a specialist who was familiar with cases like mine. After my transabdominal cerclage procedure to stitch the top of my cervix, I was officially TAC'd and able to carry my babies beyond the second trimester, unlike before.

Indeed, Queenie was our miracle child, and we both loved her so. Still, there was no doubt about it: she was a daddy's girl. The thought of my family being fractured after all we had endured caused a lone tear to streak down my face. I quickly swiped it away before either of them saw it as we all finished up our food and then exited to prepare for church service.

———

"Tabernacle Baptist?" Quincy questioned, eyeing me as I pulled into the church parking lot. "I thought we were going to New Hope."

Before I could answer, Queenie, who had been zoned out watching her LeapFrog tablet, looked up and made the exact same assessment. "Heyyy, this is not the same church."

As I parked our Mercedes S-Class, I confirmed to them both, "No, it's not New Hope, and no, we're not attending there today. We're visiting this one. Now let's get out and go inside before service begins."

Again, Quincy eyed me strangely, but rather than grill me with a hundred questions, he simply exited the vehicle and helped Queenie out of her booster seat in the back. Under different circumstances, my husband would've definitely instituted a sidebar conversation about this impromptu church visit. Seeing as he was skating on thin ice though, he left the particulars alone and decided to roll with the punches as I knew he would.

Together, we stepped inside the vestibule of the church looking like the model family, each of us matching in our yellow and gray color scheme. It was important to me to represent a united front; therefore, I'd chosen my yellow A-line business-style dress with gray trim and my gray Zanotti pumps with a yellow rosebud. Quincy had donned a tailor-made gray suit with a yellow dress shirt and a matching gray and yellow tie with gray Prada shoes, and Queenie wore a yellow sundress with a white short-sleeved cardigan and gray dress shoes.

We slipped inside the fourth pew from the front just as the praise and worship team began leading devotion. As we nestled into our seats, my eyes zoomed to the front when I caught the side profile of the mocha-brown woman on the second pew with the bob-styled hair. Bingo. Eva "Evil" Campbell. The source of my irritation sat mere seats away from me, singing her treacherous heart out to "Praise on the Inside." *More like evil on the inside.* My internal thoughts ran rampant as I struggled to stay focused. I glanced over and apparently my husband and Queenie were thoroughly enjoying the service, none the wiser.

I had tracked down everything on Evil Campbell, even the church she *currently* attended. My intentions were a mixed bag. Part of me wanted to see if she was actually this sick, churchgoing woman, and the other part wanted her to see me and understand there was only one leading lady in Quincy's life, and that was me. I'd hoped that once I saw her, I'd feel sorry for her and then pray to God to forgive me and for my heart to forgive them. However, as I watched her as she jumped up, lifting holy hands and singing God's praises, looking as if she'd stepped off *America's Next Top Model*, it only fueled my raging fire.

Peeling my eyes off her, I refocused on the service. This "thing" that Quincy had with Evil forced me to recollect on past hurts. Hurts my first love, Zion, had brought me. I had dealt with numerous females and constant unfaithfulness from him, and I refused to do the same with Quincy, especially Quincy. Not my *husband.* So yes, I was in warrior mode and protecting my family. Our family.

I also understood that while Quincy's heart was huge and pure, he played the biggest role in Evil's disrespect because he'd allowed her to get too close. I also knew my husband well enough to know that he was being honest. Yes, I knew they'd been friends. Yes, I knew the woman had told him she was sick. Yes, I knew nothing had happened with them. Yes, I knew all the backstory—now. *But still.* We were happy and building a life together, and there was no way on God's green earth that I was going to let any woman finagle her way into my marriage.

"Say it with me: *let it go!*" the pastor shouted, bringing me out of my reverie.

I couldn't believe the pastor was nearing the end of his sermon. I remembered the offering and passing the collection plate to Quincy but other than that I was so zoned out that I hadn't heard a word. When the pastor shouted about letting it go, I tuned in.

"God is calling you to let it go today, church! Let it go!" he preached, fisting the microphone in one hand. He wiped his brow with his handkerchief as he eased down from the pulpit. "The people that underestimate you, let it go. The people who criticize you, let it go. The people who undervalue you, let it go. The people who scandalize your name, let it go. The people who do you wrong, let it go. The people who betray you, let it go." He jumped up and down as the spirit filled him. "Everything that anybody does to you that means you no good, let it go!" he shouted exuberantly as the congregation hollered in praise and worship with the pastor.

A tear trickled down my cheek and I felt the thickness of emotion swell in my throat as the pastor's words began to resonate within me. I hadn't listened for the entire service, nor sermon, yet somehow the exact sentiments I needed to hear floated out into the atmosphere at the exact time I needed to hear it. My soul felt full and lifted with those few words of confirmation.

"Now, I know this is unusual, but I feel the presence of God in this building today. Before we open the doors of the church, I need to do another altar prayer. There's somebody in this building that is unsettled in their spirit. And God is calling us to pray. If you are in need of prayer, my brother and sisters, I challenge you to grab somebody's hand and bring them up to the front with you to receive it."

Before I knew what was happening, I found myself on my feet with a few other people. Quincy stood quickly with me and took my hand as I approached the front. As I got to the second pew, I reached over and grabbed the hand of Eva, who looked over at me, startled, as Quincy looked between the both of us, panic instantly covering his face.

With a slick smile on her face, Eva stood and said snootily, "Pleased to *finally* meet you."

Without any acknowledgement of her snippy greeting, I wrapped my arm around her shoulder as all three of us walked to the front of the church together.

Leaning over into her ear, I whispered, "I know you are pleased to meet me. It was Quincy's ultimate pleasure to meet me too. Understand this, sis, the only thing my husband can offer you is prayer. And the only thing I'm offering you is this one-time pass." I pulled her into me for a warm embrace, placing the final stamp on my warning. "My husband doesn't need you as his landing pad. He's very happy on Liberty Island and I intend to keep it that way. So respect my wishes and stay away from my husband while I'm willing to… *let it go*." Pulling back, I smiled into her flabbergasted face as she blinked uncontrollably. "Amen?"

"Amen," she said shakily.

I turned to look at Quincy and held his hand. "Amen?" I asked him.

He nodded with complete understanding. "Amen."

Satisfaction coursed through my entire body as I held both their hands while the pastor prayed over us and everyone who'd come forward. When church ended, Eva couldn't face me let alone look at Quincy as we greeted some of the long-standing members on the way out of the church. *That's what I thought.*

"So, Tabernacle, huh?" Quincy said as he buckled himself inside the passenger seat after securing Queenie in her booster.

I nodded as I cranked up the car. "Uh-huh. I got exactly what I needed, and the message was well received."

"Good, because I miss New Hope," Quincy said, gazing over at me as he intertwined his hand into mine.

"Perfect, because I don't plan to have to come to Tabernacle again."

# CHAPTER 8

*January 15, 1992*

## ZION

*O*NCE CHRISTMAS BREAK was over and we'd returned to school, everything had picked up as it had left off. Since then, it'd been a full two weeks at my new school, and I was digging it. The people were cool, especially Pac-Man and Lonnie, and of course, Liberty. We sat next to each other, along with my boys and her homegirls, Shaneria and Terica. There were others, but we were the main crew. A real live Get Fresh Crew in full effect! For me, it made school worth attending because we were close. Even though I had only known them for a short amount of time, our crew was a much closer family than I was used to at home with my real one.

"You gon' catch cooties the way you be looking for Liberty," Lonnie joked. "I saw her coming down the hall with Unique."

I pushed him. "I wasn't looking for Liberty," I lied.

He and Pac-Man looked at each other skeptically. "Nah, you was looking for Liberty!" they joked in unison as we all burst into laughter.

Okay, I *definitely* was looking for her. She'd become a consistent part of my day, and I never wanted one to go by that I didn't see her. I didn't know what it was, but she made my days better. As I was about to throw a joke back of my own, Liberty walked in. Her hair was in two pigtails on either side of her head, with the rest of her hair hanging down her back. She seemed to walk in slow motion before she saw me and her lips curled upward. A dreamy-eyed smile plastered across my face immediately as she made her way over to me.

"Hey, Liberty."

"Hey, Zion."

"Liberty and Zion sitting in a tree… K-I-S-S-I-N-G," Pac-Man sang, throwing himself between us.

Liberty rolled her eyes. "Shut up, Pac."

Liberty had taken the words out of my mouth. While she was upset because of the teasing, I was upset about his interruption. I wanted to ask Liberty to be my girlfriend, and he'd killed the moment with his clowning.

"You always playing." I shook my head.

Pac-Man stuck up his middle finger. "Play with that."

"Ooh," Terica and Shaneria said about his gesture around fits of giggles.

"Yo' mama!" I joked back.

"Oh snap! You gon' let him talk about your mama like that?" Lonnie boosted.

Pac-Man slid back, eyeing Zion. "I know you're not about to come with the 'yo' mama' jokes. I know you don't wanna do that."

Never one to back down from a challenge, I stepped into his space and lit him up before he could strike first. "Yo' mama so ugly, when she went to the haunted house, they thought she worked there." All our crew burst into laughter, and Liberty high-fived me.

"That's a good one, Zion!" she said.

Pac-Man sucked his teeth. "Shut up, Liberty," he said, then turned back to me. "Yo' mama so stupid, they told her to dial 9-1-1, and she asked what's the number."

His joke garnered laughter from all the crew except Liberty. *My girl.* "Well, yo' mama so dark, God saw her and said, *'Let there be light.*'"

Again, the whole crew erupted, and Pac-Man looked a bit nervous. From what I was told by our crew, he'd been the king of the "yo' mama" jokes, but I had the jokes all day for him. What they didn't know was that I was the king of snaps, no matter the topic.

"Well, yo' mama so stupid she thought Dunkin' Donuts was a basketball team!"

"And yo' mama so stupid she returned the donut because it had a hole in it!"

"Yo' mama so fat, she has to bathe at SeaWorld!" Pac-Man laughed, yet his was the only voice I'd heard.

My attention turned to our crew, and everyone was timidly gazing around at each other.

"Umm, that one wasn't really funny, Pac," Terica pointed out with a shrug. Stating the obvious since no one else appeared to want to chime in to tell him.

"Forget you, Terica." Pac-Man waved her off.

"Well, yo' mama so ugly she scared the shit *out* of the toilet," I said, taking advantage of his weak "yo' mama" joke. Everyone fell out laughing at that one, even Pac-Man.

Conceding defeat, he slapped hands with me. "You won that one. That was good. I gotta steal that one."

We gave each other our newly developed homeboy handshake, and all was right with our world again. We were back to being boys.

After winning the "yo' mama" battle, I turned to find Liberty grinning at me. "What?" I asked, grinning back.

"That was funny. You got him real good. Pac is always bothering somebody."

"He was messing with you, so I had to get him."

The blush on her face was enough thank-you for me, but before she could formulate the words, our teacher walked inside the classroom and called for all of us to take our seats. However, before I could take my usual place next to Liberty, the teacher called me to the front of the class. Among the oohs of my classmates, which the teacher immediately quieted down, I strolled up to her desk. My mind scrambled to remember what I had done to get into trouble. Nothing popped up, so I was even more confused by the time I stood planted like a tree next to her. She asked me to walk with her out of the door, and I knew then that I had to have done something. When we stepped outside, the principal was there, and I braced myself for some type of punishment.

"Zion, we have to apologize to you, son," the principal said, causing me to stare up at him with shocked eyes.

"For what?" I stammered around the relief of not being in trouble.

My teacher turned to me and said, "Apparently, there was a mix-up on the paperwork. You're supposed to be in Mrs. Bernam's class, not mine. This isn't a fifth-grade classroom. It's fourth grade."

"What?" I asked, confused. It didn't seem like fourth grade to me. I didn't remember learning the things we were talking about at my old school.

"Our curriculum is on a slightly advanced track at this school, Zion, so it is quite possible that you are covering material that you may not be familiar with," the principal added, as if he'd read my thoughts. "However, we must move you. Rather than disrupt you in the middle of class, we'll allow you to go meet with Mrs. Bernam quickly, and then tomorrow morning, you'll report to her class."

Slowly, I walked with the principal while my teacher returned to the class. Although I should've been happy to be with kids my age, I was upset. It wasn't about moving up as I should have been in the right class in the first place. It was the fact that the move meant that I would no longer be in the same class with Liberty. She was the only reason I was excited to get up and go to school anyway. That and lunch. Those rectangular pepperoni pizzas and chocolate-covered peanut butter balls were the bomb. My head fell as we reached Mrs. Bernam's classroom. Everything else was like a blur to me after that. Even when I returned to my soon-to-be old class, I was stuck in a haze.

"Earth to Zion." Liberty snapped her fingers in front of my dazed face. "What's going on with you? Where did you go?"

Sadly, I turned my face to hers and looked up to find our teacher's back to us, writing on the chalkboard. I leaned over and whispered, "I'm in the wrong class. I'm in the *fifth* grade. I have to move classes tomorrow."

Liberty's facial expression was as distraught as I felt on the inside. Her lip quivered as she tried to make sense of this sudden and unavoidable change of circumstances.

"What? No, wait," Liberty fumbled. Her eyes seemed to gloss over as she touched my arm. "So, you're leaving, for real?"

I didn't have the heart to answer her with words, so I bobbed my head. When I heard her swallow, a second glance in her direction signaled that she was fighting off tears. She looked down at her paper. "But I don't want you to go."

If ever there was a time to express how I felt, it was then and there. Liberty was everything to me, and even at that young age, I knew I needed to speak what had been in my heart.

Thinking quickly, I pulled out my composition notebook, and on a slip of paper, I wrote: *Will you be my girlfriend and marry me?* Underneath, I drew a big box with the word *yes*, and beside it, I drew a smaller box with the word *no*. I slid it to her, and she unfolded it. Her eyes lit up like a Christmas tree. Grabbing her pencil, she checked a box and slid the paper back over to me. I hoped Liberty hadn't seen the bullets that I was sweating when she slid that paper back. If she'd said no, they could've moved me to the new class right then. There was no way I could take rejection from her. I played it cool, though, smoothly taking the paper and gradually opening it. When I saw the big check in the *yes* box, I wanted to break-dance. I was that excited. But instead, I gave her a warm smile and prayed that it didn't come off as the strong blush that I'd been attempting to hide.

"At recess, we'll do the ceremony," she whispered happily.

"All right."

My response was calm and nowhere near a reflection of how I truly felt on the inside. I couldn't let Liberty think I was soft, even though I was probably more excited than she was. How could I not be? At recess, Liberty Banks was going to be mine forever.

---

*October 5, 2014*

# LIBERTY

Time escaped me as I held my cell phone in my hand. I was still reeling from my phone call with Mama. I'd explained to her about my recent run-in with Terica and how she'd assumed I'd married Zion. *Zion.* Over the years, his name had become little more than a distant memory. He had faded so far from my reality that he seemed more like a dream to me. As if I'd conjured him in the crevices of my youthful mind. However, that conversation with Terica proved that not only was Zion alive and well, but he was real, and our destined reunion an ever-present reality.

Still, the interaction with Terica had caused a ripple effect of memories to course through my mind. Her allusion to our nonexistent marriage led to my reflective rumination of a special time. Indeed, my most memorable experience with Zion. The day we got married. Laughter emitted from the pit of my belly as the recollection of the day washed over me.

We were free-spirited fourth graders. Well, I was a fourth grader, and he was a fifth grader, but we were so sure of ourselves.

We exuded far more confidence in our union then than we had as we grew older. It was astonishing that as children, we could possess mature qualities that life had a way of stripping from us by the time we became grownups. Yet, there we were as nine- and ten-year-olds, making a lifetime commitment that full-blown adults couldn't seem to make. Sweet memories filled my mind of the day I gave my hand away in marriage—the first time.

———

I couldn't believe it. On January 15, 1992, Zion asked me to be his girlfriend and to marry him. I would've followed Zion to the end of the earth. My wildest dreams as a fourth grader had come true. I slipped a note to Terica for her and Shaneria to read. *Zion asked me to be his girlfriend and to marry him. We gotta do it at recess because he's switching classes tomorrow.* From my peripheral, I could see Terica read the note and pass it to Shaneria and Unique. They read it, both goggle-eyed and smiling. When I glanced back at Terica, she nodded with a grin a mile wide.

Giddiness overcame me, but it was also bittersweet. On the one hand, I was marrying the boy of my dreams, but on the other hand, our time together would be limited by the fact that I would only see him before and after school. He was about to be my boyfriend forever, so I wanted him by my side at all times. No matter what I went through at home or in school, knowing that Zion was there made my world better. He had an innate knack for knowing when and how to brighten my day.

Being that it was still wintertime, we would only get a few minutes of recess. Our teacher agreed to allow us outside since it was warming up, even though we still had a little snow on the ground. When recess came, we all met up outside by our favorite tree.

"What's this all about?" Pac-Man asked as he approached Zion, Unique, and me.

"Yeah, Shaneria and Terica pulled us over here, and we wanted to play football," Lonnie added.

"Liberty and Zion are getting married!" Unique shouted enthusiastically.

"*WHAT?*" Lonnie and Pac-Man asked in harmony. Their heads swung back and forth between us in confusion.

Zion looked up, offering me a smile before turning his attention to his boys. "I asked Liberty to be my girlfriend and to marry me, so that's what we're doing. And y'all gotta be my best boys."

The corners of Pac-Man's mouth lifted as he let out a boisterous bellow. "I knew you liked Liberty!"

Shaneria pushed him so as not to ruin the ceremony. "Shut up and go stand on the other side of Zion. You and Lonnie."

"Why?" Lonnie asked.

"Because, big head, that's how they do it in the weddings. The boys stand by the groom and the girls stand by the bride," Terica chimed in.

I'd been quiet as I processed the impending ceremony in my mind and suddenly let out a loud gasp. "I need flowers. The bride always has flowers." My eyes drifted around, noticing the soft white flakes covering the ground. "It's snowing though." I panicked. "I have to have flowers, or it won't be right."

Realization struck Pac-Man as he turned to address Zion. "And don't you need a ring?"

"Yeah," Terica, Unique, and Shaneria chimed in, eyeing Zion now with the same panicked expression I held.

"I got one," he said confidently. "I got it during lunch."

While we all stared at Zion in shock and admiration, Terica jolted us when she shouted out, "Wait, I'll be back."

As she ran toward the open door that led back into school, we all called out to her to question where she was going and why, but she kept her brisk pace and never gave us a backward glance. I was a little perturbed because we didn't have all day to pull off my wedding, and I wouldn't have another opportunity to marry Zion since he was switching classes and grades. However, before my switch flipped, Terica came running back to the tree with items in her hand. She handed them to me, and I looked at them as we all burst into laughter.

"Hey, it's the only thing I could find," Terica said.

"It's perfect." I hugged her tightly.

She'd swiped one of the flower pens on our teacher's desk and grabbed a key ring off her house keys. The pen was my bouquet, and the key ring was Zion's ring from me. Terica was just as stoked as I was about this moment. We'd talked about getting married once we were adults after watching one of those *Lifestyles of the Rich and Famous with Robin Leach* episodes that her mother subjected us to on Saturdays.

"Okay, so what do we do now?" Pac-Man asked.

Terica thought. "Oh wait, Lonnie, walk Liberty arm in arm to Zion."

I walked back a few paces with Lonnie, and we linked arms. We walked back toward the group as Shaneria, Unique, and Terica sang an off-key rendition of "Here Comes the Bride." When we reached Zion, I unlinked my arm from Lonnie and stood in front of Zion.

"Now go stand back by Pac-Man," I directed Lonnie as he hurriedly reclaimed his original position.

Zion looked at me with questions on his face. "What do we do now?"

"We say things to each other. I think they call them 'vows.' Like stuff to promise each other," I explained. "You have to go first."

"Uhh, I promise to always be your boyfriend. To buy you whatever you want. And… treat you like my Mrs. Forever… because I really really like you."

I blinked a few times and felt the butterflies as they swarmed in my belly. It was the sweetest thing I had ever heard.

"I don't know what else to say," Zion said nervously as Lonnie and Pac-Man tried to stifle their laughter.

I shot a glare at them so hard that it shut them down immediately. They weren't about to sabotage my wedding day with their tomfoolery. My eyes found Zion's and while neither of us couldn't stop smiling, I knew then it was something truly special about our connection.

"I promise to always be your Mrs. Forever. To bake you cupcakes when you want them. And to call you my king... like in the fairy tales."

"*King?*" I heard Pac-Man echo. "Well... King Zion, is y'all gon' kiss now or what?"

"They have to give each other the rings first!" Unique yelled.

"Oh yeah," Zion said, reaching into his jacket pocket. He pulled out a Ring Pop packet and ripped it open. Placing the cherry-red flavored ring on my finger, he said, "There you go."

In turn, I placed the key ring on his finger. "And there you go."

"So, I guess we're married now?" he asked.

"No! You gotta kiss first," Pac-Man said, blowing out a frustrated breath.

"Weirdo," Shaneria said, rolling her eyes.

Terica ran in front of me and Zion and shouted, "I now pronounce you husband and wife! Mr. and Mrs. Zion and Liberty Mitchell!" She clapped and then leaned in close to Zion. "Now you can kiss her."

We all looked around for Mrs. Dexter, who was talking to another fourth-grade teacher. Zion went the safe route and quickly kissed my cheek, but Pac-Man wasn't having that.

"Man, *kiss her*. Geez," Pac-Man fussed.

We stared nervously at each other as Zion licked his lips, and

I bit mine. Our timid energy proved that we were both unsure how to proceed. All sorts of questions swirled in my mind, but as Zion leaned forward, I had a feeling that he would guide me in this and that it would be all right. So, I closed my eyes and when I felt his lips touch mine, we both jumped back from the shock of the connection.

"That's what I'm talking about," Lonnie said as he and Pac-Man slapped hands and howled.

Shaneria and Terica jumped up and down and clapped for us, then all of them stood around us making jokes and talking about how we were now a married couple. All the while, Zion and I could only stare at our crazy friends while we basked in the moment. It wasn't long before they all took off to play and left Zion and me by ourselves.

Zion picked up one of the decorative stones around the tree and started making markings on the tree.

"What are you carving?" I asked.

"'Z and L forever.' This way, if our hearts are ever apart, I'm going to be the one to find you and bring us back together."

I smiled.

Soon, it was finished, and I rubbed the spot on the tree that commemorated our forever union. Zion walked up beside me, looked me in the eyes, and whispered, "Mrs. Forever."

My head fell to the side as I briefly leaned on his right shoulder. "For always."

———

The glint of light bouncing off my ring reflected in my eyes, bringing me out of my reverie. Gone was the plastic ring of the Ring Pop. It had been replaced by a 14K gold band, and in the center a ruby stone. Along with it, another man had replaced Zion, too. Along the way, I had transformed from Zion's Mrs. Forever to

Quincy's Mrs. Eternity.

I began to peck away at the keyboard, then found myself deleting the entire paragraph. And the next. And the next. I had to get my next "Soldiers of Love" column written and over to the *Love & Lifestyle* staff editor in three days to make the magazine's print deadline, and I hadn't written one single word. Then it hit me. It was time our 1.2 million subscribers knew where the inspiration behind my radical "Black Love" undertaking came from. I began to type: Forever doesn't last always...

# CHAPTER 9

*December 15, 2015*

## LIBERTY

I LOOKED OVER AT the clock on the wall as I put down the second magazine that I'd read from cover to cover. A sigh of frustration pushed through my lips. Against my better judgment, I had scheduled this doctor's appointment on my birthday of all days. My obstetrician was one of the best in the state, arguably the country, which was why I was still waiting to be called to the back a full hour after my scheduled time. The tugging ache in my lower back and the numbness in my rear were confirmation that I'd worn out my waiting room welcome. I rubbed my swollen belly and quickly came to appreciate this moment. We'd been waiting on this second miracle for a lifetime, it seemed, and here it was.

Having Queenie was the center of our joy. After miscarriage number six, dreams of having a child of our own had died until an onslaught of early-morning nausea and late-night heartburn. Forty weeks later, Queenie had made her grand debut. Now here we were with baby number two in sight.

My phone buzzed as I sat staring at the television drone on and on about different experimental drugs that would more than likely be the focus of later class-action lawsuit infomercials. I fished my phone out of my purse. It was a text message from Quincy.

**QUINCY:** Hey baby. Leaving work and on my way to you.

**LIBERTY:** Okay. Still in the waiting room. Drive safely.

**QUINCY:** I will. Love y'all.

**LIBERTY:** We love you, too.

As I was about to pick up my third magazine on parenting, my phone buzzed again. As always, she'd beat me to the punch.

"Hey, Mama Jackie!"

"HAPPY BIRTHDAY, LIBERTY! How's my favorite girl?"

"I'm great! How are you?"

"Awww, I'm doing okay. The old Arthur starting to kick in, but I'll live," she cackled, although I was sure there was nothing funny about the painful effects of arthritis. "How's Nana's baby doing?"

"Queenie's good. Getting big on us."

"Well, you oughta make time for me to see her, baby. It's been too long."

"You're right. I'll be sure to do that soon."

Though Zion and I didn't last, my relationship with his mother had stood the test of time. We didn't talk often, but on December 15th, Zion's and my birthday, the universe always reconnected us. And while I shared the special day with her son, Mama Jackie and I had a mother-and-daughter bond that I couldn't let go of, and Quincy was cognizant of that. He might've even been a tad jealous, considering my mother-in-law and I didn't share the same relationship.

"What have you been preoccupied with these days?" Mama Jackie inquired.

"Oh my goodness, Mama Jackie! Are you ready for *your* surprise?"

"Yes! Spit it out."

"Quincy and I are pregnant again!" I said enthusiastically.

"REALLY! Are you serious?"

"As a heart attack, honey. That's why I didn't beat your call this morning. I was trying to get to my prenatal appointment. I'm here now."

"Oh my goodness! Congratulations, Liberty! This is wonderful news. I know Quincy must be beside himself."

Her thoughtful words warmed my heart. "Thank you, Mama Jackie. And he is. We both are."

"So, do we know if we're having a boy or girl?"

"Not yet. We're supposed to find out today, actually. If I can ever get called to the back."

"Those doctors can take forever, child. I know. It makes it worse when you're anticipating news. Don't worry yourself. You'll find out soon enough. And when you do, call me and let me know. I have my fingers crossed for a little boy. Quincy deserves a namesake," she chuckled.

"That's what we are hoping for, too," I replied. My attention shifted once I spotted my husband, who was coming down the corridor and headed in my direction. "Hey, Mama Jackie, I hate to rush off, but I'm going to go check with the front desk regarding this wait time."

"All right, baby. I will talk with you later, sweetie. Love you."

"Love you too," I returned.

"Hey, baby. Thank God they haven't called you back yet," Quincy said, planting a kiss on my lips before taking the seat next to me.

"Liberty Bridges?" the young lady in blue scrubs called out.

Quincy and I took each other's hand, our twinning smiles illuminating the room. I said a special prayer as we followed the nurse to the sonogram room.

---

# ZION

"Finally, you answer the phone for your son on his birthday, huh?" I did not hide my irritation.

"Happy birthday, son," she said. "I'm sorry I didn't click over.

I was talking to …"

"So, whoever you were on the line with was way more important than your son on his birthday, huh, Mama? See how you treat your lastborn?" I said jokily, giving her a hard time.

"You oughta quit, Zion," she chuckled.

Though Mama and I had our differences, I loved her dearly. She was the only person who never turned their back on me. Even when she knew I was wrong, she stayed in my corner.

"And if you care to know, I was actually on the phone with Liberty."

Hearing her name alone shot off a signal in my brain, and a calmness swept over me.

"Mmm-hmm. I bet that piped your ass right on down," Mama joshed.

"How she doing, Mama?"

"She's doing well. Gonna find out today if she's having a son or another daughter."

"Wait, what? She's pregnant? Again?"

"Ain't that what I said?"

Silence.

Mama was still talking, but I had instantly checked out.

My throat closed as I struggled to suck in air and, at the same time, attempt to appear unbothered. I told myself that one baby was likely a fluke. But *two* babies. Nah. That was more like an official fuck-you-I've-moved-on-with-my-entire-life kind of notice. And it wasn't that I'd expected Liberty to wait around for me to get my shit together back then. Well, a part of me had. But that day hadn't come fast enough for her. She wasn't the type to sit around and wait for a man to see her worth, and she damn sure wasn't chasing his ass either. She was all woman, about her business, consistent with her goals, and constantly leveling up. I knew back then she'd never gamble her future on my maybes. And truth be told, I didn't want her to. Not because I didn't want her for me and only me, but because I knew I wasn't good enough for her. I didn't deserve Liberty, and I should've made peace with that, but I couldn't. I floated on memories of a past that continued to haunt me as much as it brought me happiness.

"Well, good for her and Quincy."

"Yeah, it was time. Queenie needs a sibling."

"It didn't do me any good. Hell, me and Janet not close."

"Zion, why would you say that?»

"'Cause it's the truth."

"Psssstt."

I was the black sheep of our family and Mama knew that. When she looked at me, all she saw was my absentee father. She took her anger for him out on me. And that anger eventually bled over into my and Janet's relationship.

I stood from the hood of my souped-up Chevy and straightened my white tee down over my distressed jeans.

"Aye yo Mama, Ima get at you later."

"Zion," she said barely above a whisper.

"Nope. Don't do that," I said sternly. "I'm up. Holla at you later, Mama. Love ya." Before she could respond, I disconnected the line.

I slipped my cell into my pocket and forced the emotions that my mom had stirred up down my throat.

"What's up, Zion!" my OG podna, Brian, from back in the day greeted as he walked up. We slapped hands and I pulled him to me with a one-armed embrace.

"'Sup, kinfolk," I said.

"Ready to run it up?"

"And then some."

"Already. Shit, let's go get it then."

# CHAPTER 10

## LIBERTY

WITH MY LIPS pursed, I examined the layer of berry-flavored Lip Smacker balm in the mirror. Satisfied with the results, I winked at my reflection as I stepped back to glance over my finished product. My ensemble was fresh to death. The straight, ankle-length jean skirt, black mule sandals, and double-layered black and white tank awesomely complimented the black and white bandana headband pulled over the front of my bone-straight hair. Spotting my science textbook on the bed, I grabbed the brown paper bag-wrapped book with doodles drawn on it and shoved it into my overstuffed book bag. Before I headed out, I slipped on my bangle bracelets and gold-cursive-name chain necklace, and then slipped on my hoop earrings. I smiled down at my little jewelry box and pulled out the mood ring that Zion had given me for our birthday last year and slipped it on my forefinger.

I grabbed my white zip-up hoodie off the wooden coat rack in the corner and used it to disguise my upper attire from my stepdad. I zipped it halfway before heading out of the front door.

"Have a great day at school, Liberty!" Mama shouted as soon as I cracked the door open.

"Thanks, Mama! Love you!" I shouted back.

Eugene appeared out of nowhere with a scowl on his face as

he stared me up and down. He wore that familiar malice-laced look in his eyes. I froze in place, giving him the same blank, emotionless stare, and hoping he'd simply let me out the door without incident.

My stomach sank because I knew he was about to be on one, as if there was ever a time when he wasn't. And if there was, I wasn't ever a witness to it. He had been medically discharged from the Army because—in the words of Grandma Sadie Pearle—"he ain't right in the head." And she was right. The mountain of prescription meds, a monthly measly disability check, and his constant anger was proof positive of that. I guess that's the reason Mama put up with him the way she did, but it didn't mean I should have to.

Slowly, a frustrated sigh breezed through my lips. I was in a good mood and didn't have time for his overbearing attitude.

"Hmph," he grunted. "Yeah, have a good day at school, and don't be hanging around that little thug. I've seen him over there at B-Jay's Cutz hanging out with them OCGs," he stated matter-of-factly. "Think I don't know what his lil' ass into." He pointed at me sternly. "You keep your lil' ass away from that thug."

Ignoring him, I looked downward and zipped my hoodie up a little bit more, then rolled my eyes. Instead of acknowledging what he'd said, I hoisted my backpack higher on my shoulder to create a bit more separation between us. It didn't help because as soon as I moved to go out of the door, he grabbed my forearm.

"Did you hear me?" he barked.

"Eugene!" Mama hollered from the end of the foyer. Without letting my arm loose, he turned his head to face her. "Let that girl go on. She's got to get to school on time."

"I was only trying to have a quick chat with her, but she's acting like she don't hear me."

Mama looked at me as if pleading with me to address Eugene so this little standoff could be over. Despite biblical quotes bouncing from his lips, we both knew how out of control he could become when he didn't get his way. Since I wasn't going to be at home for the aftermath, I decided to help ease the tension so he wouldn't turn his anger toward me onto Mama.

Shrugging my shoulders, I huffed and let out, "I heard you. Okay." With that, he let my arm go, and I rushed out of the door without another word.

As soon as I trotted down the steps, my girl Terica walked up to the sidewalk to meet me. I unzipped my jacket so that the front of my tank top could be revealed. She grinned when she saw my attire.

"Ooh, my girl, looking like all that and a bag of chips!" she howled, covering her mouth with her hands. "Got that Aaliyah joint going on!"

"*Who? It's the Li-ber-tyyyy, rippin up the stage. I got jazz personality, G-mentality, beats from soul train,*" I sang, belting my version of the latest new banger, "Back & Forth" by Aaliyah.

We met up, high-fived each other, then interlocked hands as we doubled over in laughter. Terica looked up as we eased on down the street. "Yeah, and Zion will '*keep on groovin and don't stop groovin*'"with you looking like a hottie!" she complimented again.

"Girl, please." I blushed. "Look at you. Out here looking fly in your acid-washed denim short overalls and that off-the-shoulder top! I see you, girl!"

She flipped her Chilli from TLC-inspired hair off her shoulder and wagged her finger at me. "Don't even try to change the subject. You know the homie is insane in the membrane over you, and you are coo-coo for Cocoa Puffs over him too!"

Thankfully, the bus pulled up before she had a chance to rag on me anymore about Zion. Once we'd boarded and were seated, I completely removed my hoodie and stuffed it inside my book bag. I tried and failed miserably to play off how in love I was with Zion, but apparently, I was only fooling myself if I thought no one could see straight through me. There was no denying it. Zion Malik Mitchell was it for me. He'd stolen my heart at nine years old, and he'd held it in a vice grip ever since. We completed each other and he understood me in a way nobody could. It was beyond some schoolyard crush. What we shared was otherworldly. There were times when I'd be upset, and he'd call knowing that something was wrong with me. We finished each other's sentences, understood each other's corny jokes, supported each other through our family drama, and we even shared dreams of going into the music industry. Most importantly, I felt safe with Zion. No matter the situation, he always had my back.

"What lyrics are you writing now?" Terica asked, removing the headphones of her Walkman.

Her voice and the sound of "Poison" by Bell Biv Devoe blasting from her headphone speakers brought me back to my current reality. I looked down at the paper inside my Trapper Keeper. Every bus ride, I wrote anything that was on my mind, from poetry to music lyrics. With thoughts of Zion zipping through my mind, courtesy of Terica's taunting, all I'd managed to write were doodles of *Zion and Liberty forever* and *Mrs. Liberty Mitchell*.

Closing it, I looked over at her and said quickly, "Nothing."

She giggled as she put her headphones back on and sat back. "Zion oh Zion," she teased, continuing her banter about him.

As soon as we stepped off the bus, I looked up and saw him. My breath hitched as he stood in a circle with his boys, Pac-Man and Lonnie, shooting the breeze and joking around. He looked so fine in his brown-, blue-, and white-striped shirt and white AJ 10's and dark denim jeans by this fresh new designer Karl Kani. It was as if my presence created a magnetic pull on him and his honey-hazel eyes automatically found me. Standing there, he still laughed at whatever Lonnie had said, but his eyes never left me. I slowly glided my way over to him; Terica and the rest of the world, or at least T.W. Brown Middle School, were nonexistent.

As I approached, he stepped to the side, and I could fully see his caramel face with his new fresh short box fade. I didn't like it as much as the Caesar cut, but I couldn't bring myself to tell him. Butterflies skirted across my stomach when he rubbed his hands together as if he had been anticipating my arrival. I thought I'd take flight when he winked at me and slowly sucked in his bottom lip. He was so fly without even trying.

"Lil' Mama, you looking good." He reached for my hand and pulled me into him for an embrace. "I've been missing you," he whispered, placing a soft kiss to my lips.

"I missed you, too."

You'd think we hadn't seen each other two days ago at the park. That's just how close we were though. Even a couple of days apart felt like an eternity. It may as well have been to us. It was hard to survive a day without my Zion, and now, I knew he felt the same way.

"Ahh man, time for us to go. Liberty done showed up," Pac-Man said, doing a quick wave of his hand toward us.

I rolled my eyes. "Whatever Pac. You're just mad 'cause ain't nobody trying to be with you." Lonnie and Zion snickered at that, much to Pac-Man's dismay.

"But she kinda right though." Lonnie pointed at Pac-Man.

Pac-Man sucked his teeth. "Whatever. I gets all the honeys."

Zion looked around and over his shoulders. "So, where they at?"

This caused all of us to burst into fits of laughter.

"Man, bump all y'all!" Pac-Man fussed, his irritation evident.

Zion decided to smooth things over and patted his shoulder. "We just clownin' around. We cool, bro?"

Pac-Man huffed, then nodded. "We straight. I guess me and Lonnie gonna give you and Ms. Liberty y'all time." He turned and looked at where Terica had joined a few of our other girls and rubbed his hands together. "Yo Liberty! I'm gonna go rap to your homegirl Terica."

"Yeah, you do that."

Lonnie put on his most dazzling smile as he walked with Pac-Man over to the group of girls while Zion and I watched them for a moment. Then I turned to face Zion with my arms wrapped around his waist. "You know Terica is gonna shoot him down. Don't nobody like Pac's stank-ass attitude. Besides, she really feeling Lonnie."

Zion looked down at me, his brows knitted at this revelation. "On the cool?"

I gave him a serious eye. "Real talk."

His mouth formed an O as he covered it with his balled-up fist. "Damn! I did not know that."

Playfully, I slapped his shoulder. "And you *still* don't know. So don't go bumping your gums to your homeboys."

He looked at me and agreed. "A'ight. A'ight. I won't say nothing. I promise." Stepping back, he took in my full ensemble. "But back to you, Miss Fly Girl. You look so beautiful."

I blushed. "You digging it? For real? I got my Aaliyah look going on."

"Nah, baby, you puttin' Aaliyah to shame. No diss to her, but the way those hips rocking in that jean skirt, you all that and a bag of chips."

"You're looking pretty fly yourself."

"'Cause we fly together," he said.

Holding hands, we walked around the building to our favorite spot. It was a quiet little nook away from pesky teachers and overbearing staff administrators who enforced strict "no fraternizing" rules with boys and girls. Everyone knew it was their attempt to keep the raging hormones down, but that rarely stopped anyone. It especially didn't stop Zion and me.

As we walked, what Eugene had told me came back to my mind, and I confessed what he'd relayed to me to Zion, hoping that what Eugene had said wasn't the truth. "Zion, I need to tell you something," I said, nervously tucking my hair behind my ear.

With his hands resting on my waist, he gave me his undivided attention. Softly, he asked, "What's up, baby?"

Clearing my throat, my eyes lifted to him, and I nervously informed him, "Ah, Eugene told me not to hang out with you this morning."

His facial expression turned into a screwface. "Why'd he say that? What'd I do to him?"

Pursing my lips, I admitted, "He said he saw you hanging out at B-Jay's Cutz with the OCGs."

He paused for a beat but kept his gaze straightforward. "Oh yeah?"

"Yeah," I answered as I nestled into him on our spot on the corner of the building. "Eugene is a jerk, though. You know he throws the Bible on everything, even when he's doing wrong. He was probably the one hanging with the OCGs and using it as an excuse to try to get my mama to yank you away from me. He doesn't want to see anybody happy."

Peering down at me with a serious expression, Zion lifted my chin and stared me in the eyes. "That's never gonna happen. I would never let it. *Never*."

The way he said it... with such certainty... made me believe every word he said. It was as if he was transporting his feelings and his heart into me. Soon, our hearts felt like they were on one rhythmic beat. He leaned down as our stare turned intense. Sparks were going off in my belly as our lips met. Deepening our embrace,

Zion planted the softest and gentlest kiss on me. It was a kiss that claimed me. It was a seal. A guarantee that he'd never allow anyone or anything to come between us. And I felt the same way.

---

# ZION

"Come on," I said to Liberty as I held her hand and led the way.

"Where are we going?" Liberty asked as I practically dragged her over to the bleachers in the small football stadium.

"Here. With your impatient ass," I said kiddingly, causing a grin to spread across her face.

Both of us knew that patience was not a virtue of hers. I knew Liberty like I knew the back of my own hand. I knew her, and I loved her. True story. Being in love was tough to admit for a youngsta, so I never verbalized it. I couldn't tell her because it was hard enough to admit it to myself. And copping to love put an automatic "lame" tag on you. With that came the irritation of getting ragged on by my boys.

But personally, I couldn't admit it for reasons that stretched beyond hiding it from my boys—the fear of not being the guy she wanted me to be, the fear that she didn't love me back, but most of all, being scared to love. Love wasn't an emotion that I was raised on, so I wasn't necessarily sure if what I felt *was* that, and even if it was, could I love her right? And saying that out loud made it feel permanent. I was scared of anything permanent with Liberty. I was scared of not being able to hold up my end of the bargain. I didn't want to let her down. Ever. So, I tucked those words away in my heart and tried to show her through my actions.

"Why did you want to move to the bleachers, Zion?" she asked, faking anger, folding her arms across her chest.

"You cute when you fake mad." I poked fun at her before

pecking her on the lips. She melted and put down her fake resolve. I loved when she did that shit.

Reaching into my book bag, I pulled out a block eraser and a permanent pen. On one side of the eraser, I drew a huge letter *L*. I made sure that it was thick and darkened it in. Once I was finished, I placed the eraser with the *L* side down on my skin and pressed it for a few minutes.

"What is that?"

I lifted the eraser to show the *L* on the underside of my forearm near my wrist. "This is an eraser tattoo." The explanation came out as I refocused my attention on her. "I put this L on my arm to represent you, Liberty. My brand. That means you're mine. Everyone will know that Liberty is Zion's. This means that I'm never going to let anybody separate us. Eugene or nobody." Her eyes widened with understanding. "'Cause you know I don't let nobody take what belongs to me." Eugene's warning to her bubbled in the pit of my stomach as I spoke.

Suddenly overcome with emotion, her hand flew to her chest, and her eyes watered. "Zion," she cooed before crashing my lips with a deep kiss.

My teenaged insides started going crazy with that kiss. Liberty smelled so good and looked even better. I was trying my best to be a good guy, but my man below had a different plan. We had known each other since grade school, and she had always been beautiful to me, but fourth-grade Liberty was not seventh-grade Liberty. Seventh-grade Liberty had breasts and ass and my eighth-grade parts were struggling to keep this thing innocent. As my mama would say, my nose was wide open. She was right because right now I was itching for a scratch.

Liberty's hand landed on my thigh, and she jumped back when she felt the result of her luscious kiss. "Zion!" She gasped.

I laughed. "You did that to me."

Her face changed into an amused expression, letting me know that she was proud of her little conquest. All I could do was adjust myself and shake my head. She thought she was funny and slick. She was though.

Taking the eraser and pen off the bleacher, she began drawing a Z. I watched in amazement as she filled in the letter and placed her Z on the same area on her arm as the L was on mine.

"And now, you're mine." Her starry-eyed gaze found my eyes. "Liberty and Zion forever."

As the school bell rang, signaling it was time for everyone to file inside, we made our way off the bleachers back to the crowd. With the teachers and staff now present, we dropped holding hands, and soon, Liberty's friends made their way over to her. They began talking it up as I fell to the back.

I appreciated watching Liberty in her element. She fit in so well with the school scene. She was the American dream personified. Taking her in, I knew in my heart of hearts that she'd be someone one day. She'd do major things and her name would ring bells. She just had it. Those thoughts made me wonder how a guy like me would fit into her world. I barely fit in it now. It was part of the reason I'd thought of the tattoo. It was my way of trying to hold on to her for as long as I could. I'd had no clue she'd want to hold on to me right back. That move was like Cupid's arrow straight to my heart. Truth was, I needed her to feel like she was mine because Eugene might have been a jerk, but he was an accurate jerk. My world was different from Liberty's. She was intelligent. She'd get out of the hood with her mind. Me? I was merely surviving school. Hell, I was trying to survive home. There were limited options for people like me. So yeah. I'd been hanging out with the big homie Abel, the head of the OCGs. I hadn't decided to join, but the OCGs treated me like real family. They looked out for me, laced my pockets, kept me fed when I was out with them, hooked me up with the dopest clothes and shoes, and made sure that nobody laid a hand on my mama and sister. Mama and Janet may have treated me like shit at times, but I cared about them. It was the young man in me. I felt a need to protect what was mine. The same way I was going to protect Liberty. Because she was mine.

# CHAPTER 11

DID I FEEL guilty? A little bit. Not about what I did, but rather, my half-truth to Liberty. When she confronted me about what her stepdad, Eugene, had said, I knew I had to distract her. Had it been anybody else except Eugene who spilled those beans to Liberty, she would have been flaming hot. The fact that it was Eugene's snitching ass bought me a little leeway because she didn't like or trust him. He'd been at her neck since we were in elementary about hanging out with me, so his accusations felt premeditated, so to speak. Still, I knew she'd brought it up because she had a slight feeling it might be true. Though I meant what I'd done with the tattoo from the heart, it was still a diversion from the truth. The truth was I wanted to be an OCG. Hell, I needed it. I needed money, power, and a street family.

Liberty was the one with a good head on her shoulders. She had talent. She had fight. She was different. She was that one in a million that would make it. And I'd never ride her coattail, but I felt like that's what I was doing. Riding. Holding her back. I needed to get stable enough to where I knew I could be in the driver's seat. I had to stack my paper. Provide a proper life for myself. That way when it came time for me to scoop my shawty, I could say that I had her and not the other way around. Sure, we had each other's back, but regardless, I didn't want my girl taking care of me. It was my job to take care of her. Protect her. Provide for her. If I couldn't do that, then who was I to her? Dead weight. A bum. Being a part of the OCGs was my come-up. She'd never understand that though. That's why I couldn't tell her nothing until I was in. She wouldn't be happy about it, but she wouldn't leave me. It may have been a selfish thought, but it was the only way to keep her from trying to interfere or talk me out of it.

"'Sup, Abel?" I slapped hands with him.

He pulled me into a one-armed hug. "Nu'n, lil' homie. You ready for this?" He eyed me intently.

"Yeah," I answered with a nod.

Looking over his shoulder and then back at me, he asked again. "You sure?"

Unlike a lot of other young boys who were just looking to be down, Abel often said that he "saw more in me." At that age, I had no clue what that meant. As I grew older, I understood that he saw my hustle and my relationship with Liberty as me wanting to do more with my life. OCG wasn't a way out of poverty. It was a way into the streets. Damn shame I never saw it like that before. To me, it was a brotherhood and a means to an end. What he saw was my dilemma between doing what I had to do and doing what I wanted to do.

"Yeah, I'm ready."

At least that's what my mouth said. My insides were jacked up as I stood there praying that the sound of my heart thundering inside my chest cavity couldn't be heard by Abel. The last thing I needed was for him to feel like I was a busta. He'd let me do a few boosting jobs and be a lookout here and there for the OCGs, but nothing heavy. I couldn't make any real money until I was an official member. Abel was a little different from the rest of these other gang leaders. He wouldn't recruit anybody under the age of thirteen, and they had to prove they were built for the life before he'd grant them a pass to be involved. I'd proved myself. Now it was time. All I had to do was make it through this part of the initiation, and I was in.

One of the other dudes, who was a year older than me, showed up. He looked even more scared than I felt. Before long, different teenage members of the OCGs pulled up and greeted each other with their sacred handshake and threw up the OCG gang sign.

"A'ight OCGs, it's time," Abel called out as all the laughter and chatter stopped and all attention focused on him. He turned and pointed in my direction. "We have the lil' homies, Trei and Zion. They up. Y'all know what to do. Keep it clean. It's over when I call it."

Instinctively, Trei and I both shuffled backward, shifting our eyes around the other men as members of the OCGs began to circle around us. I'd hung out with many of them previously, but none of that mattered now. Right now, they eyed me and Trei as if we were members of the Greedy Grove Kingz, the rival gang to the OCGs.

Out of nowhere a swing came and connected with Trei before we knew it. Twisting around, Trei swung back, landing a blow of his own before two members jumped on him. Rather than stand there, I raced to Trei and pulled him up. My interference caused blows to land on me too as a few more members jumped in, landing haymakers on me and Trei. At that point, it was me and Trei for ourselves left to fight until the end of this initiation.

For a minute, I stood toe-to-toe landing blows on a few of the guys and holding my own, but when someone grabbed me from behind and slammed me, it was over. All I could do was cover myself in protection as stomps, kicks, and punches landed on my face, stomach, back and legs. I dared not ask for mercy. Mentally, I zoned out so that I could take the blows. It was no different than the ones I had absorbed at the hands of my mama's new live-in boyfriend, Calvin. The only difference was I felt a sense of acceptance and love from the OCGs that I never felt from him. They were my real family.

"That's enough," I heard Abel call out in the distance.

Instantly, the brutal beating stopped. Abel and his right hand, Dame, walked over to Trei and me. Dame helped Trei up and Abel helped me up. I was woozy as hell, and I could taste blood in my mouth. My ears were ringing, and my body was hurting from head to toe.

"You good, lil' homie?" Abel asked, standing in front of me as I struggled to focus. I stumbled backward, and he caught me. "Hey, hey. Easy. Try to focus," he directed. "You good?" he asked again as my eyes finally cleared up to where I could see him clearly.

I nodded slightly. "I'm good."

He walked me over to where Trei and Dame stood, and if Trei was any indication of how I looked, we were fucked up. Abel lifted two blue bandanas out of his pocket and handed one to me and Trei.

"To the newest members of the OCG, Trei and the lil' homie Zion!" Abel shouted out.

The rest of the members roared, throwing up the OCG gang sign as Trei and I did the same. Abel took the bandana from me and wrapped it around my head as Dame did the same to Trei and then all the members came up to each of us one by one, touched knuckles with us and showed us love by signaling with the gang sign again.

"Aye yo, Abel!" Big G, one of the older members, called out. "Real talk, lil' homie Zion got hands. Nigga knocked my back tooth loose with that uppercut."

Everyone laughed and agreed.

"Yeah, Juke's eye is swole shut," Dame added with a chuckle.

"Lil' homie caught me, for real," Juke laughed.

Abel patted my shoulder. "Respect, lil' homie." He turned to face me as everyone started going into the trap. "If you need a place to hang out for a few days until that bruising and swelling goes down, you welcome. This is your place now too. We got you, G."

Even though I knew I couldn't go home, I didn't want to stay there with them. I needed space to clear my mind. It's not like my mama would care anyway. She'd kicked me out two days ago for what seemed like the millionth time. I had been at Abel's, but I needed a break from the constant flow of traffic, stench of weed, sounds of sex, and smell of beer. I craved my peace.

Immediately, my mind went to Liberty. As much as I wanted to run to her, I knew that I couldn't go there either. Liberty would have my head about the initiation, and I couldn't risk being caught by her mother, brother, or that bastard Eugene. Freddie's spot was a no-go because his T-Jones was a stay-at-home mom, and second to my own mama, I didn't want to face her. And Freddie's dad was an electrician for the city and had a side hustle installing car speakers. He would always pull up at any given moment. Besides, I'd never bring my activity to their doorstep. They'd been too good to me, and Freddie—much like Liberty—was headed places. So, my mind went to my next best option. Pac-Man's house. His mama worked third shift so I could at least have a decent place to stay, shower, eat, and sleep.

"I'm going to head over to my boy's house. I'm good."

"A'ight. If you need me, you know how to get at me." Abel touched knuckles with me before we did the OCG handshake. "One."

"One."

I made the painful trek to Pac-Man's house. As my luck would have it, I couldn't stay there because his mama had switched shifts that week and would be home. While she was at work, Pac-Man let me hit the shower and gave me a change of clothes to wear. He told me he'd throw mine in with his to wash and bring to school for me. Pac-Man was an asshole to most people, but he always had my back. Aside from the OCGs and my homie Freddie, he and Lonnie were my family. I stayed for as long as I could, which was until eleven o'clock that night, and then headed out.

"Zion? What the hell?" Liberty whispered angrily as she eyed me up and down.

"Can you sneak me in? My mama kicked me out again a couple of days ago, and I can't go back there like this."

I stood outside of Liberty's bedroom window. She'd been asleep, and I'd woken her up by tapping on her glass with pebble rocks from the flower bed. I'd known she'd be upset, but I had nowhere else to go.

"Wait here," she said, and left her bedroom. A few minutes later she returned, moved the curtain out of the way, and lifted the blinds. "Everyone is asleep, so you have to be quiet."

After I climbed inside, I sat down on her beanbag in the corner of her bedroom. It was the first chance I had to see her in anything besides school clothes, and I seized the opportunity. She was looking so damn fine in pink cotton boy shorts and a matching tank top. My eyes roamed her body, but when my gaze met her face, I felt bad. She was worried out of her mind because she didn't know the truth.

"Who did you get into a fight with?" she asked, walking over and holding my face.

I shrugged away because even that slight touch ached. "Nobody."

The eye roll she gave me came before her words. "So, you swole up and blackened your own eye, busted your lip, and bruised up the side of your face?" She sighed. "Zion, you have bruises and cuts all over your hands and arms. Who did this to you?"

Her concern was so loving. She cared so much for me, and it pained me to tell her that Eugene was right. I'd hoped she'd leave it alone, but I should've known she wouldn't. My body went stiff as I braced myself for her wrath because I'd already promised myself that I wouldn't lie to her.

"Don't be mad at me, please."

Attitude. That's what was on her face in an instant. She folded her arms and pursed her lips. I knew then that this would not go over well with her.

"What did you do?"

The easiest way was to show her. I pulled out the blue bandana and fisted it. She took one look at the bandana and gasped, covering her mouth with her hands. Rather than go off as I'd thought she would, tears filled her eyes as she struggled to blink them away.

"No, Zion. Tell me you didn't."

I brought my hand to her face and wiped away the lone tear that trailed down her cheek. Putting my head down, I nodded. "I'm OCG now."

She snatched the bandana out of my hand and threw it at me. It hit me in the face as she stood, walked over to her bed, and plopped down.

"You lied to me."

"Liberty, I didn't lie." I looked at her with pleading eyes. "I never told you."

"We tell each other everything."

"I didn't tell you because you would've tried to stop me."

"That's what I'm supposed to do. You're better than that."

"It's not about that—"

"Yes, it is!"

"No, it ain't," I said a bit louder than I should have or wanted to. We glared at each other before I blew out a deep breath. "Liberty, my mama stays kicking me out. I'm thirteen. I can't get no job. I don't have nobody outside of Freddie, Pac-Man, Lonnie, and you. I need protection. I need money. I need a place to be where I can lay my head at night. I need to survive. I need OCG."

She sat there for a long time, casting her eyes between me

and the ceiling before she spoke again. "Why didn't you just tell me? I could've talked to Mama Jackie for you. I could've done something."

"You can't do everything and save everybody, Liberty. You shouldn't have to. I got me. I can take care of myself."

"That's not what your face says."

I sucked my teeth. "You know how it works. This was my only way in." I sat back on the beanbag and dragged my hands down my face. "If you gonna fuss at me, can you at least do it tomorrow? I'm hurtin', and I'm tired."

Liberty stood up and opened her walk-in closet. "Get up." I stood confused until she grabbed the beanbag and sat it inside the closet, then grabbed a blanket off her top shelf. "You can sleep inside my closet. If my mama gets up before I do and sees you in here, just know, she'll kill us both."

I walked over to her and kissed her left cheek. "Thank you."

She smiled up at me. "You're welcome."

She left the room as I settled on the beanbag, and when she reentered, she had an ice pack wrapped up in a towel in her hand. "For your face. I'd start with the eye first, so it doesn't close completely."

I accepted it. "Thank you, baby."

She tried to stop the smile, but the corners of her mouth turned upward. "You're welcome," she said before climbing into her bed. "Goodnight, Zion."

"Goodnight, Liberty."

―――――

The next morning, I was awakened by Liberty's sweet voice. "Good morning, sleepyhead."

With a yawn, I stretched and sat up. Immediately, I felt beat to hell. I winced from the ache in my rib cage. It was going to take all weekend for me to recover. At least today was Friday. I would just skip school and hang out with the crew.

"Good morning."

"How are you feeling?"

"Worse than yesterday."

"I'm sure. At least your eye isn't swollen. It's still black though. Your lip went down, but it's still busted, and the bruising is still there. But, you're alive, and that's all that matters."

"Yeah, I'm alive. My stomach hurts too though." She lifted my shirt to reveal a nasty bruise on my side. "I caught a few kicks."

"My mom has some bandages. I'll wrap you up." She handed me some sweatpants and a T-shirt. "You can change into these. They are Eugene's so I had to pray over them. But don't ever wear them again because I'm convinced that even prayers have an expiration date."

"Where is everybody?"

"Eugene took Mama to work, and then he's going to pay the light bill. And you know Justice has to be at school before me, so he's gone too. It's just me and you. Are you going to school today?"

"Naw." I shook my head. "Ima be with Abel and them."

"The OCGs, huh?" she asked, more as an attitudinal statement.

"Don't be like that."

Huffing, she waved me off. "Go shower so we can eat breakfast and leave before Eugene gets back."

With that, she handed me a washcloth and towel, and I headed to her shower. The warm water felt soothing to my aching muscles, and when I was done, I felt brand new. When I walked out into Liberty's bedroom, her mouth dropped open and she swallowed.

"Sorry, I left the clothes in here. I need some lotion and you were going to wrap my side."

Her eyes blinked rapidly before she lifted the bandages. "Yeah, sure. Yeah, uh, right," she stammered.

I laughed at her for being flustered for seeing me basically naked. The only thing shielding me was the towel wrapped around my waist. I waltzed over to her bed and sat down as she retrieved the lotion and handed it to me. She sat down beside me, quietly staring down at the floor while I lotioned my body.

"Can you lotion my back for me?"

Liberty's eyes shot up at me in shock. Instead of protesting or shying away, she took the bottle out of my hands and crawled behind me on the bed. I heard the squirt of the lotion and the thud of the bottle hit the bed beside me. The next thing I felt was her warm and trembling hands on my back. I leaned my head back so that our eyes met.

"You don't have to be nervous, Liberty. Nothing is going to happen." I smiled at her, but her face remained serious.

"What if... what if I want it to?" she asked softly. "I mean wanted something... to... happen."

Those words were music to my ears, but I couldn't risk it. She had to be in school, and I didn't know what her mama and stepdad's schedule was. Besides, I wanted our first time to be something special, not something we did on a whim. I couldn't do her like that. Not my Liberty. Even if I wanted to take her up on her offer.

I turned to the side and caressed her face with one hand. "Not now and not like this. One day, I'm gonna make you mine, and that moment will be special for both of us. I'm all beat up and hurt, and you have school. Now ain't the time. When that time comes, I promise you'll never forget it."

The sweetness of the moment drew us near, and as I stared into her beautiful eyes, I knew that there was no one else for me except her. Our faces pulled near each other, and when our lips met, I felt like my heart exploded. Ain't no way I could tell her what I was feeling, but at that moment, I *knew* it was love. Liberty had a brother messed up. The kiss grew deeper when I slipped my tongue inside her mouth. She jumped with surprise briefly before she gave into it, and our tongues danced with each other until we found our rhythm. I couldn't help it, and my hand found its way underneath her shirt to her breasts. I massaged a handful. When she moaned into my mouth, my man down below thumped with anticipation, and I broke off our kiss. Otherwise, I'd break my own promise and find myself in between her legs, fulfilling the urge.

"I think you should wrap my side so I can put these clothes on," I said to her, both of us panting heavily from our mutual heated emotions.

"You're right," she mumbled, then finished lotioning my back before she bandaged my side.

To my surprise, she brought me a plate of eggs, bacon, and toast with a glass of orange juice. I tore into the food like I hadn't eaten in years. I was happy to have a home-cooked meal. After I ate, I dressed, and it was perfect timing for Liberty to make it out of the door to catch the bus.

"I'll see you later, okay?" I said to her.

She nodded. "Be careful, Zion," she said nervously.

"I will." I leaned down and kissed her lips, and then I rolled out. It was time to go put this work in with my fam.

# CHAPTER 12

MY EYES FLUTTERED open to the sound of loud-playing gospel music. I rolled my eyes as old-school Lee Williams & the Spiritual QC's floated through the house. Not that I had an issue with gospel music, but rather I knew who was playing it. Eugene. To the outside world, he probably seemed like the most holier-than-thou person walking. God's human version of Gabriel. Instead, he was more like Lucifer. God's human version of a fallen angel. A converted demon. Straight from the pits of hell.

Kicking the covers off my feet, I planted them firmly on the floor as I made my way into the hallway to get ready for school. As I was about to cross the threshold, I heard what sounded like groaning and moaning coming from Mama's room. Everything inside of me told me to let it go and get dressed, but concern overwhelmed me. I found myself in front of Mama and Eugene's bedroom. I pushed the door open and peeked inside. Mama was holding her side, and her face had a fresh bruise on it. My feet took off toward her.

"Mama!" I squealed, seeing her face and visible pain. "What did he do to you?"

Her flailing hand motion signaled me to stay back. "It's nothing. It's all right. Get ready for school. Don't worry about me."

"Don't worry about you?" I snatched the handheld mirror off her nightstand before she could answer. "Have you seen your face?" I turned the mirror to her so she could see her reflection.

Without looking up, she huffed and fell back against the pillows. "It's going to be fine. We just had a little argument. I hurt myself trying to get my medicine."

My head snapped to the nightstand to see her diabetic medicine. I grabbed the insulin and held it in my hands. "I got you, Mama. Lift up your shirt."

Her eyes popped open, and she hesitated, giving me a cold stare.

My head cocked to the side. "Mama," I whined. "I know how to give you your meds. Lift your shirt."

When she didn't move, I launched forward to lift the shirt, and she swatted my hands away. I knew something was off then. For a few moments, I tried to lift the shirt, and she continued swatting my hands. On the last swat, I gripped her wrist and lifted her shirt slightly to see the bruise on the side of her stomach. Evidence that Eugene had escalated from slaps to punches.

"Oh, hell no, Mama!" I fumed.

"Let it go," she said firmly, staring me in the eyes.

"Mama, he knows you're a diabetic, and bruising is bad for you. Why would you let him do this to you? Why don't you kick him out?"

"You better lower your voice before he comes back here."

Defiantly, I folded my arms. "I don't care. He can't keep doing this to you. He keeps promising you he won't hit you again, and then he does it again. It's getting worse."

She flashed a stony expression my way that chilled my bones. It gave me pause, so I stepped back still with a slight attitude. It wasn't enough to test her but just enough to let her know that I was far from done with the subject.

"If you're gonna give me my shot then do that, but leave that other shit alone, Liberty. It ain't got nothing to do with you. Stay in a child's place and mind the business that pays you."

"But Mama—"

An irritated gasp left her mouth. "Girl, if you 'but Mama' me one more damn time…" she warned, allowing her words to taper off.

I motioned for her to lift her shirt after I released a frustrated sigh. She obliged, and I administered the insulin through a shot on the uninjured side of her stomach. After I was done, I discarded the needle and alcohol pads, and without another word, I headed toward the bathroom to get ready for school. The entire time I was getting dressed, I fumed over what Eugene had done to my mother. I'd never liked him anyway, and the fact that he was beating my mother and she was accepting it fueled my internal rage. She may have subscribed to his brand of bullshit, but I didn't. Hell, I flat out refused.

Deep down inside, I knew that the only reason my mother was putting up with his raggedy, no-good ass was because we needed the money. If I had to reach inside of myself and find one positive trait about Eugene, it was that he was solid about contributing his entire disability check to the household. Solid in the sense that our rent was paid and our lights stayed on, but we still struggled from month to month to make ends meet. It was why I was constantly thinking of opportunities to earn money. And at times when there wasn't an opportunity in reach—I created one. I sold snacks at school, bangle bracelets and mood rings, helped our elder neighbor pick up cans to recycle, and I even charged to create custom T-shirts with personalized sayings using iron-on letters. I did whatever I could to flip a profit so that I didn't have to ask Eugene or Mama for one red cent. And I only wished I could hustle enough to pay all of the bills, that way Mama wouldn't need Eugene, and we could be rid of him.

As I glanced at the alarm clock on my nightstand, I knew I wouldn't have time to eat at the house. I had been so inside my head with thoughts about Mama that I'd moved slower than I intended. I used the little time I had to finish up my hair and examine my outfit. I eyed my knotted T-shirt, acid-wash jeans, and ballerina shoes before securing one final colored scrunchy around my high ponytail. *Perfect,* I silently assessed with thoughts of Zion on my mind. He loved when I wore tight jeans.

With my book bag in tow, I made my way to the living room to head out to the bus stop when Eugene turned down the music which was now blaring out a Georgia Mass Choir song. He eyed me, and I eyed him as I turned the corner and headed toward the door.

"Your little sassy ass. And where you think you going with them tight-ass jeans on?"

Before I knew it, I turned on my heels and spewed, "Buy me some jeans then."

He flew off his La-Z-Boy before I could move a muscle. "Who the hell do you think you're talking to like that? I'm your father. I'm in charge. I'm the man around here."

"Act like one!"

The slap met my face before I realized it happened. My body crashed backward into the wall from the force of his hand, and I had to grab the edge of the wall to keep from falling over. The taste of blood filled my mouth as I brought trembling fingers to my lips. He had busted my lip. As I tried to catch my balance, I heard hurried footsteps scurrying down the hall.

"Eugene! Let her go to school. Please," my mother begged.

Tossing her an accusatory glance, he spat, "You're the reason she thinks she can talk to me like that. It's you! She around here hanging with that gangster-ass little boy and thinks she tough. I'll show both of y'all tough."

He went to take off his belt, and Mama yelled out, "Please! No, let her go to school. She's gonna miss the bus."

Justice, who had stayed home because he was sick, came scurrying out to the front and yelled, "No, Daddy, don't!" His short and athletic body was still tiny enough to maneuver past Mama and Eugene as he ran to me and wrapped his arms around my waist. I hated that he was witnessing this. He was used to his dad's hateful words, but he'd never witnessed him laying hands on us—until now.

Justice's presence must've been enough for Eugene to rethink the torture he was prepared to rain down because he paused before sucking his teeth and re-buckling his belt. He pointed in my face. "We ain't done with this conversation."

My chest heaved up and down as fire burned through me. After sliding Justice away from me with a reassuring pat on the back, I slapped Eugene's finger out of my face, and before he could react, I flung the front door open and rushed out, slamming it behind me.

The door opened as I reached the bottom step. "And don't you slam no goddamn doors around here. You don't pay a damn bill in this house. Ima deal with you when you get home, Liberty! You wait and see."

The front door slammed back as I continued down the block. Tears prickled at my eyes and stung as I struggled not to let them fall. All I wanted to do was to go to school, and I couldn't even do that in peace. Eugene had been a plague for years, but now, he was unbearable. Swiping at the tears that fell, I sucked up all of my emotions and bottled them up inside. I paced at the bus stop to try to ease my frustrations. I was pacing so much that I didn't even see Terica walk up to me. Her presence startled me, and I jumped, clutching my chest.

"'Sup, home skillet? What's got you twisted? Dang! What happened to your lip?" I tossed her a look that matched the level of anger consuming me. "Eugene… again? He stay trippin'!"

"'Trippin'' ain't even the word for him." Leaning forward, I whispered to Terica, "He punched my mama in the stomach and then slapped me when I got smart with him."

"Aw hell naw! Somebody needs to open up a can of whup-ass on him!"

"I want to tell Zion so bad, but I know if I do, he'll confront

Eugene."

"You should tell him then. When he sees your lip, he not gon'
let up until you tell him who hurt you anyway."

I stopped pacing and shook my head. "If I told him the truth,
he'd kill Eugene, and then I'd be responsible for him going to jail."

"It'd be jail time worth serving," she stated matter-of-factly.
"But I feel you."

Noticing the heated angst on my face, Terica reached out and
hugged me tightly. I melted into her. Although I was still pissed
off with Eugene and the entire situation with my mother, Terica
soothed the raging waters within me, at least enough to make it
through the school day.

"Thanks, Terica. I really needed that."

"We're best friends. And real homegirls hold each other down."

My grandma always told me the way your day starts is the way it
will end. I never knew what she meant by that until today. Ever
since my confrontation with Eugene that morning, nothing had
been going right for me that day. I lost one of my bracelets, my
shirt got ripped on the bottom from getting stuck on the door
of the restroom stall, I broke a nail, I got in trouble for talking in
second period—when it wasn't even me—and I failed a pop quiz.

On top of everything else, I hadn't seen Zion all day, which
wasn't like him at all. Usually, we met up at the lockers and had
lunch together. I knew he'd come to school because I saw when
Abel had dropped him off as I was going inside. I didn't have time
to go back and talk to him because I would've been late for class,
and I didn't have time for Mrs. Benson's talking-self to run off
to tell my Mama. For as populated as Dallas was, Mrs. Benson
seemed to know everybody personally, my mother included.
Unfortunately, she was my first-period teacher, so needless to say,

I was in bit of a funky mood.

"Let me borrow this right quick," Simone said, snatching a pencil off my desk.

I snatched it back before she could walk off. "Uhh, that's my pencil. Excuse you."

She turned back, rolling her eyes. "You have two other pencils on your desk, Liberty. You can let me hold one for this assignment. I lost mine."

"I could if you knew how to ask me."

Simone cocked her hip to the side. "You act like I stole your damn lunch money or something girl. It's a pencil. It ain't even worth all that." She rolled her neck.

"It's *my* pencil, and it's one you need. You need to ask like you need it," I spewed before turning back around and adding, "with your stuck-up ass."

A collective "oooh" sounded through the classroom.

"Simone, girl, I know you not gon' let Liberty dog you out like that!" one of her friends poked.

Today was not the day for Simone. I barely liked her as it was along with half the school. At least I could tolerate her, but she was pushing it with me. There was only so much of this bad day that I could and would take, and especially not from the likes of Simone Little.

She smacked her lips. "She just mad because Zion ignored her today."

"Ahh shit," Terica said around an exasperated sigh. "Let it go, Liberty."

I stood up and turned to face her.

"Girl, you think you're the only one for Zion," Simone said. "Please. Why you think he ain't been around you today?"

"You know so much, and you got so much to say then why don't you tell me why he wasn't around me today like he is every day?"

She laughed and walked up in my face. "'Cause he was with me." She smirked. "You ain't Zion's girl no more. You're only *one* of Zion's girls."

I had no clue what came over me, but the fact that she'd tried to take my pencil and I was already upset and having a bad day coupled with her claim to having been with Zion, it all pushed me over the edge. I snapped. My fist connected with her face before she could finish whatever else she was about to say.

"Oh snap!" I heard someone say. "Fight!"

It was more like a beatdown. I was on top of Simone so fast she couldn't even defend herself let alone fight back. I was on the floor clawing, punching, and snatching her like a rag doll. One of the PE coaches snatched me off her, and I barely realized who it was as I landed a kick to Simone's face when he lifted me.

"Enough!" he yelled. "Stop fighting!"

"She started it!" Simone screamed, crying and holding her face.

"You started it!" I yelled back, struggling to calm down.

"Both of you are going to the office," my teacher said as the coach marched us both down the hall into the principal's office.

As we made the walk of shame, other kids eyed us, and I could see the whispers. I knew the rumor mill was imminent. By the time we entered the office, I had no doubt that the talk of the town would be that Simone and I were fighting over Zion. That thought alone caused me to plop down in the chair to wait on the principal. I'd resolved that this was partially Zion's fault. While I didn't believe a word that came out of lying Simone's mouth, I couldn't help but feel that if Zion had met me like he'd normally done then it wouldn't have bothered me, and we wouldn't have ever come to blows. Well, I came to blows and she caught all of them, let her face tell it.

Sulking and slouching in my chair, I sat there in my thoughts until Vice Principal Walker's door swung open. I glanced over and saw Zion sitting in the chair in his office. He had a scowl on his face, and soon, I saw Mama Jackie and a police officer. I became nervous. Zion had been an OCG for a few months, and he'd been in and out of trouble already. I'd tried to talk to him about it but gave up because it was like talking to a brick wall. Still, we remained together, and he took care of his family and even me at times with whatever he did with the OCGs.

"And don't think I'm coming down there to visit you either," Mama Jackie fussed as she walked out before a man in a suit and the officer walked out with Zion in handcuffs.

My curious eyes turned to him, and he put his head down. His expression caused Mama Jackie to look in my direction. "Hey, Liberty," she said gruffly.

"Hi, Mama Jackie." I waved.

"Young man, you really need to get your life together. If not, you're headed to a long stay in prison. You don't want that, and your mother doesn't deserve it," Vice Principal Walker lectured before he shook the guy in the suit's hand.

"We'll keep you all abreast of the situation," the suited man informed the principal.

Zion looked into my questioning eyes and said, "I violated my probation."

"Yeah, and now his little badass is headed to juvy," his mother finished under the uncomfortable scrutiny of the vice principal.

My heart broke into pieces. I couldn't believe he was going to juvenile detention. There was no telling how long he was going to be there and when I would get the chance to see him again. What was worse was that I didn't have the opportunity to talk with him before he was sent away. It was the worst feeling in the world, except for getting summoned into the vice principal's office to find out I was suspended for five days because of my fight with Simone.

The ride home with my mother was a somber one. As expected, she'd ripped me a new one for the suspension and iterated and reiterated the laundry list of privileges that had now been stripped from me including not being able to see Zion. Normally, that restriction would've been the one that hurt the most, but I had information that she wasn't privy to. I wouldn't be able to see Zion anyway because he was locked up in juvy. There was no way I was going to divulge that information to her though. If she found out that he was locked up, then the punishment of not seeing Zion would become a permanent fixture.

"And I'm telling you right now, you better not fail one class. And don't think that just because you're at home for these five days that you get to chill. The house will be cleaned from top to bottom on the inside and out by the time you're done," Mama fussed as we pulled into the driveway. "When you get in, change clothes and start on that kitchen."

All this extra made me want to beat Simone again. I snatched my backpack out of the car and ran up the front steps with my house key. I didn't want to wait on her, I wanted to go straight to my room, change, and get started. As soon as I opened the door, the impact of a hard slap sent me crashing into the wall so hard that my head bounced off it, and I fell to the floor.

"So, you want to end up like that good-for-nothing thug, huh!" Eugene yelled. "You ain't 'bout shit!" He snatched me up by my arm.

"Let me go!" I screamed, trying to jerk away from him.

My futile attempts were no match for his strength. He gripped me by both arms and turned me, slamming me into the wall like a rag doll. My back arched with pain before he slammed me again. "Who the fuck do you think you're talking to? That's your damn problem." He pointed in my face, mushing my forehead with his forefinger. "But I'm about to teach your little fast and disrespectful ass a lesson."

He unbuckled his belt and slipped it off as my mother entered the house. "Eugene!" she cried out. "No, stop!"

Her words startled him as he flung the belt backward, knocking her in the jaw with the buckle instead of it striking me. The shrilling screech that emanated from Mama caused me to clasp my ears with both hands.

From the corner of my eye, I could see Justice running toward us, but this time, the situation was too dangerous. I didn't want him to get hurt. I put my hands out, halting him.

"No, Justice. Stay back!"

Eugene was so enraged he didn't even pay attention to me or Justice.

"If you stayed your dumb ass out of the way, it wouldn't have happened!" Eugene boomed. He looked at me. "A disobedient child's days will be short," he cursed, before rearing back to strike me with the belt. Mama caught it in her hand.

"That's enough goddamn it!"

Staring into his face seemed as if I was peering into the soul of the devil. His chest heaved up and down and sweat poured profusely from his face. His rage was off the Richter scale. "Lucille, I'm only going to say this one time: let… it… go!"

"No, Eugene. She's already been punished. She has to clean the kitchen. Let her go and serve the punishment I gave her."

The scoff that Eugene released was sinister. He flicked his nose and turned to face her. "Punishment that you gave her. *You?* You're the reason she's running around doing God knows what now." He pointed to himself. "I'm the man of this house and I've sat back too long. You're gonna let me discipline her unruly ass, or I'm just gonna have to whip both of you!"

He went to snatch the belt from her hand, and she gripped it in place. The anger seemed to bolt through Eugene like a jolt of electricity. "Bitch!" he roared before jerking the belt forward. The movement yanked my mother off her feet and she slammed into him.

"Daddy! Please stop!" Justice yelped with tears in his eyes.

A sense of primal fear invaded my body, and all I could think about was our safety, beginning with my baby brother. "Justice, go back to your room! Now!" I demanded. His feet took off in the opposite direction toward his room.

Without warning, Eugene threw Mama back into the corner by the door. As my mother tried to maintain her balance, she let the belt go, and instead of coming for me, he charged forward toward her.

"I told you to let me deal with it. Didn't I? Now, you're gonna get it!" he yelled, spittle flying from his mouth into her face.

The crack of the belt slashed into my mother's face with a force that snapped her head back into the door. It split her face, and blood poured from the cut and mixed with the tears that poured out of her eyes. She wailed out in bloodcurdling screams that shook my fear-frozen stance. It was as if a switch had flipped, and my soul felt like it was astral-projecting itself. I knew I was moving, but I couldn't stop myself or grasp what was happening fully. All I knew was that somewhere amidst the beatdown being issued against my mother, I'd moved to her bedroom and retrieved what I was searching for from her nightstand.

*BOOM!*

The sound rang out like a cannon amid Eugene's and my mother's screams.

*BOOM!*

A second shot rang out, and a wounded Eugene was gripping his thigh as my mother propelled from her huddled position over to me as if Eugene hadn't been beating her to a bloody pulp.

"Liberty!" Mama shouted as she approached me, holding my hand. "Give me the gun, sweetie." She lifted a hand to my cheek as fear danced in her eyes.

Her touch brought me back to reality, and my body began shaking. Slowly coming back to the moment, I realized what I'd done, and the fear that was in Mama's eyes gripped me. She snapped into mommy mode and slid the weapon from my hands and held me close to her bosom.

"Did I kill him?" My teeth chattered as I nervously asked the question.

"Hell no! You didn't kill me, but you should've!" Eugene shouted angrily, wincing in excruciating pain.

My mother turned to face him and shot the gun right above his head, rendering him speechless. She turned to me, cupping the side of my face with her free hand. Her slight head nod and slowed breathing were an unspoken directive to mimic her calmness. We fell into a single rhythm.

"Go and pack your clothes and call your grandma. Do the same for Justice. Y'all going over there." The look she gave me garnered my complete attention. "Listen to me. You and Justice were over at your grandma's the entire time. I dropped you off over there with her and Justice after you were suspended. You were never here."

"But—"

She snatched my chin and gripped it in place. "Listen to me. You were with your grandma the entire time. You don't know what happened here. You were there the entire time."

Nodding, I took in what she'd said and, more importantly, what she was doing. Alibi. She was giving me a way out so that she could take the blame for what happened to Eugene. My soul hurt because I didn't want my mother to get in trouble, especially for something I'd done. However, I knew she'd never let me take the fall for what occurred, and there was no use fighting her about it. She was protecting me as only a mother would. Protecting my future.

Without another word, I took off for the phone and called grandma, then packed my bag and Justice's bag, and got him dressed as instructed. Eugene lay on the floor yelling at my mother to get him help and cursing me the entire time. When my grandma arrived, I rushed Justice to our grandma's car so he didn't have to witness too much of what happened. Then I ran back into the house to gather my things.

Reentering the house, the pit of my stomach lurched. It felt like I'd walked upon a murder scene; there was so much blood. My senses suddenly went into autopilot. As my mother finished explaining what had happened to my grandma, Eugene sat there groaning in pain, and I watched, gripping my book bag and suitcase, terrified into complete silence. All I could focus on was my mother's lips moving and my grandma's head bobbing. Reality didn't snap back into focus until I felt my grandma's hand ushering me toward the door. Before we left, she turned around, giving Eugene a stare so threatening that he probably wished I would've killed him so he wouldn't have to face her wrath.

"God rules over the just and the unjust. Your sins finally caught up to you, I see," she sneered at him. I could tell he wanted to attack her, but all he could do was grit his teeth as perspiration from the agony sheened his forehead. "Since you like to Bible-thump, lemme put this on yo' spirit... '*you live by the sword, you die by the sword.*' Remember that 'fore you think 'bout spreading lies about my grandbaby."

Eugene's eyes widened as big as mine behind my grandma's direct threat, and without another word, she wasted no time hauling me to the car.

As we sped off down the street, my fear shifted from me to

Mama. After grandma's threat, I doubted Eugene would go against the grain because everybody knew that when Sadie Pearle spoke, she meant it. That bit of peace did nothing to quell the anxiety I felt over Mama.

Finally finding my voice, I mumbled, "Will Mama be okay?"

She patted my knee with one hand without breaking her focus on the road. "Let's hope so, Liberty."

# CHAPTER 13

*August 18, 1995*

"MAN, SLOW DOWN when you turning!" Zion yelled as I zipped through the streets.

Shaking my head, I said coolly, "I've got this."

"A'ight... *you got this*... flip my shit over and have us both fucked up, Liberty."

The song on the radio served as the perfect distraction for Zion's niggling. Besides, many things were on my mind. At the top of that list was my mother. It'd been five months since the incident with Eugene. My mother took the rap for me as she promised. Surprisingly, Eugene took heed of my grandma's warning and did not try to implicate me. With gunpowder residue on Mama's hands and witness statements from her, my grandma, and me all corroborating the same story, they sewed it up as an open and shut case. Both Eugene and Mama were arrested for a domestic dispute and disorderly conduct. My worst fears came true when Mama's charges were upgraded from disorderly conduct to assault with a deadly weapon.

Mama's only card was the one she led with when the police had arrived at our house—self-defense. Since the police had been out to our home on previous calls, the investigators were inclined to believe her version of events. To help her case, she'd filed charges against Eugene for abuse to ensure the self-defense theory would hold up before the courts. For once, her war wounds worked in her favor. As Sadie Pearle would always say, "God will make your enemy your footstool." I'd never understood that until then. One look at Mama's face and all the stitches she'd needed, and the state dropped all charges against my mother and pressed formal charges against Eugene. Simple battery. It wasn't enough to keep him in jail long term, but it was enough to give Mama time to get her life together so she could get away from him when he returned.

Throughout that entire ordeal, I stayed with my grandma. A better neighborhood by all accounts. To visit my friends, I had to trek across town on two different bus transfers, but it was all good if I had the opportunity to be away from the belly of the hood and the threat of Eugene. Things got better once Zion was released from juvy by the end of summer. Part of the reason I'd hop to the hood was to check on his mother and so that we could talk on the phone. A couple of times Mama Jackie took me to the detention center to visit him without Mama or grandma's knowledge. She felt guilty for doing so, but between Zion's pleas and my own, she gave in twice. That was it though. We had to learn to deal with being satisfied with each other's voice until his release.

Although I missed my old neighborhood, my grandma did allow me to continue going to my current school. She'd either take me, or I'd pretend to catch the city bus and let Zion pick me up for school. We were very careful about that because if my grandma caught me, anything Eugene ever did to me would pale in comparison to the punishment that she would dish out.

At any rate, that day was one of those days Mama was on my mind heavily. I missed her. I missed the hood. I didn't miss living there, but I felt displaced like a fish out of water. I knew Mama longed to have me back in her custody again. We both needed it. I just didn't know if it would ever happen again. Grandma didn't play no games about me, not even with her own child.

"I'm not trying to explain to your grandmother why you were in a car accident. You know Ma Pearle is a thug," Zion joked.

His joke brought me back into the moment, and I couldn't help but snicker. Zion could pretend he was worried about an accident all he wanted. We both knew that was a lie. He just didn't want to get caught teaching me how to drive because neither one of us was of the age to drive and because his mom would literally kill him if he damaged her Buick Regal. He loved her '88 Regal Turbo-T so much you'd think it was his, but I understood that. But man, how could you not speed a little bit in a Turbo-T.

"You're just trying to look fly in front of your little friends in the eighth grade, but we ain't gon' look fly on a stretcher. Slow your little cute ass down."

A grin spread across my face. "So, you think I'm cute, huh?" I asked, ignoring the rest of his little lecture.

He huffed and leaned back in his seat. "You already know this. Stop trying to change the subject." I came up to the red light and he leaned over and buried a kiss in the crook of my neck. "I actually think you're fucking gorgeous."

My breathing nearly stopped at Zion's touch. My hormones were going bananas, and it didn't help when he did things like that. I was trying my best to hold on to my virginity, but I could also see the pressure building in Zion.

To make matters worse, we had to sneak around since his mother kicked him out. Zion was in the ninth grade and one of the youngest members of the OCGs. When Mama Jackie found out that he was affiliated, she bounced him right up out of her house, but not before her boyfriend Calvin went a couple of rounds with him over it. I don't believe he cared about Zion's affiliation seeing as how he'd never treated him like a son, but rather it was an excuse for him to lay hands on him again.

For the time being, I lived with grandma. The first couple of nights, I was able to sneak him into the house so that he could stay. After that, he'd been staying between Lonnie and Pac-Man's house. The key was trying to keep him out of Pleasant Grove and far away from the Greedy Grove Kingz' territory. Other nights, he crashed at an unknown spot with some of the OCG crew. He and his mother were on better terms, mostly because he wasn't under her roof. It was hard on us, but we stayed connected and we met up wherever we could, every chance we got.

Zion fell back on his side of the car once the light turned green, but his hand found its way to the apex of my legs and his finger glided in between, against my jeans. With his head leaned back and his eyes closed, he hissed, "Libertyyyy."

To calm the sexual tension between us, I leaned forward and turned up the volume on the radio.

"'*Back in elementary, I thrived on misery,*'" I rapped along to Tupac's latest banger, "So Many Tears," throwing a glance over at Zion.

"Hell, I'm in misery now," he fussed as he moved his hand and massaged his temples.

"Come on, babe, you know you like this song. Show me those skills." I jogged my eyebrows and rocked my head to the beat.

"'*Is there a heaven for a G? Remember me… shed so many tears.*'" He bopped his head to the beat as we fell into a rhythm together.

Just like that, the moments before were forgotten as we continued our ride to my school, blasting Tupac and rapping the lyrics like we were performing at the Coliseum.

As we pulled up to the school, my friends Terica and Shaneria met us at the car. Zion and I both got out, and he hugged and kissed me before dapping Terica and Shaneria up and leaving. As soon as I turned to face my girls, they went in on me, of course.

"Look at Zion teaching his boo thang how to drive the whip!" Terica jived. "When are you going to take me for a spin?"

"Girl, when I get a license! I'm crazy, but I ain't that crazy!"

Shaneria fanned her hands. "That's when you better take her for a ride. You nor Zion ain't got no business driving anyway."

Before I could even respond, Terica gave me that I-told-you-so look. Shaneria was my girl. We'd been cool as long as me and Terica, in fact, all of us had, but sometimes, she was so negative. It was like she always had an issue with anything that anybody else was doing if she wasn't benefitting from it. Terica and Shaneria's relationship had demised a long time ago because Terica had maintained that Shaneria seemed a bit shady to her as we grew older, but I chalked it up to the fact that they were different. They were both my friend, so off the strength of me, they remained cool with each other.

"Dang Shaneria, what's up with you? Are you the po-po are something?" I asked, trying to joke, but deep down, I was a little perturbed by her comment.

Sneering, she lifted her eyebrows, stunned. "You buggin'! You know I ain't nobody's snitch. I'm just saying. You act like I'm telling you something wrong."

Sensing the comeback, I gripped Terica's forearm. Her mouth opened and closed, and she waved her hand in the air as if she were sending up praises. "Girl!" she dragged out, then leaned close to me. "That's *your* friend." She shook her head in irritation. "I'm gonna catch up with y'all later. 'Cause I cannot!" With that, Terica sashayed off with her short denim skirt swishing from side to side.

Shaneria snapped her head around. "Whatever! With that fake hair in her head. She's always got something to say about somebody."

"Yo chill, Sha." Her feet stopped moving, and I knew she was gawking at me for intervening on her little diss she was about to spit on Terica, but I wasn't about to have that. Shaneria and I were cool, but I felt a way about what she said which was directed toward me. There was no way she was about to talk junk about Terica when Terica was only trying to have my back. "Y'all might not get along, but Terica is my friend, and her hair is real."

"And I'm not your friend?"

Groaning, I snapped, "You know you are, and you know that's not what I meant. I just want my friends to chill."

As she began to walk again, she admitted, "You're right. My bad."

Just like that, all was forgiven, even if it wasn't forgotten. It was our last year in middle school, and all I wanted to do was enjoy our "senior" year and my friends. They could save that drama for their mamas. It was not in my forecasted future. Next year, we'd be high schoolers at the bottom of the totem pole, so this year called for us to parlay! Heck, we'd earned it.

The rest of the day had been pretty copacetic. The teachers didn't pour a ton of work on us, there were no fights, and everybody, in general, got along. In the words of Ice Cube, today was a good day. It was so good, in fact, that I couldn't wait for Zion to pick me up so that we could hang out. The last thing I wanted to do was go home and be holed up at my grandma's house all weekend.

Despite all that had happened, Eugene was right back in the house with Mama and Justice, and back to his same old dirty tricks. In fact, Eugene's antics had finally taken a toll on Mama. Like him, she'd succumbed to heavy drinking and smoking. Unlike Eugene, it was not good for her to indulge. Besides the fact that she couldn't hold her liquor, her body couldn't withstand it either. Mama suffered severely from chronic asthma and diabetes, or "the sugars" as my grandma called it. Eugene didn't suffer from anything except being the world's greatest loser, so whereas he could possibly withstand all the poison he was pushing into his body, mama could not. With a man like Eugene around, who could blame her for needing a crutch to make it through the day? And I didn't blame her because I knew firsthand the stress that Eugene could impart, but I wanted better for her because I saw her slipping, and there was nothing I could do about it. Hence why I was in no rush to get back to my grandma's crib. I wanted to keep an eye on Mama.

"You're not riding the bus?" Terica asked me as I met up with her outside after school.

"Nah, Zion is gonna come scoop me up." I tapped her arm, thinking of an idea. "Hey, you wanna ride? We could go and hang out at Big D Bazaar."

"I wanna hang out!" Shaneria's voice and body plowed into me with a soft thud, making me hop a few steps to keep my balance.

"Yo' crazy self almost knocked me off the curb," I fussed, before playfully bumping her with my hip. Suddenly, Zion pulled up. "Sure, you can come with us." I turned to look at Terica as the late buses filed in. "You coming?"

Looking back and forth between Shaneria and me, she shook her head. "Nah, I'm goody."

Zion jumped out of the car and tapped the roof. "'Sup, Sha, Terica! Hey babe! Let's roll out before I get stuck behind these buses."

Throwing my finger up to give me a sec, I eased up to Terica. "She's not gonna act a fool on you. I already handled that. You can come with us. Lonnie might be there," I said, trying to coax her with the presence of the Bizzy Bone look-alike aka Lonnie.

She laughed at the Lonnie portion of the comment and waved her hands. "Girl, you go and have fun. I promise. I'm good."

For some reason, I wanted Terica to come with me. The internal tug felt more like a need rather than a want. So rather than accept her answer, I pressed once more. "Are you fo' sho' fo' sho'?"

"I'm sure!" she said with exasperation as she pushed me toward Zion's car. "You better hurry up too. Don't leave that chick alone with your man for a second," she half joked, referring to the fact that Shaneria had already made her way to the car and was waiting on me along with Zion. For someone who was against underaged driving, she was the first to hop in the car.

We made silly faces at each other. "Girl, stop it. You're a mess." Briefly turning to face her, I pulled her into a quick hug. "A'ight. I can't force you. I'll call you later, okay?"

"A'ight. Later!" She threw up the peace symbol with her fingers before jogging to our bus. "Peace out!"

We went to eat ice cream and were met with Lonnie and Pac-Man as well as some of Zion's OCG crew. I hated that he was affiliated but what could I do? I'd been upset when I first found out because Zion was better than that. However, he needed a reminder that he had people outside of OCG who loved and wanted the best for him, so I didn't stay angry too long. I had to love him through this, and hopefully he'd one day get the courage to walk away. Until then, I was riding with him until the wheels fell off. We all hung out and had one of the best times of our lives. I felt horrible that Terica wasn't there to enjoy the day.

As promised, later that night, I called Terica, and she didn't answer. When she hadn't called back in a decent amount of time—thirty minutes, to be exact—I called her back. In fact, I called her repeatedly to no avail. By now, I figured she was upset with me for allowing Shaneria to tag along, so I stopped calling. That was a stupid reason to ignore me, but I guessed that once she was over it, she'd hit my line, and when she did, I was going to let her have it. We were the best of friends, so we'd argue, and then it would be like nothing ever happened, so I wasn't worried.

The rest of the weekend was uneventful, but now, I was a little bit peeved that my best friend hadn't attempted to call me all weekend. I knew she didn't care for Shaneria, but this silent treatment was way beyond uncalled for. I could barely wait until I got to school so I could give her a piece of my mind. When I got to school and Terica wasn't there, I grew concerned. I couldn't concentrate all day, and no one had seen or heard from her since

Friday. I decided not to ride with Zion after school that Monday. Instead, I rode the bus to Mama's house and hightailed it up the block until I reached Terica's house. After what seemed like an eternity, Terica finally answered the door. *Oh, she's sick,* was the first thought through my mind gathered from her appearance. She wore sweats and a robe tied tightly around her with flip-flops. Her hair was up in a headscarf and her face looked like she hadn't slept in weeks.

"Hey girl. I wanted to check on you," I said softly as she backed away from the door and started walking back to her bedroom.

She didn't say anything, only kept walking. I followed her, remaining quiet because this was not at all my best friend. By the time we got to her room, I shut the door and before I could sit down good, she jumped up, ran to the door, and locked it. That's when I knew something wasn't right.

"What's wrong?"

Those words set off an avalanche of tears. I had no clue what to do. Once the water spigot was turned on, it was like it was unstoppable. I felt horrible because I didn't know what was wrong, or how I could help. I'd do anything to help.

Reaching over, I wrapped my arm around her shoulder and brought her against me. "Terica, whatever it is, it'll be all right. We've made it through so much, and we'll get through this."

Terica snatched away from me. "No, we won't. You haven't been through this. You don't know what this feels like!" she seethed.

"Well, let me help you through it then. I can't do that if I don't know what it is."

Terica swiped the tears from her eyes. Her hands trembled uncontrollably as she pulled her robe tighter to her chest. Emotions gripped her and it was as if she transported back in time. Head-shaking, lip-quivering, and body-quaking overtook Terica as I climbed in the bed, sat behind her, and held her. For what seemed like hours, all I could do was rock my friend in my arms as she wailed and I whimpered. Repeatedly, I whispered in her ear, "I got you." The weight of her sorrow was so heavy that my body was tired. Still not knowing what had happened, I did all I could to assure her that I was there, and I was never letting her go.

"I should've gone with you." The words drifted out of her mouth so softly I barely heard what she'd said.

"What?" I asked, completely confused. "What are you talking about?"

"Friday," she answered simply.

My heart dropped instantly. Something in my spirit had kept telling me that she needed to be with me. Droplets pooled at my lids. *Please don't let nothing have happened to her on Friday.* It was a vain request. Even as the thought came to my mind, I knew whatever was going on with Terica had taken place on Friday evening.

With a shaky voice, I asked the inevitable. "What happened on Friday?"

There was a long pause before she spoke again. The pause let me know that whatever she was about to divulge to me was something that she may not ever recover from. In that moment, I vowed that whatever Terica needed from me, she had it.

"My mom's brother... the one who be in and out of here sometimes..." She glanced up at me, and I gestured, letting her know that I knew who she was referring to. "He... uhh... he... he... he was over here 'cause he'd lost his job, and he was drunk and he... uhh... he..."

I couldn't stop shaking my head if I tried. I couldn't believe it. Not that I didn't believe what she was about to say, but I couldn't believe that it had happened to her, and by her *uncle*? No. This could not be true. *Please, God, say it's not true.*

With her head bowed, she confirmed my worst fear. "He raped me." The floodgates opened again as she tried to explain. "I tried to fight him. Tried to remind him of who I was. He said that I was fast. Wore all those short skirts. Said my hair smelled like flowers. Said my skin felt like satin. Cotton candy. He said I smelled like cotton candy." Her words came out jagged between gusts of breaths and sobs.

Climbing down off the bed, I kneeled in front of her and gripped her shoulders. My tears were clouding my own eyes as I pleaded with her. "You have to tell your mother. She'll fix this. She'll get his ass locked up. She won't let him do this to you and get away with it."

The stoniest expression I'd ever seen in my life reflected back at me, and it caused me to shut up in an instant. "I did," she bit out. "She told me not to say anything. Not to go to the police. That she and my grandma would deal with him. She took me to the hospital, and they gave me an exam. She lied and said it was some random man on my way home from the bus. No description. I got pain pills and was discharged. She said I needed a couple of days off school to feel better. He's at grandma's house. Told her he'd never do it again. And now…" She couldn't finish from being overcome by tears.

I could've been knocked over with a feather. How could her mother do this to her? This was her child. I was devastated, but not like Terica. Never like Terica. All I could do was grab her and hold her again. There were no words of comfort that I could possibly give when her own mother had discarded her feelings like yesterday's trash.

"But I'm not fast. I'm a virgin. *I'm a virgin*," she whimpered. "I'm not fast."

I held her face in my eyes and agreed. "I know. I know. You're not fast. I know." She nodded with me and then fell apart in my embrace.

We stayed like that for hours. We stayed like that for so long that even Zion called to check on me after my mother finally reached out to him to inquire about my whereabouts. I decided that I needed to leave before grandma and Mama put a missing person's report out on me. There was no way I could let Terica's secret get out. I didn't want to make matters worse for her. She didn't deserve that. She didn't deserve any of this. My poor Terica. Reluctantly, I left, and I'd never felt more lost in my life.

# CHAPTER 14

*October 24, 2014*

MY PHONE CHIMED, and I smiled at the text I'd received from Terica. She wanted to link up for family introductions. My family and hers. The thoughts of her family made me reflect on who her family was. She had a whole wife out here. I accepted her new lifestyle, but I couldn't help but remember a time before her change. Would she have still led the same path had it not been for what happened with her uncle? Her incident had even impacted me. It had forced me to switch up how I approached relationships. I'd even second-guessed Zion's sexual advances behind what happened to her. How could I not? Intimacy on any level was a sensitive subject to me after what my best friend had endured. I remembered the time that I revealed my trust issues to Zion. That conversation had led to the beginning of the next phase in our relationship. The grown phase.

---

*August 11, 1996*

Ever since I'd learned of Terica's rape, it'd affected me. Sex was the most intimate act, and it should be shared with someone special. Her opportunity to experience it the right way with the right person had been stripped from her. The thought of someone doing that to me ran rampant in my mind. It made the mere mention of sex highly uncomfortable. The desire I once held to experience this moment was stripped from me through Terica's pain. In essence, I was walking this lonely path with her. When I said I was walking it, I meant that in the most literal of terms. I could barely kiss Zion without Terica's ordeal running through my mind. With Zion not knowing what was going on, it drove him completely insane. He never pressured me for anything physical, but he wasn't used to the way that I'd been withdrawing from him.

Also, those words that Simone had spoken still sat with me, all this time later. No doubt fueled by what happened to Terica. *"You're only one of Zion's girls."* I wasn't naïve. Zion's caramel complexion, honey-hazel eyes, LL Cool J lips, and muscular build had many of these young girls—and older ones too—doing whatever to get a piece of him. My concern was if he was taking the bait. We were as close as ever but there was a part of him that was now closed off from me. The OCG side. He didn't want me involved nor did I want to be so I understood, but for as long as I could remember, Zion and I had shared everything until we didn't. He still had total access to all things Liberty, but me, not so much. A part of me felt that there was now a part of him that I no longer knew and what bothered me most was that he seemed okay with that. In fact, he seemed *comfortable* with that. It was that comfort level that caused doubt. If he was comfortable with me not knowing certain aspects of his life, then what other parts of his life was he comfortable with me not knowing?

That feeling was never more prevalent than when I entered my freshman year and enrolled in the magnet high school I had been banking on attending with my real friends. It was my first day. The big ninth grade. The only difference was I was now back living with Mama—who'd finally divorced Eugene.

In middle school, I was the quintessence of everything being bigger and better in Texas. But in high school, I was simply average.

Most of the girls, especially the older ones, looked like grown women. Breasts, hips, and ass slung from the left and swished to the right in skintight jeans. Zion had been exposed to all that temptation for a full year without my presence and that reignited that old fear that Simone had set ablaze back in middle school. How could I compete with these girls when everyone seemed to be vying for Zion's attention?

Negative thoughts danced around in my head as I waited in the quad for Zion like we'd discussed. When it was almost time for the bell to ring, I went in search for him inside by my locker to no avail. He hadn't hit my pager at all to let me know what was up, and I was both worried and pissed off.

"Hey girl. I was looking for you," Terica said, falling into the lockers beside me. "What's wrong?"

Throwing my book bag into my locker, I released a frustrated sigh. "Girl. It's Zion. He's MIA."

"Liberty, it's our first day. Don't worry about no Zion," Terica fussed, rolling her eyes. "Bump all dat!"

I turned to face her, and my eyes nearly popped out of me head. "Your hair!" I screeched. "Terica, you cut your hair?"

Patting the T-Boz inspired hairdo, she agreed. "Yeah, I needed a change. So whatcha think?"

Spinning her around and side to side for inspection, I squealed, "I love it!"

"Thank you." She smiled. "Just a little something something new."

"Speaking of, I wish Zion was here. I wore my favorite new outfit, and he hasn't seen my new hairdo. It's just like him to kill my grand moment."

Terica cast sorrowful eyes at me and then clapped her hands together. "Work the runway, girl. You better show me that 'fit and those shoes."

Giggling, I walked three strides in front of her, modeling off my Mary J. Blige-inspired baseball jersey with a matching skort, bamboo earrings, and combat boots. My two fishtail-braided ponytails completed the look. Terica followed suit, showing off her jean overall shorts with a bold orange T-shirt and combat boots. Our styles made it appear as if we were about to grace the cover of *Vibe* magazine as she matched my fresh. We slapped high fives just before the bell rang, signaling that we had exactly five minutes to spare before the late bell caught us. Since we didn't have the same homeroom teacher, we walked with each other until Terica had to break off in the opposite direction to her classroom, and I walked into mine.

The rest of the day was eventful. They tried to make the first day hype for the freshmen. The fanfare was exactly what the doctor ordered to take the edge off being the newbies. I wish I could say that I enjoyed it as much as I would've wanted. The fact was I couldn't. Zion hadn't shown up on the first day of school, and I had no idea what had happened to cause him to skip. I didn't know whether to be nervous or upset. So, I stayed in limbo the entire day, zoning in and out of the happenings surrounding me, because while it was a memorable and enjoyable moment, it wasn't special without having Zion to share it with.

After school, Terica, Pac-Man, Lonnie, Shaneria, Unique, and I stood around the bus loading zone, talking and tripping out about our first day in high school. Our bus was late as usual, so we had a little time to kill, joking and freestyling among ourselves. I was in the middle of them, about to spit a hot sixteen, when I felt arms wrap around my waist and scoop me off my feet. Bellows of laughter rang out as I started to swing. The culprit held my arms in place and whispered in my ear.

"Stop wildin' before these teachers think I did something to you."

That voice. The one that made my heart go pitter-patter. The one that I'd longed to hear all day. The one that made my blood boil because I'd had to spend my entire first day of high school without his solace. He placed me back down on my feet, and I spun around and swung on him anyway. The hit landed on his arm, and he rubbed the pain away, eyeing me in disbelief. He deserved it for scaring the life out of me and for missing my first day.

I narrowed my eyes to slits and pursed my lips. I was faking the funk on the outside, but internally, I was mush. He held the keys to my heart, and I didn't think he realized it.

"Come on, Liberty," Zion ordered, reaching for my hand. Irritation ruined his handsome facial features.

"Where have you been, Zion?" I pressed.

"Lovers' quarrel," Pac-Man joked, trying to bring lightheartedness to the moment. "Gon' kiss the man and quit trippin'. You know you want to."

I turned and glared at him, then rolled my eyes. "Shut up, Pac."

He threw his hands up and backed away as a show that he was out of it. Shaneria, Unique, and Lonnie recoiled in a corner together and Terica rubbed my back.

"Calm down, girl," Terica whispered calmly. "Go see what your man wants. Don't be making no scene out here, especially in front of these vultures."

Zion's patience was wearing. I scoffed before relenting. Grabbing my backpack, I stormed off in the direction that he'd tried to take me. He fell in step with me and reached for my hand again. I pulled away before he could grasp it and folded my arms as we continued to walk toward the parking lot.

"Hurry up, before I miss my bus."

"You know good and well I'm taking you home."

I stopped in the middle of the parking lot. "I'm not getting in the car with you."

He walked up to me so that we were face-to-face. "Listen, I've been through a lot of bullshit today. I'm entertaining all yo' rah-rah because I deserve it, but Ima need you to pipe it down. This…" He fanned between him and me. "It ain't us. Don't let these hood hos at this school gas you up."

My head snapped back. The arrogance. It was a characteristic I loved and hated about him. Right now, it wasn't working in his favor and only served to set my attitude ablaze. "'Gas me up'? The only person that's gassing me right now is you."

Zion swiped a hand down his face, and before I could say another word, he gripped me about my waist and delivered a tender kiss to my lips. It wasn't long. It wasn't nasty or overtly sexual. It was just right. Sweet. Soft. Gentle. Enough to take the sting out of my disappointment in him and the steam out of my kettle. Yeah, that kiss brought my boiling waters back down to a slow simmer. The power of Zion.

Casting my eyes downward, I bit my lip and shook my leg. Zion's laugh was sinister. He knew what he'd done, and he relished in the effect he had over me. He offered me his hand and I accepted without hesitation. He led me to a souped-up Caprice.

"Whose car is this?" I asked, pausing to enter when he opened the door.

"Don't worry about whose car it is. Just get in."

The neck roll was immediate. "Uhh, whose car?"

"My man's, Abel." He huffed. "Can you please get in now?"

Reluctance washed over me, but still, against my better judgment, I slipped into the passenger seat of the car. Once I was tucked away inside, Zion closed the door and then placed my book bag in the back seat of the whip before walking to the driver's side and getting in. Cranking up the car, he peeled out of the school parking lot as we rocked out to the hip-hop tunes of UGK.

"I'm sorry about today."

Cutting my eyes over at him, his face was focused on the road, but his eyes were filled with something. It appeared to be a mixture of worry, frustration, anger, and, most of all, sadness. With his elbow propped on the armrest of the driver's side door, his forefinger rubbed his temple as he steadied the car with his right hand on the steering wheel. Whatever was eating at him was on his mind heavily. That was the only thing that made me soften toward him. It was his way of saying he didn't mean to stand me up on this day. Warmth covered my heart and chipped at the iceberg that had been building around it all day.

"Why did you miss today?" The question came out soft as I turned my body slightly to face him.

Shaking his head, he flicked the tip of his nose before exchanging hands on the steering wheel. "Moms kicked me out."

My heart shattered. I loved Mama Jackie. She was like a second mother to me, but her and Zion stayed in arguments, and it was driving me insane. She hated the life Zion lived, and understandably so. However, the constant arguing coupled with Zion always feeling like he was never good enough, combined with the constant kickouts were enough for anyone to resort to the alternative so that they could fend for themselves. Especially Zion. He wasn't old enough to hold down a job yet, and even if he was, he wouldn't make enough to afford his own place.

I gripped his hand. "No. Not again. But I thought you all were getting along a lot better?"

His jaw clenched. "We were. But I can't compete with her old man. She chooses him every time." He released a deep groan. "We got into it, and I slapped him. Wasn't even a hard slap. Just a tap. He couldn't take the L so he wanted to lay hands on me, but he didn't. That worked to his benefit because when he told Mama that I had to go, or else he would leave, she agreed to kick me out. No hesitation. He played his deck of cards right. He baited me, and I bit the bait. Now, I'm out."

"I'm so sorry, Zion. When did this happen?"

"Last night."

"Wait. Last night. Where did you stay?"

"Where else? Abel's."

My head fell in dismay. I already hated when he had to be with the OCGs, but when he was embedded deep with them twenty-four-seven, it was worse. At least when Zion only had to put in work or only wanted to hang out with them, his presence was manageable. Being around them on a constant basis was a recipe for trouble. Anything could pop off, and anyone could come around.

"Why don't you try to stay with Freddie, Lonnie or Pac?" My feeble attempt to get him away from Abel and the entire gang affiliation.

"You know that's only temporary. Freddie's parents ain't having it. Hell, we barely talk now because of my lifestyle. Lonnie and Pac's mamas can barely afford them, let alone adding another mouth to feed. Pac's mama barely wants Pac there, and Lonnie's mama, she is just like Freddie's folks; she ain't cool with the whole OCG thing. She thinks I'm bad news for Lonnie as it is. Staying there is definitely a no-go. Abel is cool with me being around whenever for however long I need."

My stomach dropped at the "whenever for however" part of his comment. Rival gangs and the police were in a heavy rotation in those areas, and I didn't want to get any black dress calls from Mama Jackie. I'd die right along with him if anything ever happened to my Zion.

Another thing that turned my stomach was the exact thought that had plagued me all day—the number of females that tracked in and out of Abel's house. He had a stable of hos that paraded through there all times of the day and night. I knew Zion loved me, but I wasn't convinced that love would help him resist temptation. Aside from Simone's words haunting me, there was no pressing matter that plagued me that I'd yet to face. Lately, there were rumors of females laying claims on him in the bedroom. I never asked. Never wanted to. Zion made me feel like I was his one and only. I didn't want to make it seem like I distrusted him or make him feel like I didn't believe he loved me. Still, it bothered me. I held it inside because no one had proof.

With his hand in mine, I used my thumb to run across his fingers. His tattoos. Each finger bore a letter and one number. *O.C.G.4.L.* His brand. Zion pulled up into my driveway and killed the engine. He moved his hand from mine and wrapped the palm of his hand onto the side of my face. I leaned my face into his hand as he caressed it.

"You look beautiful. My fly girl." My face lit like the rays of the sun. His eyes narrowed as he gazed at me. "Ain't none of them upperclassmen try to hit on you, right?"

I shook my head. "No!"

He licked his lips before the corner of his mouth turned up into a satisfied grin. "Good. I'm already missing school. I don't need a reason to get expelled."

"Stop." I blushed.

He eyed me again, this time seriously. It was like he had a sixth sense. He knew me without me having to tell him a thing. "You seem sad. I know I missed today and all, but it seems like it's something more. What's on my baby's mind?"

My earlier fears hadn't dissipated but rather manifested in Zion's mind. I didn't want to broach the subject, but he'd asked and with no backup plan to leave Abel's, I had to tell him what was on my mind before it blew up in our faces.

Shrugging, I gave a partial truth. "I don't know. I guess I just worry about you over at Abel's so much."

"I'm straight, shawty. You know my boys got my back and ain't nobody gon' do nothing to me. I put that on us." He bent his head toward me, searching my eyes. "I don't like the way you looking right now, Liberty. Nah. It's something else. Don't hide things from me."

There it was. It was that statement that did it. He'd opened the doorway for me to address the rumors and my discomfort about the girls at Abel's. If he didn't want me to hide anything from him then the same respect should be given.

Leaning back, I closed my eyes and took a deep breath. "It's just…" I paused before he urged me to speak my mind. "I hear rumors. Girls saying you been with them… sleeping with them. Then you're at Abel's, and we both know Abel have girls running all up and through his house and his traps. It makes me wonder. I mean we haven't, ya know, and I know you been waiting on me. But have you ever, ya know, been with other females?" I forced myself to look at him. "Just tell me. Please."

He was quiet for a moment, causing my breaths to cease. My heart raced and slammed against my chest like the resounding beat of a bass drum, and then he spoke. "Don't be listening to these hos out here. I love you. I want to be with only you. I need you. There ain't but one Mrs. Forever, and that's you."

Relief washed over me like rushing waters, and that did it for me. That reassurance was all it took for me to believe Zion and deduce that the rumors were just that: rumors. Girls wanted to separate me and Zion to lay claim to him. He'd said it. There was only one and that was me.

Smiling, I leaned over, and we met each other for a passionate lip-lock. When I felt his tongue slip inside my mouth, I pulled back. He kept me near, leaning his forehead against mine.

For a moment, I was speechless and breathless. When I finally found my bearings, our eyes connected, and there was something swirling in his eyes. A storm.

"Mama is helping a friend. She'll be gone for a minute. You wanna come in for a while?" I wanted more time with him. More time for myself. More time before he was the property of the OCGs. More time away from the trouble, both street trouble and the girl trouble.

A smirk graced his face. "Of course. I got all the time in the world for you."

Happy that he obliged, I did a little shimmy and jumped out of the car. Opening the back door, I pulled my book bag out and grabbed my key. Just before I put the bag on my shoulder a few items were knocked out of the back seat. I handed my book bag to Zion and bent down to pick them up. Rolling papers. A copy of *The Source* magazine. A pack of Newports. I shook my head as I threw them back inside, but the next two items made my breath hitch. A photo, a Polaroid picture of my Zion with Abel sitting beside him, throwing up the OCG gang sign with Black & Milds hanging from their lips and two half-naked women sitting in their laps. The next was an item that I slung and hit Zion in the face with. A lace thong.

"I'm your one and only, huh?" The anger sizzled on my tongue. "Then who the hell is she? Two and a possible!" The picture and thong hit him in the chest. I whizzed past him, up the front steps, and fumbled to get in the house. I had to get away from Zion.

"Liberty!" He stopped the door from slamming in his face. "It's not like that. Let me in so we can talk, please."

"No, Zion. It's exactly like that! I asked you, begged you, to tell me the truth and you lied to my face. How could you? I believed you. I would always believe you, and you lied!"

"I didn't lie! Let me in."

"Hell no!" I screamed, tears falling down my face. "Go to Abel's or whoever's lace panties those are."

"I don't know who they belong to, Liberty. It's Abel's car! It's some girl he was messing around with, I guess."

"Maybe. But that picture showed the girl you were messing around with!"

"I didn't mess with that girl, man!"

"Then why was she all cozy on your lap with short shorts and no top?" He dropped his head at my words. "Exactly! Goodbye, Zion!"

His foot in the door prevented me from closing it all the way. "Liberty, please let me explain. Please. Just hear me out, and if you want me to leave afterward, I promise I'll bounce." Bringing his steepled hands to his face, he begged again. "Please, baby."

*Baby.* The name he called me when he was really sweet on me or in the doghouse. He was both now. Either way, it was the name that always made me putty in his hands. As much as I wanted to slam the door shut, a part of me wanted to hear him out. I needed an explanation behind the photo, the rumors, and the lies. I prayed that there was some type of misunderstanding that he'd reveal and that we could continue—Zion and Liberty against the world. I'd ride to the ends of the earth for him… with him… but I had to know if he was riding for me and with me only.

I opened the door and he sauntered in with my book bag in tow. I snatched the bag from him and headed to my bedroom. He followed me into my bedroom as if he were afraid of giving me additional space to reconsider his presence. When I turned around, he closed my bedroom door.

I stood with my arms folded. And whereas we were close in height in elementary, Zion now towered over me. His perfect Caesar waves were back and naturally he brushed his palm over his head. Pulling up his baggy jeans, he took a seat on my bed.

"Sit down." He patted the empty bed beside him.

"I'd rather stand because this might not take long."

He turned sad eyes to me, and I swallowed back my emotion. "*Baby*, sit." A simple two-word command that only he could make.

Begrudgingly, I sat down beside Zion but close to the other edge of the bed. I needed space between us, room to process his words.

"I'll admit that we were wildin' in that photo. It was a night with the homies. My man's G-day. Liquor, loud, and ladies were on the menu. We partied into the wee hours of the morning, listened to music, played spades, and dominos. The ladies got a lil'… out of control… just the way Abel loved it. I can't deny what you saw. Like I said, we were wildin', but what you saw was it. They wanted to hop in the photo with me and Abel. They did, and afterward, they went back to dancing and drinking. It wasn't much, but it was wrong, and I apologize."

I took in his explanation. Still, I wasn't convinced. "Then why didn't you tell me?"

He shrugged. "You think your reaction would've been any different if I had?" When I didn't respond, he pointed at me. "Exactly."

"What about the rumors?"

"That's just what they are—rumors. Every female wants to be down with some member of the OCGs. I don't entertain them because the only female I want is the one that was already down with me before OCG. You." He slid closer to me, closing the gap between us, and lifted my chin with his forefinger so that we were eye-to-eye. "I love you, baby."

Whatever words I was going to say were lost when his lips descended onto mine. That kiss was pleading and hopeful. That kiss aimed to set all the wrongs committed right. Indeed, that kiss was so potent that it doled out a lifetime's worth of apologies, and damn if it didn't suck an eternity's worth of forgiveness back. And I folded. Every rumor, every sneer, every doubt was erased from my heart and my mind under the spell of that kiss.

Just as I thought Zion was going to come up for air, he didn't. He felt the shift in my attitude. He knew that all had been forgiven, and now, he was working on the forgotten. His kiss deepened as one of his hands caressed the back of my neck, and the other pulled at the bottom hem of my baseball jersey, bringing me closer to him.

# CHAPTER 15

THAT KISS WAS one of longing. That kiss was one of desire. That kiss turned the corner of puppy love, away from the "big box for 'yes' and little box for 'no' with no 'maybe' box," so there was no room for indecisiveness. That kiss was the difference between *USA Up All Night* and *HBO* and *Cinemax After Dark*. Zion had been given reentry, and he hit the throttle. All gas. No breaks.

With his lips still pressed to mine, he dragged his forefinger down the middle of my heaving chest. "Where is your brother?" he whispered.

"At practice. He won't be home until later." The words came out jagged.

It was only then that Zion lifted from me and made his way to the bedroom door. I thought he was going to leave. He should've left but he didn't. Instead, he turned the lock on the door and waltzed back over to me. His lips were on mine before I could even attempt to retreat. We leaned back on the bed, and Zion's body intertwined with mine as we kissed with wild abandon. I jumped nervously when I felt the stiffness between his legs pressing against my thigh.

"I want you so bad, Liberty," he groaned as if he was in physical pain. "I want you but you gotta want it too. You're my wife. A man needs his wife, baby."

He wasn't playing fair. Bringing up our impromptu elementary wedding was a slick blow. He was giving me the option to walk away, and at the same time, making it damn hard to do so. Bringing

131

up memories, that one in particular, touched me deeply. He knew that. He was trying to score brownie points and eat the whole pan of brownies at the same time. He knew what he was doing. But if he was slick, then I was motor oil. The unfamiliar throb between my thighs and the heat of my skin were in uncharted territory, but I wanted to glide right into it because on the other end of this was a shared moment with the one guy who I'd vowed only to share this moment with.

"Are you ready for this? 'Cause I'm ready for you. But only if you say yes."

Fear consumed me but love drove out fear, so even though I was scared out of my mind, I nodded. "Yes."

Not another word was spoken as Zion unbuttoned my jersey one by one. He eased it off my shoulders and down my arms before tossing it on the floor. Following suit, he lifted his T-shirt above his head and tossed it beside my jersey. I unzipped the matching pleated skort and Zion eased it off me. I lifted for easier access as he tugged the fabric down and around my petite cheeks and down my legs. Clad in only my matching bra and panty set, I covered my privates out of habit and shivered from the fact that Zion was about to see my naked glory.

He leaned down so that his mouth was to my ear. "You can tell me to stop at any time, and I will. It may hurt a little bit at first, but I'll go slow. Just focus on me. I'll make you feel better."

I nodded and gripped his face. "I'm scared, but I trust you."

Something flickered in his eyes, and he blinked it away. He stood and dropped his pants and briefs, and my eyes widened. He couldn't be about to stick that thing in me. Geez. *Might* hurt? I could already see myself in the ER. How in the world could I explain that to my mother?

"Is it supposed to look like that and be that long?"

He smirked. "Yeah, baby."

I eyed him suspiciously. "How do you know?"

"'Cause I've had it all my life," he joked, and our laughter broke up the nervousness at the moment. Laying against me, Zion whispered, "I'll take my time with you. I love you."

My heart swelled. "I love you, too."

Zion pulled my bra down, and his lips enveloped my nipples. My hands pressed his face against them. It felt so good. I withered underneath him from the feeling. It was like electric jolts shooting through my body. My hands freed my bra from around my chest, and Zion returned to my breasts, then kissed my nipples and kissed down my chest to my stomach. When I felt his hands tug at my panties, I tensed. He paused and glanced up at me, waiting for my approval to keep going. A few seconds passed before I relaxed and allowed him to proceed. Zion came back up my body and kissed me deeply.

"I'm going to put it in, okay?" he said softly.

"Okay," I said nervously.

"Trust me." The words floated out of his mouth before he kissed me again.

He worked for a few minutes pushing against me. He never let my lips go, and though I was a little tense, I let him keep pushing. It hurt, but Zion's gentleness was the calm. An unfamiliar object felt like it nestled inside of me, and he paused.

"Do you feel that?" he asked.

Timidly, I nodded. How could I not? It felt massive. My feminine parts were throbbing. My nerves were on edge. Yet, somehow, I relished this moment. Zion began to move his body in and out of me nice and slow. The first few times, the pressure and pain felt almost unbearable, but then I felt myself open down below. My legs wrapped around his waist, and my arms found their way around his neck.

"Ohh, Zion," I moaned in his ear.

"Liberty, you're so tight. Damn, you feel so good."

We rocked slowly at first and then a little faster as Zion glided inside my warm folds. It felt good. Too good.

"Zion," I called out in confusion and ecstasy.

His eyes fell on mine. His face was a mess, contorting with pleasure. "You're coming. You can't stop it. It's supposed to happen. Come, baby."

As if on cue, my body exploded, and wetness poured out of my womanly parts. I screamed in pleasure. "Ziooonnnnn!"

"Oh, Liberty! Baby!"

His screams matched mine, and he snatched himself up off me just in time for me to see him grip himself, pulling once as white thickness oozed from the tip of his manhood.

"Oh shit. Oh, that feels good," he wailed before collapsing beside me.

My breathing was jagged, and so was his. When I finally looked over at him, he gazed at me with sweet eyes. He brought his hand to my face and caressed it. I kissed the palm of his hand.

"How was it for you?"

"Beautiful."

"Just like you, baby." He pecked my lips. "I love you, Liberty."

"I love you, too."

"And thank you for giving that to me." He rubbed between the apex of my thighs.

A lazy giggle escaped my lips. "It's sore, so don't even think about it."

He smirked. "I know. I'm gonna clean us up and make it feel all better."

He stood, already knowing where I kept my wash cloths. I watched him exit the bedroom and go to the bathroom as I reflected on what had just happened. I'd given up my virginity to Zion. Our relationship had always been real to me, but this moment made it serious. I was connected to him now beyond a schoolhouse crush. He was my man, and I was really his woman. When he reentered my bedroom, he carefully spread my legs and gently washed me off. I saw the little blood splatter from my cherry pop. Surprisingly, it didn't freak either of us out. We were bonded by the moment. It signified us having pieces of each other that no one else had.

"If we're going to keep doing this, you have to get condoms. We see how not using protection worked out for Shaneria."

Alarm flashed in Zion's eyes, but he calmed down. "I got you. Whatever you want me to do. I'll make sure you don't end up like your girl. That's my word."

Our thoughts went briefly to the fact that Shaneria had gotten pregnant during eighth grade using the infamous "pullout" method. I didn't want that for Zion and me. One day, I'd marry him, and we'd have a little boy and a little girl, but my freshman year in high school was not that time. After what I'd experienced with him, I was certain many more times would come, but they would have to come with protection.

Once we were cleaned and dressed, I walked Zion to the front door. He turned to me and kissed me, holding me close for a while.

"Ima be at Abel's."

"Be at school tomorrow."

He grinned and nodded. "Yes, ma'am." He gazed down at me. "You good?"

"I'm great." I kissed his lips. "I love you."

"I love you more." He pulled out his keys and exited the house. "Lock up and dream pretty dreams about me." We smiled at each other, and then he was out.

# CHAPTER 16

*September 20, 1997*

"ARE YOU NERVOUS about tonight?" Unique asked Liberty as we all sat around the lunch table.

All eyes fell on Liberty. "A little bit." She wrung her fingers.

Pulling her hand into mine, I winked at her. "Nah, my baby is good. She got this." She blushed and popped a French fry in my mouth.

Shaneria huffed. "Y'all are so disgusting," she said with an eye roll.

"Yeah, well, better to be disgusting with one man than a slew of them," Terica smarted, pursing her lips.

"Ooh burn!" Liberty giggled as she and Terica did the girly finger dap.

"Or a slew of females," Shaneria countered.

"Dammmnnn!" All the guys at the table said in unison.

"You know what—"

Liberty stood up, blocking Terica from swinging on Shaneria. "You know what, Terica, you should help me get ready with these lyrics for tonight. Come on."

Terica scoffed and walked away, and Liberty turned to me. "Let me go calm this chick down, babe. Okay?"

I hit her with the head nod. "You good, baby. Go get your girl."

She pointed at Shaneria. "You wrong. Deadass." Shaneria's only response was to shrug.

"Damn, Shaneria, I know you and Terica don't see eye-to-eye, but this rivalry brewing between y'all is getting kinda bad," Unique said.

Shaneria scoffed. "It's her fault. Terica always got something slick to say about stuff that ain't her business."

Lonnie, Pac-Man, and I looked at each other. "That sounds a lot like—"

Shaneria threw napkins in our direction. "Shut up! All three of you!" Everyone burst into laughter while Shaneria pouted.

"Anyway, girl, you just need to chill out some," Lonnie said. "Leave that girl alone."

Shaneria shrugged. "Anyway, let me go find out what my homegirl doing. You coming, Unique?" Unique nodded and stood with her. "See y'all tonight at JC's."

When the girls left, Pac-Man turned to me. "So, man, your girl is about to blow up performing at JC's. How'd she land that? You put her on?"

I held up my hands. "Nah, man. All her. Liberty got talent and negotiation skills. My baby a boss. Like her man," I smiled.

"I just know you better not miss it behind no crew shit," Lonnie said. "Liberty will kill you if you miss her showcase."

"Ima be there."

"All right, don't get fucked up like you did on our first day of ninth grade. Liberty was about to knock your block off for skipping school," Pac-Man joked.

"Shut the hell up, Pac! Why you always gotta bring up old shit?" I threw a balled-up napkin at him. "It's a new year, and we worked that shit out."

"You ain't have no choice. You done had your nose up Liberty's ass since the shit was flat," Pac-Man joked.

"Bro, don't worry about me and Liberty, and damn sure keep my baby's ass outta ya mouth."

Just then, Liberty walked back over to the table and reclaimed her seat beside me. I wrapped my arm around her shoulder and glanced at her.

"Terica straight?"

Liberty sighed. "It's all good." She grabbed her water, opened it, and took a swig. "I don't know why those two can't get along. Speaking of, where are Shaneria and Unique?"

"They bounced," Lonnie offered up.

"I'm kinda glad. I get so tired of the back and forth," Liberty admitted.

Lonnie nodded. "I feel you. Hey Liberty, real talk, you ready for tonight?"

"No lie, I'm a bit nervous."

I turned her to face me and held her hands. "No need for all that. I'm gonna be right there, front and center, cheering you on. With me there, that's all the encouragement you'll need."

She smiled sweetly at me, and I could see the nervous energy in her smooth away at my words. All I ever wanted to do was make her feel safe and secure. It made me happy to see that I had that effect on her.

Pac-Man groaned. "See what I mean, Lonnie?" He pointed at me. "Love-struck-ass."

"At least he has someone to love on," Liberty snapped with a scoff.

"Oh snap!" Lonnie and I said in unison, laughing at Liberty's comeback.

Pac-Man shook his head. "You always gotta go there."

"And you stay flapping your jaws. Kill that." My words came out searing.

Usually, I was good at ignoring the back-and-forth between Pac and Liberty. It had been their thing since elementary, but whenever Pac got upset with Liberty, I always deaded it. He wasn't about to get upset over some comebacks, and he damn sure wasn't about to get disrespectful to Liberty. Not on my watch. Better not be *off* my watch, either.

"We all good." Pac-Man raised his hands in surrender. Then he looked at Liberty. "My bad. Besides, I don't want to mess up your vibe for tonight. I talk a lot of shit, but real talk, I'm proud of you, Liberty. Like Zion said, you've got this."

Liberty's face lit up. "Aww Pac! That's the nicest thing you ever said to me. Thank you," she cooed.

He waved her off with a shoulder shrug. "Stop all that. You know Ima go right back to tagging your ass with these jokes after tonight."

We all laughed, and it seemed to be just the therapy Liberty needed to shake her nerves for tonight. Pac-Man talked major cash shit, but one thing he was correct about: Liberty had this rap thing in the bag, and she needed to know that we believed in her just as much as she believed in herself. I knew tonight was going to be the best for her, and I planned to make sure it was.

# CHAPTER 17

JC'S WAS PACKED as usual. Typically, no one under seventeen was allowed inside the joint. However, being as such, the owner was down with the OCGs, and the fact that Liberty helped pass out event flyers and promote the club meant he made an exception for her and her friends. She was able to reserve a table right up front, and when I strolled in ten minutes before showtime, I spotted our whole high school crew at the table already: Unique, Shaneria, Terica, Pac-Man, and Lonnie.

I'd already been there an hour ago to drop off Liberty, but I had to go and handle some OCG business and then change. By now, I had my license and was able to purchase my own car. I liked the classics: Buick Regals, Novas, and Caprices. My big body Chevy was nice. It was blue inside and out, and sat on twenty-fours. The street hustle was paying off big-time.

"'Sup, bro!" someone called out to me before I entered.

Halting my stride, my attention turned to the side of the building, and I spotted Freddie. Jogging over to him, we slapped fives.

"'Sup, fam! I didn't know you were working at JC's tonight."

"Yeah, JC got me out here posting these flyers trying to catch some passerby patrons for tonight." He turned his full attention on me, and that's when he caught a glimpse of my outfit and iced out chains. He placed a balled-up fist to his mouth. "Ooh, that boi fresh! Lemme guess, you here to see Liberty."

A megawatt smile spread across my face. "You already know. You gon' have time to catch the show?"

"Oh yeah. I'll have to leave right after, but you know Ima at least check out ya girl."

Nodding, I dapped him up. "Respect. I appreciate it, and I'm fo' sho she does too."

I didn't ask why Freddie was leaving right after because I already knew. Curfew. His parents did not play. Never had. Never would.

"No doubt." Inhaling deeply, he changed the subject. "You know T-Jones been asking about you for Sunday dinners. She knows it's a losing battle to get you in the church," he joked, taping the last flyer to the building.

"I know, mayne. Say, I will try my best to get by there next Sunday. Dinner is still at 6 p.m., right?"

"Like clockwork," he said, turning to dap me up again.

"Bet. I'll see you inside and at dinner next Sunday."

"I'll let her know." He pointed at me. "Don't make her come looking for you."

I held my hands up. "Hell nah. I know T-Jones ain't nobody to play with."

I walked inside JC's joint fresh to death with my all-blue Karl Kani T-shirt, Karl Kani denim jeans, and Timberland wheats. My all-blue baseball cap was turned backward, and I was iced-out with gold links and a big face watch. When I made my way to the table, I sat right in the middle. Pac-Man was to my immediate right, and Shaneria was to my immediate left.

"Zion!" they all greeted me as I sat down.

Once seated, I hit the girls with the head nod and gave Pac-Man and Lonnie some pound. After the banter of small talk, Pac-Man looked over at me and playfully hit my arm.

"Boi! You clean."

"I had to get fresh to death for my baby's showcase tonight."

Shaneria leaned in and bumped my shoulder with hers, which made all of us direct our attention toward her. I looked over at her, showing all her pearly whites. But it wasn't just the curve of her lips. It was the way she peered at me. She smiled with her eyes not just her mouth. Shaneria was a lot of things these days, but she was still Liberty's friend, so I brushed it off.

"Well, your effort shows." She eyed me up and down. "You are definitely fresh to death, Zion." She popped a fry in her mouth and chewed slowly. Her eyes never left mine.

The shit threw me off, and while I would never entertain Shaneria, it made me blush a little bit. "Uhh, thanks."

She grabbed my forearm and leaned in. "You're so welcome." Her words came out airy around a girlish giggle.

My eyes shot past Shaneria because I could feel the other girls damn near burning a hole into me. Unique's mouth was hanging wide open, and Terica was shooting so many daggers at Shaneria and me that we would've been stabbed to death if it were real. I glanced behind me, feeling the eyes in the back of my head, and Lonnie shook his head warningly while Pac grinned sinisterly. It was then that I realized that Shaneria still had a hold of my arm, and I turned back to her and gently lifted her hand off me. I had no clue what she was up to, but I was there to celebrate Liberty. I wouldn't ruin her night with Shaneria's foolery.

Pac-Man leaned into me. "Man, you hittin' that too?"

"Hell nah! I wouldn't do Liberty dirty like that. I don't know what the fuck Shaneria's problem is."

Pac-Man and Lonnie eyed me suspiciously for a moment, and I hunched my shoulders with my hands pointed upward. Hell, I didn't know. Lonnie shook his head, and Pac-Man waved it off. I glanced over at Terica and Unique, and both of them shot me those sista-girl neck-roll looks, and I gave the same motion that I'd given to Lonnie and Pac, hunching my shoulders with confusion. Terica rolled her eyes and sat back, and Unique gave me one more warning glare before she followed suit.

Before anything could jump off, the showcase started. As the first two acts performed, we all had fun together, bopping and dancing to the music. Shaneria started grinding in her chair but it got uncomfortable when she winked at me and licked her lips. Terica looked like she was two seconds off Shaneria's ass, and Unique kept whispering to her, I was sure pleading with her not to create a scene.

Finally, Liberty took the stage. She looked nervous as the crowd hushed around the floor, giving her our undivided attention. Her eyes were cast downward, and at first, I thought she wasn't going to be able to go through with it, but our eyes connected the moment she looked up, and it was as if a switch turned on inside of her. Her eyes flickered, and I saw the sexy and confident girl I knew appear, but it seemed like something more. That was no longer my girl, Liberty. That was Libby B, the artist. I winked at her, and that demure smile crossed her face. She was good now. As soon as she grabbed the mic, I knew she was about to rock out, and she did. She rapped her original song lyrics across dope beats, performing three numbers, each one more hyper than the next. We were going crazy in JC's rooting for her—even Shaneria—and the remaining crowd seemed to join our infectious energy. By the time she finished, she was the only act to receive a standing ovation.

There were two more acts left, so after Liberty grabbed her belongings from the back, she ran out to the front with us. When I saw her coming, I made sure to get up out of my seat and move around Lonnie so that I was the first face she saw. As soon as she saw me, she ran straight into my arms. I scooped her and bear-hugged her. When I put her down, I kissed her.

"You did great, Libby B," I said, gripping her by her waist. "That's my girl."

"Thank you, baby. For that and for earlier. I couldn't have done this without you." She kissed me again, then slowly pulled back. "I love you."

"Forever?"

"For always."

"I love you, too, baby."

"A'ight, a'ight, enough with all that mushy shit," Pac-Man called out. "You did a'ight, Liberty." He approached us as we pulled apart, and he dapped her up.

"But I saw you rocking in your seat to my songs."

"Catchy beat," Pac-Man joked, and Liberty swatted him. "Nah, real talk, you ripped it!"

Lonnie followed up with his praise before she ran to her girls, who hugged her and praised her for how well she'd done. Pac-Man pulled up another chair for Liberty and sat it beside him, then he and Lonnie moved down a seat to make room for Liberty.

Before she sat down, Terica said, "You might wanna let Zion move down one, and you sit on the other side of him." Liberty looked at her confusingly, while at the same time, Shaneria shot a glare at her.

"I'on think it really matters," Liberty said, about to sit down.

"Oh, but it does matter," Terica shot back.

To avoid conflict, I stood and slid into the new chair and motioned for Liberty to have a seat. As Liberty walked around, she eyed me and Terica suspiciously before taking the seat. She didn't say anything about it, though. Instead, she sat down, and we started talking about her showcase before the waitress reappeared. I ordered Liberty and me some food and drinks. While we waited for the food, the next act came on, and we all partied it up. Our food came, and Liberty and I fed each other and enjoyed our time out together. There was a small intermission before the last act came on—who was the headliner—so mostly everyone ate, laughed, and talked. It was a chill vibe. At least with everyone except Shaneria. Apparently, Shaneria had let out one too many of those loud-ass sighs she kept throwing out and Liberty finally turned to her.

"Shaneria, you good? You sound irritated. All that huffing and puffing gonna blow the damn building down."

Most of us tried to stifle our reactions but Terica let out a loud and boisterous wail of laughter that caused a few heads to turn. Unfortunately, Shaneria took the bait and went in on Terica.

"You always got your mouth open when it comes to me. That's why I don't like your ass right now," Shaneria spewed.

Terica leaned forward, one eyebrow cocked up. "Maybe if you kept your mouth and your legs closed, nobody would have a reason to keep your name in their mouth. You probably just mad because I don't want a taste. Which yo' nasty run-through ass."

"Hating ass broad!" She pointed at Terica. "I wouldn't want your nasty-ass lips on me anyway, but I bet you'd like it. Come out the closet. Dyke ass! That's why you mad. You want some of this Shaneria juice."

"What closet?" someone asked.

Terica stood up, and Liberty and Unique stood between them as the altercation caught the eyes of everyone in the club. Terica pointed at her. "You lucky I'm not trying to fuck up Liberty's night. And best believe if I wanted a taste, I could have it, with the way you dish it out. I know about all ya activities. I'm tryna keep my composure and not lay hands on you, but you pushing it."

"Well, push it to the max then! Ain't nothing but space and opportunity."

Terica damn near leaped at Shaneria, and it was all me, Unique, and Liberty could do to hold her back. While we tried to contain Terica, Pac and Lonnie jumped in front of Shaneria. I didn't know who Shaneria was fooling. Terica would mop the floor with her bone-thin self.

"Hey, hey, y'all calm down, damn," Unique pleaded.

"She's right. It's not worth it. Y'all can hash this shit out later. Chill," I added.

Pac-Man pulled Shaneria's hand. "You can sit by me, and we can chop it up, Sha."

She snatched away and slung her hair over her shoulder. "Boy bye!"

Pac-Man pointed at her. "I was trying to be nice to your funky ass."

Terica shook her head. "Nah, Pac, she don't want you to be nice to her 'cause she too busy skinning and grinning up in Zion's face! That's who she wants. Got a baby daddy and a man of her own, but she trying to make moves on Zion every chance she gets. Skank-ass ho."

The moment it came out, I sensed that Terica regretted it. She'd been so heated that she'd forgotten that she'd spoken the words in Liberty's presence. A hush seemed to fall over us and the entire club. Everything seemed to happen in slow motion. Liberty turned Terica loose and stared at her.

"What did you just say?" Liberty asked Terica.

"Ahh shit," Unique added, throwing her hands up and moving back toward Pac-Man and Lonnie. "I'm out of it."

I reached over and touched Liberty's arm. "Baby, don't even trip off Terica. She mad right now. Let that shit ride."

Liberty snatched away and looked at me. "You got something you wanna tell me, Zion?"

I lifted my hands in surrender and shook my head. "I ain't got nothing to say baby."

Just then, a few of my OCG crew, whom I'd invited, strolled over—Trei, G-rock, and Montay. They posted up beside me, each of them hitting me with daps. Trei stepped forward with his hands in his pockets.

"What up, folk?" he said to me. "Ya lil' shawty was fire, mayne. You need us, fam?"

I flailed my hands, motioning that I didn't need them. "Nah, fam. But I 'preciate that, folk."

JC, the owner, popped up out of nowhere. I guess since he saw more OCGs come over he wanted to end things so they could get the show over with and keep his club intact. He dapped up all the OCGs and then turned to Liberty.

"Liberty, you know I appreciate everything you do for the club, and I know this is your premiere performance but Ima need y'all to take that shit outside. Now, when things cool off, you're welcome back inside, but if something pop off then you know Big E and the security crew gotta step in and…" He looked back at me and my OCG crew. "I don't want no problems in my establishment."

"Ain't no problems, JC. We gon' bounce," I said, putting the order down so that the OCGs knew to stand down.

He slapped fives with me and pulled me into a brother-man's hug. "'Preciate that, folk."

"Aye, y'all, let's take it outside," I said.

Everyone listened as we all grabbed our things and headed for the exit. I was glad nothing happened. Liberty's mother would never let her go out again. It was bad enough she didn't know she was at the club. Let alone hanging with known gang members."

However, no sooner than we got outside, Liberty snatched Shaneria by the arm, spinning her around so hard she was now facing Liberty. "Now, what the fuck is Terica talking about?"

"So you gon' believe that trash bucket over me? You always take her side, Liberty! Always!" Shaneria yelled; the vibrato in her voice made it seem like she was about to break down.

"You know, I felt bad for telling Liberty, but now I don't." Terica turned to Liberty. "Liberty, her scandalous ass has been after Zion since middle school. She don't never push up directly but when you not around she always grinning and smiling up in his face. Finding ways to touch up on him. He ignores her, and you too close to her, but I see it. Tonight, we *all* saw it." She looked at Shaneria. "Deny it. Go 'head." Terica turned back around. "If I'm lying, I'm flyin'. Y'all back me up."

Liberty looked around at us. Nobody agreed, but nobody denied it either. Finally, Liberty looked at me. Her arms folded across her chest and her hips jutted out to the side. My head fell back in surrender.

"Terica ain't lying," I confessed.

"So why *you* didn't tell me?" Liberty asked, anger rising like heat off the concrete.

"I didn't think nothing of it. I mean, it's Shaneria. *Your* friend. I know she likes to get a lil' free with the flirts. But I don't pay that shit no mind."

Pac-Man and Lonnie spoke up.

"He really didn't, Liberty," Pac said.

"Real talk," Lonnie agreed.

Without warning, Liberty lunged at Shaneria and stole a lick straight to her face before I pulled her off her, and Trei grabbed Shaneria.

"You bitch! What did I ever do to you? I've always been your friend. I used to get on Terica about coming at you, but you ain't innocent either. We've been friends since sandboxes, and you coming for my man? Mine! How you do something like that to me? They drag your name at school, but I've never fronted on you. Despite all the shit that I know, I still remained your friend." Liberty shook her head. "Put me down, Zion! I'm calm," she screamed at me. She eyed Shaneria hard. "I swear bitches ain't shit but hos and tricks!"

"So that's how you really feel, Liberty? I'm a ho and a trick now?" Shaneria pointed at herself with tears trickling down her face. "Wowww."

"If the shoe fits." Liberty shrugged nonchalantly as I shielded her behind me.

Shaneria looked around at everyone. "If that's how you feel, then fuck all y'all!" She stared at Liberty. "I just be playing, but you know it's good to know how you really felt about me this whole time. Since I'm just your ho-ass trick-ass friend, we can cancel this friendship. Ever since I got pregnant back in middle school, you've treated me like shit anyway. Like I'm beneath you. You ain't shit, Liberty. Don't forget you from the hood, too. With your bougie ass!" She stormed off, all of us yelling for her to come back. Even Liberty.

We might've been angry, and it might've been the end of their friendship, but nobody wanted to see her walking home at almost ten at night. She'd ridden with Unique, so she didn't have a ride to get to wherever she was stomping off to.

"Aye yo, Sha!" Trei yelled out to no avail. He turned to me. "Get G-rock and Montay back to the block. Ima holla at y'all," he said before jogging off.

"Where you going, mayne?" I yelled after him.

He turned, backpedaling. "Ima catch up with lil' shawty and give her a ride home."

I shook my head. Trei was trying to get in the panties. The sad part was Shaneria would probably let him. He knew that, so that's why he was playing Captain Save-A-Ho. But I guess it was a compromise. As long as she got home safe, that was good enough.

I turned back to see Terica and Unique consoling Liberty. She wasn't crying but she was visibly upset. I reached out and pulled her into my arms. "It's gonna be a'ight, baby. Let it go. We all know how hard you rode for that girl."

"I ride even harder for you, but you can't have me out here looking stupid."

Looking down at her, I licked my lips before offering a sincere apology. "I'm sorry, Liberty. On the real. I didn't say anything because I wasn't paying that girl no attention and because y'all were friends. It was your big night, and I just didn't want to mess things up."

Liberty was quiet for a long while, and I could visibly see her mind turning over my words. I hated that her special night had come to this, but everything I'd told her was the God's-honest truth. I hoped she could see past Shaneria's antics and not let it come between us.

After what seemed like forever, Liberty smiled up at me. "You were being considerate. I get it."

"You know damn well I ain't gonna have you out here looking stupid with your friends. Come on now, I'd never do you like that." With that, we hugged it out, and everything was settled.

As we milled around, Trei drove by us with Shaneria in his car. He pulled to a slow creep and yelled out of the window. "Y'all be easy. I got lil' mama. Ima take her home."

Being the kind of person she was, my girl tried to smooth the issues over with Shaneria. Yes, Liberty was mad as hell, but deep down, she loved Shaneria. We all wanted better for Shaneria than it seemed she wanted for herself.

Liberty stepped forward. "Shaneria, we should really talk. You could stay, and we can work it out."

Shaneria rolled her eyes. "What for? I'm just a ho and a trick, remember? Gonna go do what I do best."

Trei eyed us with a smirk on his face. "She about to be a little preoccupied right now, Liberty. I'll take good care of her and see if I can fix this lil' situation between y'all."

"A'ight, big homie. She gotta dude," I warned.

"Shut up, Zion! Ain't nobody ask you," Shaneria hollered through the window.

Anger flashed in Trei's eyes, and he turned to her with a death glare. "Calm down, lil' mama. Don't talk to my mans like that. For real."

In true Shaneria fashion, she recoiled and began apologizing in the flirtatious way that she always used on dudes. Nobody said anything more. It was what she wanted to do. We couldn't do anything but let her live her life.

G-rock, Montay, and I walked over to the window and dapped up Trei. "A'ight, Ima get up with y'all tomorrow."

"A'ight, be easy, folk," I said, giving him our hand salute. He returned the gesture before chucking up deuces and driving off.

The rest of us drove over to Sonic to chomp down on burgers, shakes, and slushies instead of going back inside JC's. Liberty had already performed, so we wanted to chill and have a good time. It felt good seeing my street fam and my school fam relax together and chill out. We were having a good time joking, rapping, eating, and just hanging out. About fifteen minutes to midnight, we all broke out so everyone—well, everyone except G-rock, Montay, and me—could make it home by curfew. G-rock and Montay rolled with me and Liberty so we could head over to the trap after I dropped her off at her mother's.

# CHAPTER 18

WHEN WE GOT to Liberty's house, she said her goodbyes to my crew, and I hopped out and walked her up to the doorstep. "I'm proud of you for tonight, baby."

She wrung her fingers nervously as she looked at me with those beautiful doe eyes and bit her lip. So sexy.

"Really? Did I do good?"

I lifted my hand to her cheek. "You killed that. My baby. The coldest MC I know."

The glint in her eyes told me she was thinking the same thing I was. As much love as I had for the OCGs, for once, I regretted that my crew was with me. Trei's blocking ass. If it weren't for G-rock and Montay, I promise I would've put Liberty back in that car, got Abel to hook me up with a hotel room, and spent a little extra time with my baby, boo-loving. Consequences be damned. Liberty just would've had to face the punishment after tonight because she'd had my nose wide open ever since our first time. Surely, there would've been hell to pay, but it would've been worth it.

Wrapping her close in my arms, we held each other for a minute, lost in our own time and space. It was in these moments when the entire world was dead to me. I could've stayed intertwined with Liberty until the end of time. When she wrapped her arms around my neck, I leaned down and placed my lips against hers. Her kisses were sunbeams. They lit up my soul. Feathery, light, sexy, and loving. I loved her lips on mine. Taking the opportunity to grab a handful of her luscious behind, I pulled her into me so she could feel my need for her. She moaned, and I swear it took everything in me not to kick my homies out of that car. Just as we were about to kiss again, the blue pager hanging on my hip started chirping. When Montay opened the car door and yelled, that forced me back into the reality of the outside world.

"Hey, mayne! Check your pager. Did you get a 911 from Abel?"

I let go of Liberty and pulled my pager off my hip. "Yeah, I got it," I confirmed to Montay. He got back in the car, and I turned back to Liberty. "I gotta go."

Without a moment's hesitation, she agreed. "I know." With that, she gave me a quick peck on the lips before turning and opening her front door. "Be careful out there. I love you."

I winked at her. "I love you more." She smiled and shut her door before I jogged down the steps and jumped in the car.

With the new awareness on my mind, I floored my Caprice over to the trap to find out what was going on with Abel. Montay, G-rock, and I pulled up, and I knew it was bad. The 911 had gone out to the entire OCG crew. Cars were lined up everywhere. When we walked in, there was a mix of emotions. Some looked like they wanted to cry while others looked mad as hell.

"What's going on?" I asked as we walked into the house.

Abel immediately turned to us. "What the fuck went down tonight?" His question was directed toward Montay, G-rock, and me.

We all shrugged. "Nothing," I answered. "We went to JC's, left, and hung out at Sonic."

"I thought Trei was with y'all."

"He was," G-rock spoke up. "Zion's girl and her friend Shaneria got into it 'cause Shaneria was trying to push up on big homie. Shaneria got mad and stomped off, so Trei caught up with her and took her home."

"Yeah, but you know he was trying to tap that ass, too," Montay joked as all three of us chuckled knowingly.

Nobody else in the room joined in, and that immediately deadened our laughter. I eyed Abel. "Boss man, what's going on?"

Abel walked over to all three of us, but he put his hands on my shoulders. That's when I knew something had happened to Trei. I could sense it. Out of all the OCGs besides Abel, me and Trei were the closest. We got jumped in together. We put in work together. We were always together. Until tonight. I braced myself for the impact as best I could.

"Somebody came up in ol' girl's house and merked her and Trei. One of the detectives on payroll called me. Lil' homie gone, Zion."

In a flash, my anxiety was replaced by rage, and I screamed in angst. It seemed like every memory I ever had with Trei flooded my mind. *Not Trei. Not the homie.* Anger coursed through my veins and I kicked the milk crate nearby. My brothers banded around me. They must've known I'd take it the hardest. Trei was like my blood brother. I was pissed 'cause he was gone. Pissed 'cause I wasn't there. Pissed 'cause I didn't make him come with us. Pissed 'cause he didn't heed my warning.

"Pharaoh!" I blurted out. "Ima kill that muthafucka!"

Abel caught me, placed his arm around my shoulders, and patted my chest. "Woah. Slow down lil' homie. Slow down. I know you're angry. We all are. But I need you to holla at me. Who is *Pharaoh?*"

"Shaneria's boyfriend. I told Trei to be careful 'cause she'd been messing around with this older cat named Pharaoh. He claimed her and played daddy to her baby. I know he behind this shit. I know it. Ima toe-tag that nigga when I see him!"

Abel turned me to face him. "No, you ain't—"

"What you mean—"

"I *mean*," he re-interrupted, "*you* ain't. You too close. The detectives can only do so much. You too emotional right now. You get caught, that's hard time—life. You lay low. We got this."

Pain like I'd never felt before seared through me. My boi Trei was gone. Shaneria was gone. Then the revelation stung that I would have to tell Liberty that her friend was dead.

"Boss man, you know I'm your soldier, but I can't sit this out. I can't."

"You can and you will, Zion!" he barked before calming down. "That shit hurt right now. It does. But it's gonna get dealt with. You got a mama out here, a sister, a lil' shawty. We gon' get this Pharaoh cat for Trei, but you gonna have to let that shit breathe. We just lost Trei. We don't need to lose no more soldiers."

Rage danced in my eyes as I stared silently at Abel. I wanted to burn down the city but his words put a pause in me. Sure, Mama and I stayed at odds, but who would take care and look out for her and my sister? I definitely didn't see Calvin lasting much longer. But mostly I worried about what would happen between me and Liberty if I had to do a bid. There was no way she'd put her life on hold for me. And I couldn't cut our time short by making foolish mistakes and being taken away from her. I needed all the time I had left with her until the time came that I wasn't good enough for her anymore.

I relented. "Fine. But I got that cat's address and anything else you need."

Abel nodded. "Let me get that."

After I gave Abel the information, I told him I had to talk to Liberty. I made a promise that I wouldn't touch Pharaoh, but I had to let Liberty know what was up. I couldn't let her find out on the morning news or at school. She would know that I already knew because Trei was involved, and she would be angry that I didn't tell her first.

---

"Zion! What the hell are you doing here so late? It's one o'clock in the morning!" Liberty's mother yelled at me.

"I'm sorry, Ms. Lucille, but it's very important. I've got news that you and Liberty need to know."

Either the look on my face or the words out of my mouth changed her attitude immediately. She waved me inside and then went to bring Liberty to the living room. A few minutes later, Liberty waltzed out in her cotton pajama set, and her eyes widened when she saw my face. Her mother beckoned her over to the sofa as she tied her robe and sat down.

"Now, Zion, what is this all about? And why so late?" Ms. Lucille drilled.

For the first time in my life, I stared into Liberty's eyes, exposing my deepest emotions. The rawness of the blow I was about to deliver swallowed me whole, and I couldn't hold back my tears. My lip began to tremble, and suddenly, it felt like I couldn't breathe. I beat my chest to quell the agony.

"Oh, dear Lord!" Ms. Lucille gasped.

Liberty jumped up and ran to me, cradling me in her arms. "Babe, what's wrong? Is it your mother? Your sister? What's wrong? What's going on?" she asked frantically.

She and her mother helped me over to the sofa chair and sat me down. My head fell into my hands as I rested my elbows on my knees. When I finally looked up, both sets of eyes peered at me, waiting on the edges of their seats for words that I didn't know if I could repeat.

"Umm, I don't really know how to say this, but..." I paused and grabbed Liberty's hands in mine. I had to hold her when I delivered the news. "Trei and Shaneria... they umm... somebody... umm... killed them tonight. They're gone, baby. They're both dead."

Ms. Lucille clutched her chest. "What?"

Liberty's body began shaking profusely as a well of tears glossed over her doe eyes. The turmoil and pain wrecked her face as devastation overcame her. "No. No, no, no, no, no!" she yelled.

"It's not true. We just saw her. She was just here. It's not true."

"I'm so sorry, Liberty," I said, trying to withstand my own pain.

"But… but…" Her lips trembled as tears cascaded down her face. "We didn't get a chance to make up. I didn't get a chance to say sorry. She was just here. She was just here."

I pulled her into my arms and her mother wrapped her arms around the both of us. It was one of the saddest moments of my life.

# CHAPTER 19

AT SIXTEEN, A person shouldn't have to think about life-altering decisions. Life should be easy. The only cares should be what to wear to school, making sure grades were up to par, and chores. Teens should not have to wonder when they go outside, hang out with friends, or go to the store if they will return home. Basic life shouldn't be up for debate. It'd been three months since Shaneria's death, and the loss of her and Trei seemed to change everyone in the hood. Some of us for the better. Some of us for the worse. Either way, their deaths were like a black cloud of thick smog that loomed and choked the life out of us.

For me, it definitely changed my outlook on life. I had always been proud of my hood. It made me. And while I knew that I wanted better, OC was still home. But with the loss of Shaneria, it felt different. It was as if the blinders had been lifted, and everything around me exposed the ugliness in the area. The crime, the gangs, the poverty, the struggle, the pain. Everything seemed to repulse me. Suddenly I felt smothered and out of place. It was as if I wore the stain of the hood on me, like an itchy sweater with the scarlet letter. It was no place to raise a family. No place to thrive. No place to be. And the more that it weighed on me, the more I knew that I wanted nothing more than to escape. For all the things that the hood made me, I feared that there were a thousand more that could break me. I wanted out.

"What's on your mind?" Zion asked, his voice infiltrating my thoughts.

I shook as I sat up and leaned forward. We were chilling at Glendale Park, and even though I was cocooned in Zion's arms on top of the park table, I felt a million miles away.

"It's nothing," I lied.

"It's Shaneria, huh?" When I gazed over at him, he nodded. "I feel you. Trei been on my mind a bunch, too."

His confession weighed on me. We had steered clear of speaking about Trei and Shaneria, but now that he'd opened the door, I walked through. "Zion, be real with me. You didn't have anything to do with Pharaoh, did you?"

Pharaoh had been Shaneria's boyfriend. He was twenty years old and had been super possessive of Shaneria. He should've been locked up for messing with a minor, but he'd paid the bills at Shaneria's mother's house and helped her take care of a baby that wasn't his because Shaneria didn't know who her baby's father was. So, her mother didn't trip. Shaneria constantly cheated on him, and he always threatened to harm her if he ever had proof. At any rate, a couple of days after Shaneria and Trei were killed, so was Pharaoh. The hood was talking and saying that the OCGs were behind it because of Trei's affiliation.

"No," Zion said with irritation splayed on his face. "How many times I gotta tell you that I didn't have nothing to do with that? I thought we settled it when you asked me the first time."

"Trei was your boy. You're OCG. And I know you."

Zion huffed and sat up. "I was ordered to stand down. So, I did. I don't really want to get into the specifics; just know that I'm clean. Shit's handled."

"Just like that?"

"Damn, Liberty!" Zion's hands flew up in the air. "What you want me to say? I didn't do shit!"

"You are always so quiet and secretive about OCG. How I know you're not lying to me?"

He slid down off the table and paced around with his hands atop his head. "I'm quiet on this because I don't know anything. I'm quiet about everything else because it doesn't involve you. I'm trying to protect you from this life because the less you know, the better. Now all of a sudden, you wanna playbook of what's going down." He paused. "Man, I could tell you some shit, Liberty, that'll give you nightmares for the rest of your life. But I won't. Because you ain't built for this part and I don't want this curse on you—"

"Well you don't need to be built for it either," I challenged. "And you're right. I do need protection."

He turned to me with his face turned up in confusion. "I'm having a real hard time understanding where you going with this. What is this really about?"

I looked up into Zion's eyes. "Zion, it's just that I'm tired of all this. Shaneria's death has me thinking about my future—about *our* future. I want more than this. For us. I'm not trying to be another statistic. I want to be an exception." I released a deep sigh before I continued. "Be an exception with me."

"What you sayin'?"

"I need you to leave OCG and go legit. Do it for us."

There it was. My unspoken truth.

"And what you want me to do, huh, Liberty?" he asked, his arms outstretched.

"I don't know. You're smart, and you're talented—"

"No!" The boom in his voice forced me silent. "*You're* smart, and *you're* talented. I've already dropped out of high school. So what options do I have?"

It was true. After Trei's death, Zion dropped out. He had already been failing anyway, and the death of Trei took him over the edge. Ever since, he'd gone hard in the streets. Our time together was even limited because I was focused on school, and he was focused on getting fast money.

I walked up to him and reached for his hands. He pulled away. "Babe." My words came out softly as I gently tugged at his forearm and pulled him to me. Sliding my hand down his arm, I stopped when our hands connected, and I interlocked fingers with him and did the same to his other hand. "You're smarter and more talented than you give yourself credit for." He looked away from me, and I turned loose one of his hands and pulled his face back to me by his chin. "No, look at me, Zion. Listen to me."

"Liberty, I'm not like you."

"No, you're not," I agreed. "You're like *you*. You have to stop being so hard on yourself."

"There's a difference between being hard and being honest. I know who I am and what I gotta do to survive. You have options. I don't. And I know you want out of the *hood*, and it sounds like anything that reminds you of it. Humph. And I want that for you, too."

My head tilted to the side as I fell back a step. "Don't you mean 'for us'?"

Zion's head and shoulders fell forward. Gripping my hands, he gently shook them before gazing into my eyes. "I'm always down for us. You know that. But I want what's best for you the most. I know you're headed for greatness. And I refuse to hold you back."

"*We* are headed for greatness… together." I lifted my hand to cradle the side of his face. "You have to believe in yourself as much as I do. And nobody's holding anyone back because we're on this journey together. Right?"

Minutes seemed like hours as we stood staring at each other. My heart yearned and pleaded with him to agree. I needed him to see himself in the future and not in the right now. I needed him to let go of this street life and embrace real life. I needed him to understand that I needed him. All of him. There was no way I'd ever move on with my life without him in it. I loved him too much, and I had to know that he loved me just as much.

"Right?" I pressed.

Uncertainty plagued his eyes. I could sense that we were not on the same track. I knew the look and I knew it all too well.

"Right," he answered finally before planting a kiss to my sweet lips.

# CHAPTER 20

*March 27, 2001*

THE SOUND OF gates clinging together still annoyed me as I walked the yard. Oh, if I could turn back the hands of time. I still remembered the day that Liberty begged me to consider my future. I had no clue then what else I could do besides beat the block, but I wished like hell I would've taken her request seriously. Who knew where I would be right now. Where *we* would be. It was those moments that haunted me.

It all started with Shaneria and Trei's deaths. That night changed the entire trajectory for our whole crew of friends. Lonnie changed… for the better. He focused more on school and signed up for track and field. Though it had less to do with him than his mother, who decided she needed to fill Lonnie's time with positive activities and keep him away from his friends as much as possible. She was a single mother, and she wanted a better life for her son. Besides Freddie's mother, she was the one parent who put her heart into her child. She was determined to keep his nose out of trouble and his ass off the streets. Unique, who'd been known to be a bit flirty like Shaneria, eased up on those provocative ways. Although she still didn't care for school, or to get involved with other productive activities, she'd begun to take school a lot more seriously. Terica seemed to embrace her new normal. She never confirmed or confessed to us guys that she was into girls, it just

163

became unspoken knowledge among all of us from the way she interacted with other females around us. There was no need to pry or question it. It was her life, and she'd have enough criticism from the outside world. She didn't need her friends judging her. Pac-Man fell victim to the streets as well. With Lonnie being into athletics and his mother not allowing him to be around us as much, he began to hang out more with me. Eventually, he joined OCG and became my street fam, along with being one of my best friends. We rolled together and held each other down, until I got put in the cage.

As for me, I never realized how much Trei's death affected me. It was the first time in my life I'd lost a friend. Though I'd been satisfied that Pharaoh had gotten his, I still hadn't known how to process Shaneria and Trei's deaths. The loss had festered until my blood ran ice cold. Whatever sliver of hope I'd seen for myself extinguished. After that, I'd dived headfirst into the game. I thought my healing was to go harder in the streets. For a while, it felt like therapy, and I was a willing participant. That was the start of one of the reasons I lost my real prize: a life with Liberty. I laid all my burdens on the cross of OCG, and then that cross burned down, and when I rose from the ashes, I lifted my eyes in prison. Liberty was gone. OCG was gone. My life was gone. One thing that Abel had said was correct: prison was a lifetime. I felt the effects of it every day. I walked down my years one day at a time. I counted the hours until I could be free, and I swore on everything I would do things differently.

I looked up from the bench to see one of the OCG members approaching. I was surprised that he was headed toward me. I'd been very clear that I was no longer active, so most of the crew who were on lockdown with me didn't associate themselves with me. There were a few who carried on general conversation, but for the most part, they kept it short and kept it pushing. My heart still bled OCG, even if that lifestyle had run dry, but my OCG days were done. Still, my stomach pitted at this sudden approach.

"'Sup, folk," Yung One said as he neared me, throwing up the OCG hand signal.

I threw it up at him. "'Sup, folk."

"I don't mean to disturb, fam, but it's some news on the wire. Lil' homies on the block put me up on it and said the big homie wanted to get the word to you."

It was at that moment that I knew something had happened. There was only one person we referred to as "big homie," and that was Abel.

I nodded. "Respect. Speak on it."

"Say, a family member went home." He held his head down in respect for the fallen. "Big homie say it was important to put you on notice."

I stood up. My heart pounded out of my chest. I had no clue what was about to come out of his mouth next, but somehow my spirit knew. I leaned on the table for support. I needed anything to brace myself for the next few words that would come out of his mouth.

"Who?"

"Pac-Man."

The report jarred me, and I gripped the table to keep from falling over. For a moment, everything around me stopped. I couldn't wrap my head around it. Not again. First, Trei. Now Pac?

"You sure?" My words came out light and pained.

He nodded. "On God. Ya feel me?"

I took in a sharp breath to keep the emotion from welling up inside of me. My teeth gritted, and I sniffed. "How?"

"Say homie had words with them Cains, and they pulled up to the bando. Caught homie on the slide. Swiss-cheesed that ma'fucka. Nothing left standing, not even the bando."

The Cains were what we called the Greedy Grove Kingz, our rival gang. A reference to the rival brothers in the Bible, Cain and Abel. GGKs had snuffed out my brother, Pac. I knew enough not to even ask about retaliation. I knew that had either happened already or was on the horizon. You couldn't ring the bell and not have someone answer the door. The hood would rain red with Abel and the crew at the helm. Still, that did nothing for my aching heart. Pac-Man. This was all my fault. He never would've been involved with OCG if he hadn't followed in my footsteps, and I wasn't there for him. I couldn't even be there for him in death. I couldn't be there for his family or our friends. He was gone. Like Trei. And there was nothing I could do.

Needing a minute to myself, I slapped fives with Yung One, and he bowed his head in solidarity and respect before he left. I should've been used to it by now. But how could you ever get used to saying goodbye to the ones who meant the most to you? Out of nowhere, Liberty's words came rushing back. The thought of her brought me peace and it stalled the vengeance in my heart. Ironically, a laugh erupted from me as Pac's voice came to mind: *You still up Liberty's ass.* For the first time, I asked myself what would Liberty do? The answer was plain as day. I had to mourn and move on. Change had to begin somewhere, and what better chance to start my change than one of the most challenging times to do so? I'd gotten it wrong after Trei's death. I couldn't afford to get it wrong after Pac's.

# CHAPTER 21

*February 7, 1998*

NOW THAT I was sixteen, it was time to get on the job hunt. Independence started with freedom. Freedom started with money. Money started with having a job. I needed a job for two reasons: the money and the experience. I already had the hustle down pat. I'd been hustling with side gigs since I was fourteen. It was the reason I was able to perform at JC's. I'd met him at Big D's Bazaar when I was peddling costume jewelry. His daughter had wanted a bangle bracelet, and by the time I was done pitching to her, he'd bought three sets of bangle bracelets and two mood rings. He'd been so impressed he asked if I could hang up posters for his club events, and he'd pay me for it. Of course, I had agreed. During the week, I hung posters, and during the weekend, I sold jewelry at the bazaar.

When JC implemented the teen night at the club, I hooked him up with local teen talent to help give the night the exposure it needed. He paid me a finder's fee for each act and a promise to let me rock the stage at the "best of" showcase. After my showcase, I even became his most requested female artist. The most requested male and female artist earned a hundred dollars every performance. Between the bazaar, promotions, and performances, I knew how to get money. A *job*, however, simply provided steady cash flow, consistently.

Between my hustle, steady cash flow, the experience, and my education, there was nothing to stop me from saving up enough money to move and go after my dreams.

After only two job interviews, I landed a job at Kmart as a cashier. My starting pay was a whopping $6.25 per hour. It was chump change, but it was my steady chump change, and it meant that I didn't have to rely on Zion when I was short for things I needed. I appreciated his willingness to take care of me, but I didn't want him to think that I accepted what he did to make the money, because I didn't. In fact, I felt like the biggest hypocrite when I had to ask him for financial help. So, I stopped asking and went without.

"What time do you get off work again?" Zion asked as he pulled up into the Kmart parking lot.

"I get off at six o'clock tonight."

Zion parked and then turned to face me. He lifted a hand to the side of my face and caressed it softly. I smiled. Batting my eyes, I bit my lip, then leaned in for a succulent kiss. He drew his lips between his teeth.

"Those lips feel so good, baby," he said.

The way he stared at me made me giddy all over. I felt my cheeks heat under his gaze. "What?" I asked curiously.

He glanced over my face with such admiration. Using his forefinger, he lifted my chin so that we were directly eye-to-eye. "I'm so damn proud of you. Do you know that?"

"Zi…on," I said, stretching his name out in an appreciative singsong fashion. "Babe, that's so sweet of you."

The light rumble that escaped him, I felt to my core. "Your man can be a little sensitive. Only with you, though." We shared a knowing grin. "Real talk though, I'm super proud of you. You see something you want, and you go get it. You inspire me."

I melted into him. Zion had always been in my corner, no matter what, but to hear him make such a declaration made me feel ten feet tall. He fueled me. With him, I felt unstoppable and like I could accomplish anything I wanted in life. He believed in me so much. His words gave me the courage to move mountains and command rivers. I felt godlike under his love.

I found his lips again, and we deepened our kiss, our tongues intertwining the entire time. Before we took it to a place that we shouldn't, I pulled back. "You know I feel the same about you," I said.

He shook his head. "This moment is about you. Not me." His eyes darted over to the clock on the dashboard. "You better get up outta here. You got five minutes. Don't want you to be late on your first day at the gig."

Smiling, I nodded and kissed him again. "Pick me up at six."

"I'll be here at 5:50, ready and waiting."

I opened his car door and eased out. He slapped my behind before I could get all the way out. "Love you!"

Biting his lip, he winked at me. "I love you more. Now tuck my ass away and have a good day."

I laughed as I closed the door and made my way inside the building. The first hour of my time was uneventful. I met the manager, James, who had me complete all of my final paperwork for HR. He also issued out my work vest and gave me my name tag. After the formalities, James introduced me to Stacy, who I would be shadowing for the first week. The next leg of my first day was to take a tour of the store with the manager before joining Stacy for training.

As I walked out of the back office, I was so distracted putting on my vest, and next thing I knew, I collided right into someone.

"I'm so sorry!" I said frantically.

"Nah, it's my bad. I should've been watching where I was going."

I met eyes with this handsome young man. He looked studious with his black-rimmed glasses, button-up shirt, and jeans. He offered the sweetest smile to let me know that everything was all right.

"I didn't hurt you, did I?"

"No, I was more worried that I hurt you." His pearly whites were still on full display. I couldn't help but blush.

"I'm fine," I said.

"Good. By the way, I'm Quincy," he offered with his hand extended.

I took his hand and shook it. "I'm—"

"Liberty? Are you ready for the tour?" James interrupted.

Looking past Quincy, I nodded. "Yes, sir."

He patted Quincy on the back. "I see you've met Quincy. He's my best stocker. A hardworking young man, this one is," he said proudly.

"I appreciate that, sir," Quincy said, his eyes never leaving me.

"Well we'll let you gone and get clocked in," James said to Quincy. "How about that tour, Liberty?"

"Ready."

James and I walked off, and he spent the next thirty minutes giving me the tour of the store so I could familiarize myself with each department and the employee-only accesses. Then, I met up with Stacy so that she could train me on how to work the register. Before long, it was time to break for lunch. I had always loved the pizza from the deli, so I grabbed a slice along with a red soda pop, then sat down to eat.

"Liberty and justice for all," Quincy said, sliding into the booth opposite me.

I caught a falling slice of pepperoni as laughter trickled from my lips. "You almost made me drop my food."

"My bad," he apologized. "But you laughed, though."

I giggled. "I actually get that joke a lot. My little brother's name is Justice."

"You serious?" he chuckled.

I nodded.

"Your mom got hella creative when she named y'all."

I nodded. "Now, you know something about me, so tell me something about you."

"I work at Kmart. One of the hardest working stockers they have," he said, smiling.

My head fell back. "Good one. I hear it's a really dope place to work."

Quincy's lips curled upward. "It is now."

I shifted in my seat. My eyes grazed over Quincy as I tried not to make eye contact. That was arguably worse. His toffee-colored skin stretched over slightly muscular arms. Lifting all those boxes had done his body a lot of good. I couldn't pretend not to notice.

"I have a boyfriend," I blurted out of nowhere. It was more like my conscience speaking on my behalf.

The expression on Quincy's face showed his disappointment immediately, but he quickly recovered. "And now you have a friend that works at the dope Kmart."

We continued talking as I ate my food, and he munched on a granola bar. Afterward, he walked me back to my trainer, as we joked around the entire time. Quincy helped my first day go by smoothly. By the end of my shift, I knew how to operate the register itself and was happy to be able to check out a few customers on my own. Stacy explained that training would last the entire week, and then after that, I'd be on my own.

At the end of my shift, I clocked out and walked to the front of the store with my vest in my hand. On my way out of the door, Quincy met me.

"So, how was your first day?"

"It was pretty good, and someone made it a bit more entertaining."

"I aim to please." He placed his hand on the door and glanced at me. "Allow me."

I was beyond impressed by his chivalry. He opened the door and allowed me to walk ahead of him before he exited directly behind me.

"Thank you."

"You're welcome, Ms. Liberty."

Before we could exchange another word, the beep of a horn and loud bass pulled us into its direction. Zion was standing with one foot out of his car, his hand on the roof, and staring in my direction at me and Quincy.

"The boyfriend?" Quincy asked.

I turned to face him. "Yes. Guess I'd better get going."

"All right." He nodded. "Have a good one."

"You too." I waved goodbye and made my way across the parking lot to Zion's car. When I made it to his ride, he was already inside. I opened the door, climbed in, and leaned over to kiss him.

He glanced over at me then muted the music. "Hey. Good day?"

"Oh yeah. Work was cool."

"Mmmhmm." He tossed his chin to Quincy. "Who's your new friend?"

I followed his eyes. Quincy was heading toward his car. "Who? Quincy?"

"Yeah, *Quincy*." Zion tossed a glare over at me.

I fanned off his jealousy. "He works there, babe. Don't worry, he already knows I'm yours."

Zion bobbed his head. "Good. Just long as Poindexter knows," he said, unmuting the music and peeling off.

# CHAPTER 22

*May 8, 1998*

IT'D BEEN THREE months, and I was still thriving at my new job and school. I was happy that I was able to maintain the two because my mother had already told me that if I couldn't maintain my job and my grades that the job would have to go, and I could not let that happen. I loved my independence and having consistent pay in my pocket. But this weekend, I was off. I knew my paycheck was going to take a hit, but it was worth it because Libby B was about to bless the mic again at JC's.

Now that it'd warmed up, JC's was back and hopping. Everybody loved the local talent nights, and the teen night was just as popular. Most importantly, people wanted to see *me*. For that, I was ecstatic. JC made me a headliner, so all wasn't lost because I got to cop that hundred dollars for my performance. Besides, I'd worked hard at school and at work, I deserved the downtime to be able to hang out with my friends and my man.

"So y'all are coming to my spoken word poetry slam tomorrow, right?" I asked, standing up at my locker, facing Unique and Terica.

Unique shook her head. "Sorry, girl, I can't. I have to work."

"Aww man!" I whined, throwing my head back.

"I know. I tried to get off, but you know how Mickey D's is about weekends. Would it hurt for people to eat at home sometimes?" Unique asked.

Terica and I looked at each other. "It's the fries!" we said together, much to Unique's dismay.

"Sorry, girl. Mickey D's shouldn't be so damn good," Terica said. "Them damn fries be calling me, Scotty," she said in her best Pookie from *New Jack City* voice.

We burst into laughter, and I hugged Unique. "Aww, it's okay, girl. There will be other shows."

"You know I would be there if I could," Unique added, hugging me back.

"I know girl."

"Well, I guess I have to rep for the both of us," Terica added, high-fiving Unique.

"And I'll be there, too," Zion said, his voice sounding behind me.

I turned around and flung myself into his arms. "What are you doing here? Principal Macklin would have a fit if he knew you were in the school!"

Pointing at Lonnie, who stood beside him, he said, "I dropped him off." They gave each other dap. "Don't worry. I'll be out before the bell rings."

"You're gonna be there too, right, Lonnie?" I asked.

"Of course." He gave me dap. "Ima head to class. I'll holla at you tomorrow, homie." He and Zion touched knuckles, and he walked off.

"We are gonna let you two lovebirds have your moment," Terica said as she and Unique walked off together.

No sooner than they walked off did Zion pull me into him for a quick kiss and feel.

"Damn. You smell so good. Ya man been missing all of this. Between school and work, it seems like I never see you."

I sucked my teeth and leaned against the locker. "Well your extracurricular activities have a little something to do with our missed time too."

"Here we go." He brushed his hand down the nape of his neck. "Don't start, Liberty."

"You promised me that you'd slow down and get out the game," I fussed. "Seems like you've sped up and haven't backed off at all. Besides, I want to see you more."

He swung his arms outward. "I'm coming to the show tomorrow. I'm making time."

I stared him down. "But what about after that? When will I see you again? It's always something…" I leaned in close to him. "I can hardly get in touch with you anymore. I hit you up and it takes hours, if not days for you to return my page. I feel like you coming tomorrow is just to pacify me."

His jawline hardened, his nostrils flaring from frustration. "I didn't come here to argue. It seems like even when I try, you gotta problem. I'm about to bounce. Ain't nobody got time for this."

"Hey, *Zion*," Keisha, one of many of Zion's fans said as she moseyed past us with her friends. "When you gonna let me swing by?"

"When you want me to swing on your ass?" I came up off the locker, stepping toward her.

She rolled her eyes, and Zion stepped between us, pushing me back against the locker with his arms around my waist. "Don't do that."

"Yeah, you better tame her ass. Run up and get done up." She tossed her long black and red braids around as her friends laughed.

"Move around, Keisha," Zion barked, never taking his eyes or arms off me.

"Humph. Well, you know where to find me. My number ain't changed." She sucked her teeth, and she and her girls moved on.

My heated glare shot at Zion. "Are you cheating on me? Is

that why I hardly ever see you?"

"Get off that," he huffed. "Listen, you can't be trippin' and letting these females get to you. Especially not no damn hood rat."

"I'm not. I'm trippin' off you and the fact that I don't see you like I used to."

The first bell rang, interrupting our conversation. Zion's face warmed, and he stared at me lovingly and lifted my chin with his forefinger. "Baby, I gotta go. I'm sorry. I'm gonna do better by you. I swear." I tried to look away, but he guided my chin back to him. "Look, why don't I pick you up tonight from work, and we can kick it? Would you like that?"

Zion knew exactly how to get next to me. I wanted to be mad at him. I wanted to fuss and cuss and get him to agree to leave OCG and stop with the dope-boy antics, but once again, I was trapped in his rapture. In moments like this, nothing mattered but him. My face heated with a blush.

"That's my girl," he whispered lovingly.

"Fine. Pick me up at seven tonight from work, and we can hang out."

He pecked my lips and released me. "I'll be there ten minutes early."

I grabbed a stack of flyers. "Since you're gonna be out in these streets anyway, pass out these flyers so I can get a bigger crowd at my show."

He took the flyers. "You already know I got you." He gave me a juicy kiss. "Gotta go. I love you, Liberty."

"I love you more, Zion Malik Mitchell." I pursed my lips and watched him walk away.

Before he could exit the door, he received head nods and daps from guys who wished they could be put on, and flirtatious stares and comments from a couple of disrespectful groupies. I let it go. Besides, I had to get to class.

"Liberty and justice for all," Quincy said sweetly as he entered the break room where I was preparing for work.

Slipping on my vest, I glanced up. "Oh, hey, Quincy."

Stopping in mid-stride, he stepped back and placed a hand on my arm to prevent me from walking off. "No quirky comeback or snappy joke?"

"Not today." I shook my head.

His cheerful expression turned serious. "Hey, are you all right?"

Although my shoulders slumped, I still denied it. "I'm fine, really," I lied.

Despite my words, his reaction told me that he didn't believe me. "You know if you ever need to talk, I'm here. I give the best advice."

My eyes fluttered, and I couldn't hold back the grin that spread on my face. "Oh yeah, says who?"

"Hell, me," he chuckled, breaking up my melancholy mood.

"You are a trip!"

He stood in front of me and cleared his throat. "But you're in a better mood."

My eyes rolled around before I agreed around a blush. "Yeah, I guess I am." Placing my hand on top of his, I said, "Thank you."

Gently, he placed my hand into his, rubbing the back of it with his thumb. "Any time."

Although I knew it was inappropriate, I didn't readily pull away from him, but rather basked in the moment for a second. He glanced at me and moved closer, closing the space between us. My heart thumped and raced as my breathing hitched.

"You know I don't know who has you down, but just know that anyone who puts anything less than a smile on your face doesn't deserve your time." He brought his free hand to my cheek and gently stroked it. "Remember that."

Swallowing hard, I backed away from him. "I... uhh... I... have to... go. My shift has started," I stammered, trying to avert his gaze and whatever was brewing between us.

He released my hand. "Duty calls."

"Yep, duty calls," I reiterated before abruptly turning to leave.

I hightailed it out of the break room so fast I was surprised I didn't leave shoe tracks and a trail of fire. Quincy and I had become fast friends since I started working at Kmart. He never stepped out of line out of respect for my relationship, but he did flirt at times. I told myself it was all innocent. Otherwise, our times were filled with casual conversation, jokes, and talking about safe topics in our lives. For me, that was school, poetry and rap, and my friends. Never Zion. For Quincy, the main subjects were work, his aspirations, and his family and friends. I knew that he didn't have a girlfriend and that he lived on his own. Besides working at Kmart, he was a physical fitness trainer, which was where his physique came from. He was eighteen and had graduated high school already. Since he didn't want to go off to college, his parents were adamant that he couldn't stay at home. They thought it would force him to go off to college, but it did the opposite. It forced him to be independent. We definitely had that in common.

That commonality between us was what drew us together as friends. I was able to talk to him about my aspirations and visions in a much different way than I could with my friends and people my age. Hell, even in a different way than I could with Zion. One reason was that I hardly ever saw Zion, but the next was that it was refreshing to talk to someone who wanted similar goals in life. It felt like a relief to know that I wasn't the lone ranger who wanted better for myself. While college may not have been for Quincy, he still wanted more out of life, and he was determined not to fall victim to the streets.

My mind raced over my issues with Zion. All kinds of thoughts swirled in my head about our future and how we got so far off track. I couldn't wrap my mind around the fact that for as much as I loved him, I felt distant from him, and worse, I felt that he was pulling away from me. This was not how I'd planned for us to be. I did believe that he loved me. I felt it in his gazes and his kisses, but I couldn't help but wonder if it was enough. Could we survive this awkward place that we'd found ourselves in, or had our childhood love run its course?

Every time I felt low about the state of my relationship with Zion, Quincy appeared. It seemed he had a knack for knowing when he needed to pop up on me. He always had a joke or comment that made me laugh or that brought a smile to my face. Not to mention, he was easy on the eyes. We were teased at work about being a couple, and everyone claimed we would end up together once we revealed that we weren't an item. I couldn't see myself falling for another man. Not when Zion had already stolen my heart.

"Feeling better?" Quincy asked as we clocked out at the end of our shift.

Turning to him, I rubbed his forearm. "Much thanks to you."

We walked out of the break room, talking about the shenanigans of the day at the store. Before we reached the front, Quincy stopped me. "Can I give you some advice?"

I shrugged. "Sure. According to you, you give the best advice."

He chuckled before getting quiet. "Don't ever let anyone or anything change you. I see how you are here, and lately, you seemed to shrink around your man. If the puzzle piece doesn't fit, Liberty, don't force it."

I allowed his words to marinate.

"What if the piece fits, but it's just worn out a little? You know, requires more time and patience."

He turned to me, sincerity in his eyes. "Then it sounds like you need a new puzzle."

"Quincy, I—"

He put his hand up to stop me. "No explanation needed. I just wanted you to know that I notice." He stepped into my space. "And this puzzle, will be patiently waiting on the shelf for you." Before he opened the front door, he turned back to me. "And best of luck at your showcase tomorrow. I know you're going to show out."

I walked out and removed my backpack purse off my shoulder. Unzipping it, I pulled out a flyer and handed it to Quincy. "Here."

He took the flyer and looked it over with furrowed eyebrows. "What is this?"

"It's me inviting you to my showcase."

Shocked, he glanced up at me. "Seriously? You're inviting me?"

"Yes." I smiled. "I'd love to see you there. Besides, after uplifting my spirits today, I realize now I'll need you there."

"A'ight. Bet. I'll be there."

I jumped up and down as excitement surged through my body. "For real?"

"Yes. I wouldn't miss it for the world."

"Yayyy!" I shouted. "Thank you. I appreciate the support."

"Fo' sho," he said, and looked out to the parking lot past me. He tilted his head. "He's waiting for you."

Jumping, I turned to see Zion sitting on the hood of his car with a blunt between his lips.

Quincy tossed a hand wave to Zion, but Zion didn't return the gesture.

I turned back to face Quincy. "I gotta go."

"A'ight. I'll see you tomorrow. And remember what I said."

"I will." I quickly turned and jogged over to the car with Zion. I was nervous about how much of my exchange with Quincy he'd seen. "Hey, babe."

He killed the blunt and pulled me to him. "Hey, baby. You ready?"

"Yes."

He kissed me long and hard then opened the door for me to get in. When I nestled inside the passenger seat, I felt relieved that Zion hadn't seen much to be concerned with, and everything between us was copacetic. When he got in the car, I gazed over at him and gave him a reassuring smile, and he smiled back before he pulled off for our date.

# CHAPTER 23

M Y NEXTEL CHIRPED as I sat in my car in front of JC's. I ignored the call again. It was from Liberty. I took a few tokes on the joint and debated whether I should go inside. Truth be told, I loved Liberty, but she was constantly pressuring me to change as if the real me wasn't good enough for her anymore. I knew she meant well, but the shit was aggravating. This life was all I knew. It was all I had. She wanted to live in this fairy tale world, but I lived in the real world. And in my world, I didn't have a lot of options. I knew what I had to do: beat the block and stack my paper as high as I could, and a nigga had to keep from getting smoked.

I saw the inevitable getting ready to happen. I'd always known she'd outgrow me. I noticed the small changes in her long ago. After Shaneria's death, those changes grew by leaps and bounds. Liberty had matured and was coming into her own. Her desires for a better life, one that couldn't include me, had taken root and were coming to fruition. I was proud of her, but I was scared. I was scared because I knew the more she grew into her own, the less I could be a part of her life. I wouldn't and couldn't fit in the world that Liberty was destined to live in. I held on to the little bit of time where I got to enjoy her before I was cast out and forced to admire her from afar.

My eyes were lidded from the haze of smoke when the time reflected that the show had started an hour ago. No matter what, I couldn't leave my baby hanging. If Liberty decided to leave me, I wouldn't give her a reason, and I damn sure wasn't going to hand over my woman on a silver platter to no square who worked at Kmart. I exited the car and sprayed some Issey Miyake over me to camouflage the stench of the loud. Afterwards, I headed inside.

Freddie was at the front collecting the door fees for the night. When I saw him, we hit each other with a head nod, slapped hands, and pulled each other into a one-arm embrace.

"What's up, famo?" Freddie said. "You running late. The surprise guests—Mr. Pookie and Mr. Lucci—just rocked it out. Your girl got next."

"I know. I know. Shiidd. Had to handle some bidness. You know how that go." I whipped out my five-dollar entry fee.

Freddie shook his head. "Bro you know I got you. Gone head inside before you miss your girl."

"'Preciate that, fam," I said with a dap.

"It's all love," Freddie said, giving the bouncer the signal to let me through.

He was right. I was just about to miss Libby B bless the mic. When I entered, my baby had just taken the stage. I spotted Terica and Lonnie at the front table to the side that we always sat at. At first, I was mesmerized by the piece she was spittin'. It was about finding true love, and the shit was so poetic it damn near made my eyes leak. As I headed to our usual table, I noticed someone on the side of Lonnie. He scooted his chair over, then leaned back in his chair, smiling up at the stage. I hung back. As Liberty finished up her first piece, the crowd erupted, and they gave a standing ovation. That's when I honed in on Mr. Kmart. He stood proudly, smiling, and clapping. I followed his eyes to the stage, and Liberty's eyes were fixed on his as she shared his smile.

"Hey, bro, you leaving already?" Freddie asked, confused when he saw me bend the corner.

"Yeah, man. I needed to get up outta here." My jaw was tight as I fought the urge to check dude.

Freddie held out a hand to stop me. "Yo, you good?"

Before I could answer, a sweet and tender voice bellowed my name. "Hey, Zion."

I turned to see who had addressed me. It was Peaches—this fine honey dip stallion from around the way. Everybody wanted a spin with her. She only had a thing for big ballers and shot callers, though. In fact, she was Saint's girl. Or, at least, Saint *thought* that she was his girl.

"Whassup?" I tossed back. The effects of my high were evident in my drawl.

Her long slender legs moved in my direction, walking up on my six-foot frame. "You."

A smirk crossed my face as I finessed my chin beard. "Ain't got time for no games tonight, Peaches. You have a good one."

"Who's playing?" she questioned, running her long pink fingernails up the middle of my chest and all over my bling. "I mean, but I do have something you can play with."

I side-eyed her, but then I caught a glimpse of Mr. Kmart and turned back to her. "Is that right?" She nodded. "Let's get up outta here then," I ordered.

She took my hand and kissed my cheek. "I thought you'd never ask."

"Zion…" Freddie said, his voice and raised eyebrow issuing a warning.

I patted his shoulder with my free hand, reassuring him. "I'm straight. Besides, Peaches won't hurt a fly."

Before we got into my car, I slipped the strap from my waist and tucked it on the right side of the seat.

"Ready to pick up where we left off the other night?" Peaches asked, sliding her yellow thongs off from under that tight dress. She brushed them across my nose and my manhood woke up.

"Hell yeah." I started the engine and that turbo bass kicked in, shaking the entire car as Master P's "Burbons and Lacs" filtered through. I couldn't put the whip in drive fast enough.

# CHAPTER 24

*I* SHOULD'VE FELT HIGH as a kite. In some ways, I was on cloud 9. JC had decided to make me a regular act which meant he paid regularly. I was becoming more popular as a local artist in Dallas and doors were slowly starting to open. I had talent scouts and two record labels from Houston interested in signing me. Mama told me to be patient and stay solo until I figured out which direction I wanted to go. This way I wouldn't be handcuffed to anyone. But all in all, I knew I was destined for success. Whether I signed with a label, stayed independent, or started my own all female hip-hop label. The stars were aligning. But while I was happy and feeling the love from everyone, Zion Malik Mitchell was missing from the equation.

Peering out into the large crowd, not once did I spot Zion. When my act was over, I joined my friends. Lonnie and Pac-Man were there. Terica was there. Even Quincy was there. Yet, there was no sign of Zion anywhere.

I thanked and hugged everyone for coming out and showing their support, including Quincy. After Quincy and I embraced, I felt the cold stares of Pac-Man and Lonnie on me, but I didn't care. Turning to Pac-Man and Lonnie, I asked, "Hey, have either of you seen or talked to Zion?"

Both of them shook their heads. "Nah, I haven't seen or talked to him," Lonnie added.

Pac-Man scratched and rubbed his jaw. His gaze looked both confused and questioning. I didn't know if it was about Zion or

Quincy. Either way, he'd have to spill what was on his mind.

"I talked to him a couple of hours before the show, and he said he was definitely going to be here. I don't know what happened," Pac-Man explained.

"Pac, can you call him, please?" I asked.

He lifted his Nokia out of his jeans pocket. "Yeah, I'll hit him up."

"Thank you," I said, relief washing over me.

Terica motioned for me to come with her, so while Pac-Man was trying to touch base with Zion, I walked off with her. I led her to the back of JC's to the small corridor that led to the women's restroom. We stopped in the hallway, and she glanced up at me nervously.

"What's wrong, Terica?"

She rolled her eyes before letting out an exasperated breath. Her hand went to my shoulder, and I knew whatever she was about to relay to me was not good. "Listen, don't trip. It may be nothing—"

"Or it could be something," I interrupted. "Spill it."

"Sis, I've been hearing some rumors. At least, I hope they're rumors. But some females have been talking and saying how they been spotting Zion at different spots. One chick told me he got that community dick now."

My mouth fell open.

"I'm just saying because I can't have you going out like that. I hope you making sure he's strapping up."

My head fell in defeat. I was beyond embarrassed. "Yeah. We use condoms." Sadly, Terica wasn't telling me anything I hadn't heard or wasn't already suspicious of. Trying to save face, I said, "But we always hear foolishness. You know how these hos hate on our relationship."

"Yeah, but I heard last week he was pushing up on Peaches. *Saint's* Peaches. Saint from his rival gang, aka the leader of the Greedy Grove Kingz. And I got that word on good authority." She hit her hands together and rubbed them as if she were trying to warm them up. "And real talk, I saw Peaches in here tonight. She wasn't with nobody but her gold-digging girls, but when I went to call the waitress, I swear I thought I saw her and Zion leave out the front door—together."

My stomach plummeted. There was no way he would do something like that to me. Not on my night. It couldn't be true. Zion wouldn't do me like that.

"You must be mistaken. You probably saw her leave with Saint."

Terica gave me that you-know-better-than-that look. "I might not recognize Saint when I see him, but you know damn well, I know what Zion looks like. I'm not trying to ruin your night or nothing Libby, but I know what I saw. Granted, my vision was skewed, and it's dark in here. Hell, maybe I'm wrong, but I had to tell you what I saw, or thought I saw. Mannnn, you know what I'm trying to say."

I didn't want to believe what Terica said, not because I didn't believe her but because if it was true, it would devastate me, and I'd have to call into question everything about Zion and our relationship.

Without another word, I walked out of the corridor and back to the table. I had to. If I hadn't, I would've hyperventilated and passed out from the bombshell that Terica dropped on me. I was grateful for what she'd told me, but I couldn't wrap my mind around it at the moment. If I dwelled on it too long, I would've broken down in the middle of the club.

Quincy caught me by the arm and turned me toward him. "Hey," he said, his forehead crinkled and his eyes filled with concern. "You all right?"

I shook my hands as I paced back and forth. "I don't know."

Pac-Man and Lonnie walked over to us, and Pac-Man stepped in front of Quincy. "You good, Liberty?" Pac-Man asked.

"I don't really know," I said aimlessly before looking up at him. "Did you talk to Zion?"

He scratched the back of his head. "Nah, he didn't pick up."

I slid into a chair at our table. My head fell into my hands as I tried not to break down. My heart galloped like a harras of Clydesdales. Suddenly, I was hot, and sweat beads populated on my head. My skin felt clammy and my breathing became erratic.

"Liberty, you all right?" Terica asked.

"Get her some water," Quincy called out before kneeling in front of me and taking my hands into his. "Breathe, Liberty. Just breathe." He looked back at Lonnie, Pac-Man, and Terica, who were staring at him with questioning expressions on their faces. "Why are y'all just standing there? Get her some cold water."

Terica went to the bar and grabbed a bottled water. The next act was preparing to come to the stage, so when she returned, all of us began to make our way out of the venue. That's when it dawned on me… Freddie. Quincy helped me up out of the chair and led me to the front, and when I spotted Freddie, I gripped his arm.

His expression was defensive until he saw who was touching him. Immediately, his face softened into an expression that I couldn't readily read.

"Great performance, Libby B"

"Thanks." I cut straight to the chase. "Have you seen Zion?"

A gust of wind released from his lips, and he shrugged. "It's been a lot of people in and out tonight."

"But has one of them been Zion?"

"I wasn't on the door all night, Lib." He turned his focus to security, seemingly ignoring my question.

"Freddie!" I squealed. All eyes were on me from my irritated outburst. Onlookers looked like they pitied me, which added to my anxiety.

Quincy put his hand up to stop me once he noticed my

labored breathing return and guided me out of the door while I still belted Freddie's name, trying to get him to tell me if he'd seen Zion, although it was apparent that he was not volunteering any information.

Once outside, I paced in place, fanning myself as Quincy stayed with me, helping me breathe through my panicked state, all under the watchful eyes of Lonnie, Pac-Man, and even Terica. She handed me the bottled water, and I drank half of it in one gulp. Everyone's concerned eyes were on me, but it was Quincy who spoke up.

He stepped into my space with both hands gently gripping my arms. "Liberty, are you good?"

"She'd be better if you kept your distance," Pac-Man spat. His attitude was on full display, showing that he had grown tired of Quincy.

After recapping my bottle, I fanned myself. "Yes, I suffer from anxiety attacks. I haven't had one in a long time. I'll be fine." My words intercepted whatever argument was about to brew between Quincy and Pac-Man.

Quincy's eyes furrowed, seeking reassurance. "Are you *sure*?"

I heard Pac-Man's scoff before I could answer. "Yeah, she's sure." He walked in between us, but his focus was on Quincy. "Why are you so concerned? I thought you said you were just a co-worker. Y'all ain't on the clock. You showing a little bit too much concern for my boy's girl than I'm comfortable with."

Quincy's heated gaze flashed at Pac-Man as he stepped back. "And what concern is that of yours? If your boy was so concerned with his girl, then he would've been here tonight."

"Muthafucka, what you say?" Pac-Man bowed up and stepped toward Quincy.

Lonnie rushed over between them and patted Pac-Man on the chest. He leaned close to him. "Not here. Security will call the cops. You don't need that on you. Chill." He turned and faced

Quincy. "Besides, fuck him. We all know what it is between Liberty and Zion. Ain't that right, Liberty?"

Reluctantly, I nodded. "Quincy, it's fine. I'm sorry to be a burden. Please just let it go."

He scoffed, but his lips turned upward into a half smile. "You are never a burden to me. It's all good." His words garnered a momentary truce amongst them. "Do you need me to take you home?"

"We have her," Lonnie intervened before Pac-Man could respond or, worse, square off with Quincy.

I turned and waved my hands downward, motioning for them to chill out. "I got this, Lonnie. Thanks." I turned back to Quincy. "One of them will take me home but thank you for the offer."

He paused for a moment before he offered me the sweetest smile. "A'ight. I just want to make sure that you're good."

"I swear this mayne really trying to make me knuckle up tonight." Pac-Man flicked his nose and shook his head. His words were to Lonnie, but it was directed toward Quincy.

"You should go," I said to Quincy.

Nodding, he began to backpedal away. "Great show tonight, Libby B. I can't wait to see more of them."

I waved to him. "Thanks. See you at work."

Once Quincy was gone, I turned to Pac-Man and Lonnie. "Y'all can be so rude."

Pac-Man pointed. "Mr. Kmart can be so out of line." The disgusted look on his face was evident. "What you expect, Liberty? Zion is our mans. I'm down for him for life. We thought you were too."

Fire lit inside of me, and I flew up in Pac-Man's face. "Don't you dare say that to me!" I yelled. "I've been down with Zion before y'all even really became friends. But he ain't acting down for me. You wanna come at me, but where was he tonight, huh? Where was he last weekend?" Pac-Man put his head down, and I sucked my teeth. "Exactly! Now get that shit straight before you question *my* loyalty!"

Terica's ride pulled up, and she hugged me before leaving. Lonnie walked up to me. "Listen, let me take you home."

"You drove?"

"Yeah, my mama let me hold her car." He looked back at Pac-Man, who was leaning against the club wall with one foot propped up and a cigarette in his hand. "Besides, I'm sure you don't want to ride with Pac right now."

A reluctant chuckle escaped me, and I agreed. "You're right. I don't."

Lonnie walked over to tell Pac-Man goodbye, and he and I gave each other half-hearted waves. Once I was inside the passenger side of Lonnie's car, I explained to him what I'd heard about Zion.

"I know you're his friend, but please be honest with me. Do you know if it's true? Do you think it's true?"

Lonnie remained quiet without answering my question or saying a word. I probably burned a hole in the side of his face from staring so hard. After a few minutes of no response, I got irritated and turned on the radio to kill the silence. When we arrived at my house, I grabbed my backpack and yanked his car door open, but the force of his strong hand stopped me, causing me to glare at him.

"As Zion's friend, I can't confirm none of what you told me." He swallowed deeply and looked away from me. "But as *your* friend, I can't deny none of what you told me." He let go of my arm. "Y'all my family. Work it out."

That's all he said to me, and he refused to look at me. I knew that was his code for that being all the information that he was willing to provide. My soul was crushed because I knew exactly what he was telling me. I jumped out of his car with a swiftness. I almost bulldozed the front door of my house to keep Lonnie from seeing the tears that streamed down my face. There was no way I would let any of them witness my breakdown. I told my mom I was home and barely made it to my bedroom before the dam broke. To silence my cries, I buried my face in my pillow and released the gut-wrenching torture that plagued me. Every memory that I ever shared with Zion flooded my thoughts like a tidal wave. I couldn't stop reliving all of our special moments. Every hug. Every laugh. Every tear. Every kiss. Every touch. It seemed like the film reel of our years of loving each other was drowning me in a sea of regret.

It was well after one in the morning when I found the strength to shower and change. As I lay in bed, I tried to drift off to sleep, but every time I closed my eyes, Lonnie's words swam through my mind like an unwanted and reoccurring nightmare. Finally, I sat up and turned on my bedside lamp. Snatching my house phone up, I dialed Zion's number. No answer. I dialed again. No answer. I dialed again. Voicemail.

"Zion," I said shakily. "Why?" It was all I could manage to say before I hung up.

Placing the phone back on the cradle, I turned my light off and lay there, allowing the never-ending flow to slide down the corners of my eyes. I didn't even know when I fell asleep, but eventually I felt the sunlight on my face and heard the birds chirping outside my window. When I rolled over my alarm clock read 9:56 a.m. Mama had left a note on my nightstand. She'd tried to wake me, but I wouldn't budge so she told me that she'd left for the beauty salon, and she wouldn't be back until later. Not caring about anything, I rolled over and tried my best to go back to sleep, but slumber was a tiresome feat, and after tossing more than resting, I gave up and got up. It was only 10:45 a.m.

Easing inside the bathroom, I examined my appearance. A

far cry from my beautiful looks for my performance at JC's just mere hours ago. My red and puffy eyes were hard evidence of the tears I'd shed all night, and I wanted to rid myself of it just like I wanted to rid myself of the aching pain in my chest and the sour feeling in the pit of my belly. Using a washcloth, I warmed it and pressed it against my eyes to soothe them and wipe away the crud. After repeating that a few times, I reached into the medicine cabinet and dropped some eye drops into my eyes. That cleared up the redness. If only there was a Visine for the heart. One drop would clear all the heartache away.

Opting for the warmth of the shower, I climbed inside and enjoyed the spray washing over me as it mixed with my silent sobs. It was going to be a lounge-clothes-and-cereal type of day. The breakfast of heartbreak.

As soon as I finished eating it, my doorbell rang. I figured it was Terica coming to check on me. I walked to the door and peeped out of the peephole only to find Zion standing on my front porch. I gasped because I was surprised to see him. Part of me didn't even want to answer the door. But the part of me that loved him wanted to open it and work out our relationship.

"Liberty, I know you're in there. Open up. You know who it is."

As I unlatched all three locks for the door, including the dead bolt, my anger grew. I swung the door open and unleashed.

"What? What do *you* want?"

He put his head down, rubbing the back of it with his hand.

"Can I come inside, please?"

"Nah, you can't."

Bracing his weight against the doorframe by his hands, he pleaded, "Please baby."

Even in my anger, I was a sucker for one of his "babys". Damn him for saying it. Damn me for falling for it. As if he used the magic password, I opened the door wider and beckoned him inside. He slowly walked in, and I shut the door behind him. He was headed to my bedroom when I stopped him.

"Whatever you gotta say to me you can say it from right here."

Zion spun around. "You being serious right now? So, we can't even go in your bedroom and talk?"

"We can do that from here. Mama is gone to her hair appointment, and Justice is at our cousin's, so we have all the privacy we need right here. Now what do you want?" I stood with my arms crossed.

He slowly turned around, fidgeting and shifting his weight from one foot to the other. "I'm sorry I missed your show. I got tied up and—"

"Did you cheat on me?" The question erupted, interrupting whatever lie he'd cooked up.

He was stunned speechless for a moment. "Huh? What?"

"No, you didn't cheat on me, or yes, you did?"

"Liberty, where is this coming from? You're my girl. I love you. So why would you even accuse me of some shit like that?"

I walked up to him, not caring that he towered over me. "You didn't answer my question, Zion."

"Yes, I did," he argued.

"No, you talked around the question. I want a live and direct answer."

"Liberty, I missed the show and I'm sorry about that. Damn."

I threw my hands up. "God! You can't even answer me."

"I ain't do nothing, Liberty!"

"So, you didn't leave my show with Peaches?"

He lifted his snapback cap off his head and placed it down on the nearby table. He laced his fingers behind his head as he paced from side to side.

"Didn't think I knew, did you?" I walked up to him face-to-face. "So why don't you tell me the truth for once? Tell me where you really were while I was at my showcase."

"Liberty." He shook his head.

Suddenly, the tears that I'd been withholding resurfaced. I'd tried hard not to show any emotion but knowing that I was so close to hearing my greatest fear and worst nightmare, I couldn't help it. My body betrayed me, and I began to break all the way down. I keeled over from the pain coursing through every fiber of my soul.

"Hey, hey," Zion said as he tried to wrap his arms around me to lift me up. "Baby, please don't cry."

I shoved him. "Don't touch me!" I screamed. "Just tell me, Zion! *Tell me who she is!*"

He backed away and swiped his eyes. The look of defeat and sadness told me everything I needed to know. Still, I propped myself up against the wall and waited for him to respond in his own words.

"I was with Peaches last night."

The blow attacked me like a front kick to my heart. I clutched my chest.

"Did you sleep with her?"

He closed his eyes and the one-word answer released from his lips. "Yes."

I slid down the wall and sank to the floor. My head dropped into my hands. Tears flooded my face but my screams had somehow gotten trapped in my throat. My throat constricted, and suddenly, I couldn't breathe.

Zion rushed over to me, snatching my face between his huge hands.

"Liberty, baby, I'm so sorry."

Finally, I found my voice. "Whyyyyy, Zion?"

"Baby I—"

*SLAP!*

He looked at me in a state of shock as he held the left side of his face.

"How many times?"

"With *her*?"

Anger flew into my eyes. "With *her*?" My chest heaved. "How many others?" He got quiet. "How many?" I screamed.

"I don't know."

"You don't know!"

"I only slept with Peaches because you had Quincy at your show!"

The admission gave me new life, and I sprang up with the strength of a high jumper. Now, I was livid. "I invited my *friend*, and you take that as a pass to go cheat on me? Not with just one broad, but you're out here juggling me and a fucking community of bitches!"

"The *community*? Now that's a little extreme."

"Arghhhh!" I was enraged. "Get out!" I shook my head as a realization hit me. "That's why you knew exactly what to do with me on my first time. Coaxing me through the pain. Explaining when I was coming. Washing away my cherry-pop stains. And here I thought we were sharing our first time *together*." My voice cracked. "That's what I get for being so stupid and believing everything you say. It was all lies. All of it! You never loved me."

He walked over and wrapped his arms around me.

"I'm sorry, Liberty. Damn, I'm sorry. I can't tell you enough how sorry I am. I know I've done some fucked-up things to you, but you have my word, it won't happen again. You're who I love, and you know that. Those gold-digging broads were just something to do. It didn't mean shit to me. But *you*, you are my heart."

Pushing away from him, I swung the door open. "Get out."

"Nah, man, I can't lose you, Liberty. Don't do this, baby. You're my Mrs. Forever, remember?"

"Once Peaches and the rest of them became your 'Mrs. Right Now,'" I seethed, "Mrs. Forever got ghost. I ain't sharing my man, and I'm damn sure not staying loyal to someone who could never be loyal to me!"

"What I need to do, huh?" He gripped me in place as he pressed his forehead against mine. "What I need to do to make us right? Please, baby. Tell me."

"You can let me go."

"I can't do that. I *won't* do that." He slipped his hand to my neck and held it as he kissed my spot. "Tell me what I need to do, baby. Show me how to act right. *Please.*"

He planted more kisses to my neck. My lips. His hand reached underneath my top and found my breasts free and nipples fully erect.

"I'm sorry, baby."

I stopped resisting once his lips connected with my nipples.

"You're my oxygen, baby," he said, placing his lips against mine. "I'd die without you, Liberty."

As much as I hated him at that moment, my heart and my loins had already forgiven him. I opened my eyes when he placed his forehead to mine. Tears trickled down his face. My breathing slowed, and I got reacquainted with my good senses.

"I need some time." I released a jagged breath.

"But you're not leaving me, right?"

"I don't know. I just need time alone."

His eyes became filled with regret, concern, and hope.

"Please don't leave me, baby."

Zion swiped the lonesome tear that cascaded down my cheek.

"Okay, Zion. I just want to be alone right now."

Looking defeated, he pulled away slowly. "Okay, I love you,

and I'm gonna make this up to you. I promise you that."

He pulled his keys from his pocket, all while studying me. After a few moments, he eased out of the door with his head bowed.

"I love you," he said, heading back to his car.

Those were his final words as I closed the door behind him. As soon as I locked it, I looked up and saw his baseball cap still sitting on the end table. I scooped it before heading to my bedroom to sulk in my sorrows. I wanted to call Terica, but there was no point. She already knew. Everyone had known—except for me. I felt like a fool. I reflected on something Grandma Sadie Pearle had said to Mama after Eugene had beaten her for the millionth time. *A man will only get away with what you allow.*

How much more of this was I going to tolerate?

# CHAPTER 25

*December 9, 1999*

IN THE YEAR and a half since the poetry slam, I still hadn't gotten over what Zion had done. For weeks afterward, he'd called me every day and attempted to see me so that we could speak in person, but I'd avoided him at all costs. According to Lonnie, he'd lost his mind wondering if he'd lost me. In fact, all of our friends tried to talk to me about him. Naturally, they wanted to gauge my temperature so they could report back to Zion which was exactly why I remained silent on the subject. I didn't owe Zion a thing, and I wasn't giving him the satisfaction of knowing exactly where we stood.

After another two weeks had passed, I finally called him. He came over and begged for my forgiveness—as I'd predicted he would. He promised on everything short of Jesus's old tombstone that he would never hurt or betray me again. Truth was, I loved Zion, so I forgave him. However, forgiveness didn't equate to forgetfulness. As soon as I forgave him, he assumed that meant that everything was back to normal. I was still with him in the sense that we were together, but exclusivity was a clause that he'd broken—so I no longer held myself to that standard either. However, I didn't express that to him. I wasn't out looking for a replacement, but I sure as hell wasn't going to remain faithful to someone who wasn't faithful to me. Love had afforded Zion the luxury of my forgiveness, but he was a day late and a dollar short of my trust without a vestige of pity.

With every passing day, I withdrew a little more from Zion. Deep down, I felt he knew that too. My conversations with him became surface level. While Terica was my best friend, I had shared things with him that I hadn't confided even to her. Like the fact that I could have gotten slapped with an attempted murder charge had it not been for Mama intervening and covering up what I had done to Eugene. At the time, I was too embarrassed to tell anyone else about the incident. But Zion, I knew he'd never judge me for what I had done. And through all of my dysfunctional family drama, he'd been my emotional pillow.

My confidant.

My best friend.

We'd swapped our darkest secrets and harrowing memories— and now, where I felt the responsibility to protect him like Mama had protected me, he didn't reciprocate.

None of that really mattered as much anymore, and it changed how I operated with him. My world no longer revolved around Zion Malik Mitchell, whereas in the past, I was down for him any place and any time.

"Penny for your thoughts?"

I glanced up from snacking on a beignet and red soda pop to see Quincy sitting in front of me. I'd been so lost in my thoughts that I had not heard him come into the break room or sit down.

"Oh hey, Quincy. I was just daydreaming about some stuff." I finished off my drink and tossed the can in the nearby trash receptacle.

With a tilted head, he searched my face and asked, "Stuff… or Zion?"

He barely knew me but could call my bluff in a second. If it were anybody else, that innate skill would be annoying, but it wasn't just anyone. It was Quincy, and coming from him, it felt thoughtful. Sweet, even.

"You are not going to let me sit in my thoughts today, huh?"

"Not when the thoughts have you down. We haven't spoken about your... *man*... since the night at JC's. That same look on your face then is the same one you have now. If I'm honest, I'm tired of seeing such a beautiful young lady with ugly scowls. Your man should make you smile. Nah, he should make you *beam*. And if he ain't doing that, then he doesn't deserve you."

"You do realize he would want to kick your ass if he knew you were flirting with his girl."

"Who said I was flirting? I'm just having a sincere conversation with a friend."

It was my turn to be floored. "Ooh, nice save." I grinned, amused by his comeback. "So, friend, what else do you *see?*"

Stealing one of my beignets, he bit into it and chewed. "It's not important what I see. It's important what you see. How you see yourself and what you want for yourself will determine who you allow in your life, and how you allow them to treat you. After all, a man will only get away with what you allow."

His words resonated with my spirit. He spoke that same truth that Grandma had said to Mama. I had intertwined my existence into Zion's so deeply that I hadn't thought I could exist without him. I had always imagined we'd be together. Forever. Even if I was angry at him and hurt by him, I couldn't see a life where we didn't coexist. It seemed inevitable.

"I don't think I know how to exist without him. We've been in each other's lives so long. It seems fated for us to be together," I confessed.

"I'm not talking about being together. I'm talking about his treatment of you. Perhaps, you all will always have each other, but how you treat each other should determine how you exist together. You should only be with the person who, despite it all, treats you well and makes you happy." He sat back and flipped his name badge in his hand. "Are you happy right now?"

I didn't even need time to think on that. I wasn't. Rather than admit that, I cowardly dodged the truth. "This conversation is getting a bit too real."

"And real friends should keep it real," Quincy replied, his brows furrowed as he gazed at me. He released a deep breath before he explained, "I'm not trying to break you up. I just want you to think about yourself and for you to be happy. If that's with Zion, so be it. But it should be authentic, Liberty. Never substitute authentic happiness for promised happiness. It doesn't work that way."

Quincy's words churned in my mind. For the first time, I considered whether I was truly happy in my relationship or if I was holding on because it was Zion.

Quincy touched my hand. "Don't ponder over it. I'm not trying to add to your stress level. I'm only offering *friendly* advice."

I smiled. "Seriously, that's great advice. I appreciate it." I cast my eyes upward, gazing directly at him. "And I appreciate you."

He blushed. Although, he tried to cover it.

"Don't get shy now, *friend*," I teased.

The corners of his lips curved upward behind a soft chuckle. "What can I say? Some people bring out the best in me."

For some reason, his declaration sent butterflies through my stomach.

"Don't get shy on me now," he said, tossing my words back at me.

I pointed my finger at him. "I can't stand you."

"That means you love me." He stood up.

"I do?" I asked playfully, standing with him.

"That's the plan." His words were solemn as he stared intently at me.

My cell phone buzzed with a text from Terica. She'd been hounding me to find out what we were doing for my birthday.

"I don't know," I said, speaking my thoughts aloud.

"Hmm?" Quincy said as we walked out of the break room together.

"It's Terica texting again about my plans."

"Plans for your eighteenth birthday next week?" Quincy asked.

Stunned, I stopped and turned to face him. "Wait. You remembered my birthday?"

"December fifteenth. I'd never forget it."

My mouth fell open in amazement. "I can't believe you remembered."

"I can't believe you thought I'd forgotten." We resumed walking. "What are your plans?"

"I'm not sure."

As we reached the front, he turned to me. "Whatever they are, make sure I'm included." He winked before he jogged back off to his station.

Once he left, I walked away, ran down an empty aisle and doubled over as I held my stomach of butterflies. A silent scream ripped through me. Quincy Bridges was doing something to me. And the feeling bubbling inside of me, could no longer be ignored.

---

Shoving my hands in my coat pocket for warmth, I paced the outside awning for the third time in the last ten minutes. Zion had dropped me off at work because my mother's car was on the fritz and I had no ride. I hated riding the public transportation in the wintertime because it was freezing on the buses, so I'd given in and asked him to take me. That also meant he had to pick me up. That explained why it was thirty minutes after my shift ended, and I was pacing in the cold weather. I refused to go back inside because if my manager knew that I was still waiting on my ride, he'd ask me to work until Zion arrived, and I was not trying to do that. Two weekends in a row I'd pulled twelve-hour shifts due to the Christmas crowds and this one Saturday night that I had the opportunity to get off on time at a decent hour meant I was going to take it. It was now 6:32 p.m. and I was heated. I'd attempted to call him but received no answer and my coded beeper messages hadn't been answered either.

At 6:45 p.m., Quincy exited the store. "Hey, what are you still doing out here?"

My attitude was evident as I sucked my teeth hard. "Waiting on... my ride," I said, pausing before I let Zion's name slip out of my mouth. And there I went protecting him... again.

Quincy grimaced with a half frown. "Zion. Just say you're waiting on him. You got off at six. He still ain't here?"

"Damn, clocking me much?"

"At least somebody's clocking for you. Your man ain't."

That stung like a bee. His outburst lit a flame inside and it wasn't because of what he'd said, but because he was right. At every turn, Zion proved Quincy right, and it made me feel and appear as if I were an idiot each and every time. The hurt must have shown on my face because Quincy rushed over to me with a look of regret plastered across his face.

"Look, I'm sorry," he said as he pulled me to the side away from the steady stream of Christmas shoppers entering and exiting the building. "It just pisses me off that he's careless and inconsiderate of you, and you still defend and protect him." He bounced from side to side in disgust. "At least give that credit to a man who'll take care of your heart."

Aghast, his words made me blink at the realness and rawness of them. Immediately, I could tell that last part slipped in anger because he seemed to regret that it'd come out. Wow. Zion had literally pushed everyone to their breaking point. Including Quincy.

Quincy opened his mouth to speak, but I intercepted him before he had a chance to renege. "It's okay. I know you mean well."

Quincy stood in silence with me for a few more minutes, then he relented his original thoughts and settled on a new one. "Listen, I can drop you off at home."

I thought of the repercussions of that move and quickly dismissed it. "I can't impose on you. I'm good."

"So, wait. You're just gonna stand out here in the cold and wait on him?"

"Yes, he'll be here," I answered more confidently than I felt. When Quincy returned my gaze with a doubtful glare, I added, "Don't let me hold you up. You're off work. You should go home and get some rest before they call you back inside."

"If you're waiting, I'm going to wait here with you."

Gently, I pushed him. "No, don't do that. Go home, Quincy. I'll be fine." He went to speak, but I stopped him. "If you stay, I'm uninviting you to my birthday party."

I could tell that he wanted to argue, but instead, he hit me with a head nod and waltzed to his burgundy two-door Chevy S-10 truck. When he walked away, I walked and stood under the lights to get some kind of warmth and comfort. I tried Zion twice more, and by the time it was 7:15, I was stuck at a crossroads between being scared to death and mad as hell. Neither Lonnie nor Pac-Man had talked to him or seen him, and neither could pick me up. Terica had a license and no car, and Unique was at work.

I paced back and forth again, and once a group of people left the store, my gaze followed them to the parking lot. I was amazed to see them parked next to Quincy's Chevy S-10. I startled him when I knocked on his door.

He unlocked it, and I pulled it open and hopped inside. It was nice and toasty, and for a moment, all I could do was warm my freezing hands against the vent. After a couple of minutes, I finally spoke. "You sat here and waited for me."

"I damn sure wasn't going to leave you stranded. I've been watching to make sure you're good since you refused to let me take you home."

I turned to the side and my body was facing him as he sat looking straight ahead. "So, you were going to sit here all night waiting to see if I made it home."

It was his turn to face me. "If that's what it took."

I leaned in closer, taking Quincy in. His round brown eyes with perfect lashes drew me in. He had innocent eyes. Sweet eyes. Eyes that appeared to have never spoken a lie in their life. Without thinking, I brought my hand to his face. "Why would you do that for me?"

He picked up my hand and caressed it in his. A beat passed before he offered, "You already know why."

A magnetic force seemed to pull us together, and before I could snap out of my trance, our lips met. It was soft and sweet at first, then the kiss deepened, and Quincy's hand was behind my neck, melding our mouths in an intense lip-lock. My hand gripped the front of his shirt and pulled him closer to me. Before long, a whimper escaped from me and that's when the realization of what we were doing hit me like a ton of bricks. Instead of jerking back as my initial reaction, I slowly pulled away.

"Waiting on me. Kissing me. Was that a part of the plan?"

"One day. I'm just happy it was today."

All of my pearly whites showed as I leaned forward, and our foreheads touched. "What am I going to do with you, Quincy Bridges?"

"You can start by letting me take you home. Everything else in due time."

Surprise filled me. "You know you have me right where you want me. A normal guy would take advantage of the opportunity."

He shook his head. "Nah, I don't want that. For one, I'm not a normal guy. I'm different. My mama raised a gentleman. Second, I don't want to take advantage of an opportunity. That's lazy. I want the opportunity to present itself to me. Then I'll know I earned it." He kissed my forehead. "I'll know that I earned you, Liberty."

I was putty in his hands, groomed for the taking, but he refused. I didn't know whether to be offended or highly flattered.

He tilted my chin upward with his forefinger. "I'm not trying to steal you from your man. I'm presenting you with a better option. I choose you, Liberty, but ain't no plan until you choose me back. That way your decision is one hundred percent on you. Not as blame, but as security. For now, I'm content with just taking you home—as your co-worker."

Everything inside me did somersaults. I was so scrambled and confused about how I felt that it was the first time I considered leaving Zion high and dry.

"I think I'd like you to do that."

A sideways smirk appeared across his gorgeous face. "Good. Buckle up."

Snapping my seat belt in place, I asked, "For the ride or for you?"

He winked. "Both."

# CHAPTER 26

*LIBERTY'S GONNA KILL me.* I was supposed to be at her job to pick her up at six o'clock, but I'd been tied up with Abel. We had a little situation with a disloyal soldier, and we had to issue our brand of discipline. Unfortunately, it was one of the soldiers that was on my block. I couldn't let sticky fingers slide on my watch. It showed weakness and lack of control. I'd been in the game now for a minute, and my rep would not be tested. Abel had hit me up about the discrepancy right when I was leaving the house to go and scoop Liberty. The business I was headed to tend to had to be discreet, so I left my cell phone at the house and only took my burner. The only people who had access to the burner number were select OCG members like Abel. I tried to handle that business as fast as I could, and more than disappointing Liberty, I had to be careful. Some things just couldn't be rushed nor handled carelessly.

As soon as we finished up, I rushed to the house to shower, grab my phone, and go pick her up. I had about fifteen missed calls, eight from her and a few from Lonnie, Pac-Man, and even Terica. I knew she was upset if Terica had hit my line. I tried calling her, but I didn't get an answer. The time on my dashboard read 7:15 p.m. I tried to call again and received no answer. I didn't know whether to be worried or scared. Either Liberty wasn't answering because something had happened to her, or she wasn't answering because she had gone back in to work or gotten a ride home. Either way, she was going to rip me a new one. I opted to believe the latter of the two explanations because Kmart was extremely busy since it was the holiday season.

At 7:20, I skidded into the Kmart parking lot. I damn near had my new Buick Regal on two wheels trying to get to Liberty. I knew she was probably thinking I was off doing her dirty with some female. Nah, never. At least never again. A female could pop up in my bed butt-booty naked, straddled across my waist, and I wouldn't flinch. Hell, I doubted I'd even rise to the occasion. Nope. I was a fast learner. It only took me one time nearly losing the love my life to know that there wasn't a woman in the world worth losing Liberty for. She had me forever and always. I couldn't wait to explain what had happened and treat her to a nice dinner and a gift for the inconvenience. In fact, I already had her next gift in mind. A beautiful diamond tennis bracelet and matching earrings.

When I pulled up to the front of Kmart, I didn't see her. After I called again and received no answer, I decided to park and run inside. That was until I looked straight in front of me and saw Quincy. I froze as I watched him lean over and lock lips with Liberty. My Liberty.

I didn't know what emotion overcame me the hardest: pain, regret, or anger. It seemed like a triple cocktail and as bad as I wanted to jump out and beat the shit out of Quincy, I couldn't. The betrayal and hurt of Liberty's actions pumped like venom through my veins. I gripped the steering wheel so hard my knuckles turned white and no matter how it hurt I couldn't look away. I couldn't move. Only watch them leave, together.

I sat there for a moment until I brought myself back to reality. I started up the car and my mind floated over all the times I'd questioned Liberty about Quincy. *It's nothing. We're just friends.* Was this her way of getting back at me? Or had they been messing around long before now? My thoughts quickly turned me bitter.

I pulled off, driving aimlessly. My mind was so scattered that I didn't know if I was coming or going. The faint sound of my ringtone jarred my attention. I picked up the phone and glanced at it. The number didn't readily ring a bell, so I answered, heated.

"Yeah?"

"Daddy, it's cold outside. Can you come over and warm me up?"

I was so distraught that I didn't recognize the voice. "Who the fuck is this?" I barked.

"I should be offended, but I know you got a flock, so I'll be nice this time. Besides, I really need you to come lay that pipe down again. It's Peaches with that pretty—"

Pulling the phone from my ear, I looked at it in disgust. "Peaches. What do you want?" My mood was still in a funk, and I hadn't processed what she'd said.

"I want you, daddy." Her words started to form a melody of seduction in my ear.

"On the cool?" I replied. "So where you at?"

"My crib."

"Where's Saint?"

"He had to make a run out of town. He won't be back until tomorrow night, which leaves me all alone. So, you coming through or you gotta babysit Liberty—"

"First of all, keep her name out yo' fuckin' mouth."

"Humph. My bad. Well, how about you come and put something in my mouth to keep me quiet."

"I'm on my way." I hung up and at the light turned my car and headed to Peaches's spot.

When I arrived, I almost changed my mind, but thoughts of Liberty's lips wrapped around Quincy's invaded me.

"Hey daddy," Peaches said, answering the door half naked in purple lace panties and bra as slow jams played low in the background, setting the ambiance.

I walked inside and she closed the door. She had incense burning and candles lit, but it was the Victoria's Secret "Love

Spell" that drove my senses insane. Liberty loved that scent. The moment Peaches turned back around I pulled her into my arms and kissed her like I'd missed her. I kept kissing her and backed her up to the couch, never taking my lips off her. She could barely keep up. Once we made it to the sofa, I pushed her down until she was planted on the cushions.

"Damn baby. Hold up. You ain't even let me catch no air. I wanted—"

"Shut up, Peaches. You wanted this wood. You wanted to do some things. Then shut up and let's do some things."

Any comeback she could think of was thwarted as I pounced on her, yanking her by the thighs to the edge of the sofa and pulling at her underwear. The fabric practically shredded at my forceful tug. I didn't skip a beat as I flipped her on all fours. With one hand, I dropped my jeans and boxers to my ankles, ripped open the condom that I had in my hand, sheathed myself, and slid right inside of Peaches from behind.

There wasn't anything sensual or romantic about our hookup. My mission was to get off. I needed to sex away the memory of Liberty and Quincy, and Peaches was the unfortunate scapegoat. I beasted out on her as if it were her fault. She seemed to enjoy it as she yelped and cried my name.

"Zion, baby, let me—"

The forceful slap against her bottom interrupted her pleas. Before she could speak again, I gripped her about her waist so roughly that the smacking sound of our bodies colliding made a song. My mind was fully on chasing the pending release. The more I thought of Liberty the harder I pounded into Peaches with more force and aggression. Peaches screamed at the top of her lungs and proclaimed the pleasure of her near completion.

"Yeah, whose is it?" I barked and pounded, knowing in my depths that the question really wasn't for her. I tugged at her hair and went deeper. "I said whose is it?"

"Yours! Oh gawd! It's yours, Zion. Ziooonnnn…"

"Oh yeah!" I hollered as we both reached our climax.

"Baby, what the fuck is wrong with—" Saint boomed, breaking through the front door.

I scrambled to pull up my jeans just in time for him to realize what was really going on. Peaches jumped up between us with her hands raised.

"Saint! It's not what you think!" she exclaimed.

The fury in his eyes of a scorned lover was unmistakable, and there was nothing that either of us could say or do to prevent the wrath that was to be handed down. Unfortunately, Peaches was the first to bear the brunt of Saint's punishment. He backhanded her without a second thought, and she went flying backward as he lunged toward me.

"You mutha! It's GGK. Ima dead me a OCG tonight!"

"Try it, mayne. OCG all day!" I yelled as we fought, knocking over anything in our way and crashing into furniture.

Peaches screamed at the top of her lungs for us to stop before we killed each other. It was no use. Saint and I were in a zone. Ironically, both of us fought over disrespect. My disrespect to him and the disrespect I felt from Liberty and Quincy. I was taking everything out on him that I wanted to take out on Quincy.

We'd fought so long and hard that neither of us heard when Five-O pulled up. All I felt were a set of hands pulling me off Saint. When I finally focused, a set of police officers were surrounding us. The severity of the moment didn't even register because of my blind rage. I sat handcuffed on the floor beside Saint as the police attempted to take a statement from Peaches. Saint and I sat heaving and glaring at each other with malice in our eyes when another pair of officers eased through the door.

"What we got here?" The middle-aged Black officer asked. It

was apparent that he was a gym buff, evidenced by his bulky frame. His superiority was clear from the swift report given by the first responders as they explained the version of events that they'd been able to piece together between Peaches's woeful sobs. My assumption was confirmed when they addressed him as Sergeant Johnson.

Once they were finished with their breakdown, Sgt. Johnson patted one of the younger officers on the back. "Good job. Why don't you two take off? Me and Sergeant Bilkins can take it from here." The officers exchanged glances, but neither questioned his authority.

"Yes, sir," the younger officers said in tandem before exiting the premises.

Sgt. Johnson turned to his partner and stated, "Finish up with the young woman, and I'll go over here and question these two." His tone was hardened, casting a sneer in our direction.

"10-4." Sgt. Bilkins complied as he pulled out his pad and pen, heading in Peaches's direction.

As soon as he walked away, Sergeant Johnson headed our way. His arrogant stance with his hands on his gun belt told me he was already about to be on some bullshit. He took a deep breath as he reared back. "You two knuckleheads wanna tell me your versions of what happened, or will you make it easy and cop to it so I can go ahead and haul your asses in for disorderly conduct?"

"Yo man," Saint tilted his chin to the cop. "Lemme holla at you."

Sgt. Johnson's eyes darted backward toward Sgt. Bilkins and Peaches before he eased Saint up and shuffled him to the side, just out of my earshot. My eyebrow shot up in curiosity as the two conversed in hushed tones. I looked up when Sgt. Johnson shoved Saint back beside me. I expected him to question me next. Instead, he turned and looked around before searching the house. My senses told me that it was about to get real for Peaches. She was known to sell weed out of her apartment for Saint. That's when it dawned on me. This dirty nigga was about to set his girl up because he'd caught her with me. When Sgt. Johnson returned, all I could think was that I was glad I had left my piece at my apartment. And I never carried product on me, so in my mind, I had nothing to worry about. I could beat a disorderly conduct charge.

Sgt. Johnson reached down and lifted me to my feet. "I am going to search you. Am I going to find anything?" he asked.

I shook my head. "Nah, mayne."

He patted me down and then searched my pockets. When he lifted his hand from my right pocket, he held a small baggie of weed. "Now, I thought you said I wouldn't find anything. Look at what we have here." He showcased the bag to Sgt. Bilkins and me, who had just finished speaking with Peaches.

"Say mayne, that's not mine!"

"Yeah right," Sgt. Bilkins chimed. "That's what they all say."

"Nah, I'm serious! It's not mine. You planted that on me!" I screamed at Sgt. Johnson, panic settling into my bones. That instinctively caused me to buck against what I knew was coming next.

Both officers started manhandling me and slammed me into the wall, knocking the wind out of me. With my face pressed sideways against the surface, my eyes landed at Saint, who held a smirk on his face. It wasn't Peaches he was setting up. It was me. There was no pleading a case that was already stacked against me, so I stilled and allowed the course of action to happen because I knew all they needed was a reason to go left, and I'd be damned if I gave them one. Sgt. Johnson Mirandized me before Sgt. Bilkins led me outside.

As soon as the police car door closed with me in the back seat, Sgt. Johnson unlocked the cuffs from Saint, and I knew there had to be a monetary exchange. My head dropped in despair. Johnson was on Saint's payroll. I was in GGK territory, and Sgt. Johnson came there to rescue Saint when he heard the address on the scanner. It all made sense.

The little hope I'd held dwindled as I pondered my current situation. With my juvenile record and now being eighteen, I was about to face the inside of a jail cell for the first time. It was a hundred things I could've gotten locked up for, and yet I was going down for this. My heart sank as I saw my entire life flash before my eyes. It was over for me, and I would have to spend my nineteenth birthday locked up.

# CHAPTER 27

*December 15, 1999*

IT WAS MY birthday, and I felt horrible because Zion was locked up. We knew he would have to serve some time because of the charges. I had visited him and told him that I wanted to be there for him through it, but he was withdrawn from me and everyone who cared about him. He was also ashamed because the streets were already talking before the handcuffs were even slapped on his wrists. It was only a matter of time before his dirt with Peaches caught up with him. I was just grateful no one got hurt. Yet, he still couldn't bring himself to tell me the truth of that night. Either way, I was committed to stand by his side. I wasn't going to leave him hanging when he needed me more than anything right now.

In light of everything going on, I wasn't in the mood to celebrate. I had always celebrated my birthday with Zion and this year I couldn't. My mother had tried to make it special for me by having Unique and Terica come over with my favorite chocolate cake. Everyone could tell I wasn't up for company, but we still made the most of the day. Later that day, I sat in my room writing poems, trying to pass time and keep my mind off Zion.

I heard the doorbell, but I assumed it was someone for Mama until my bedroom door opened and it was her alerting me that I had a visitor.

"Hey, Liberty. You have a guest. A very good-looking one at that," she smiled.

Confused, I hopped up and walked into the living room. Quincy stood up from the sofa the moment he saw me. "Hey Liberty."

"Quincy," I said surprised. In his hands were two huge balloons that said *Happy 18th Birthday*. My hands flew to my face in shock. "You remembered?" I walked over to him.

"I don't know why you keep thinking I have short-term memory."

My mother cleared her throat. "Oh, Mama, this is Quincy. He works with me at Kmart. Quincy, this is my mother, Lucille."

They shook hands. "Very pleased to meet you, Ms. Banks."

"You as well," Mama said. "This is a very nice gesture for my daughter."

Quincy smiled, but it was directed toward me. "Your daughter is an extraordinary young woman. She deserves this and so much more."

"I *really* like him," Mama said playfully, eyeing me. "Well, I'm gonna give you two your privacy. It was good meeting you, Quincy. Don't be a stranger now."

"Oh, I won't," Quincy replied, looking directly at me as Mama nodded approval before heading to her bedroom.

I lightly bumped his shoulder, eyeing all the gifts in his hands. "Flowers, balloons, and a card. You really outdid yourself."

He lifted a bag from behind his back. "This one is yours, too."

"Quincy, stop. You didn't have to do this for me."

He extended his hand with the gift. "I know I didn't have to. I wanted to. Here."

I accepted the gift, sat down, and removed all the colorful tissue paper. I hollered as I pulled out a box of beignet mix and a bottle of red soda pop. I couldn't stop smiling. There was also a CD. I stared up at Quincy. I flipped it back and forth. He sat next to me, and I side-eyed him.

"What's this?" He took the CD from me and opened it. On the outside of the CD, it read, For Liberty with Love.

"This," he said, handing the CD back to me, "is you. I recorded your performance and had my boy put it on a CD. That way, you'd always have a copy of your poetry slam. Your first spoken word CD."

Tears sprang to my eyes. Whatever strings Quincy had been pulling on my heart finally worked, and I caved. The emotions ripped through me, and I fell into his arms, unable to speak. I was filled with such joy and happiness. Then it hit me. It was the first time in two weeks that I'd smiled. Quincy made me smile. Quincy gave me joy and happiness. Quincy gave me peace. Tears slid down my cheeks.

"I didn't mean to make you upset—"

I raised my head and looked up at him. "No, this is the most thoughtful gift I've ever received, Quincy. I'm not upset. I'm happy. You make me happy. Very happy." I placed the gift bag and CD on the coffee table. "You make me beam," I admitted finally, reflecting on his words to me.

Placing my hand against his face, we couldn't tear our eyes away from each other. I leaned into him for a kiss. It was so passionate and glorious. When we finally parted, he leaned down and kissed me again.

"Look at opportunity presenting itself," he declared.

I couldn't help the joy that spread across my face. "And the decision was all mine."

He wrapped his arm around my shoulders. "So does this mean I no longer have to wait for you?"

Lacing my fingers with his, I said, "I'm ready to start on a new puzzle."

He exhaled for the both of us. "What about Zion?"

"He made his choice. Now it's time I make mine. You're here in this moment with me. And you make me happy."

"I make you *beam*," he corrected.

I nodded. "Yes, you make me beam."

"And you make me beam, too."

This time I exhaled for the both of us. "I feel like I'm at the State Fair and I finally won my prize."

"No, Liberty, you're the prize." He kissed me tenderly. "My prize."

# CHAPTER 28

*May 20, 2000*

"GIRL!" TERICA SCREAMED as she ran up to me in the line. "Can you believe this? We're about to be up out this bitch!"

We embraced warmly, with me playfully rubbing her new hairdo—a short curly fro. "Girl, no! I can't. It seems like we waited all of our lives for this moment, and now that it's here, it seems like it snuck up on us."

So much led up to the day we crossed over from teenagers to adulthood. It was May 20th, and the graduating class of 2000 was lining up and getting ready to walk the stage. We were a far cry different than the hip-hop-loving teens that had bounced through those doors as freshmen. So much had transpired throughout high school, but we made it, and I couldn't be prouder of all of us.

Terica had enlisted in the military and Unique was enrolled in cosmetology school and working at one of the local salons as a wash girl and braider. Lonnie had received a track scholarship to Grambling State University, and Pac-Man had dropped out our senior year and dedicated his days and nights to hustling. We noticed the change in him early on, and once he got a taste of the fast money and the perks that came with it, he was as good as gone. I blamed Zion the second Pac showed up one day with OCG tattoos and teardrops on his face. I knew he was in way too deep by then. But I kept my nose out of their street business. Because as Zion used to tell me, the less I knew, the better off I was.

As for me, I got accepted into the University of North Texas, and I hung my Kmart vest to be a part-time receptionist at the bank, making double the pay. I didn't enjoy writing music and poetry as much anymore, but that didn't mean my creative flames had been extinguished. I'd found new love in journalism and creative writing. And I was so lucky to have a supportive boyfriend like Quincy. We were still together and going strong. Terica and Unique were happy about our relationship when I first shared the news that we were official. Pac-Man and Lonnie on the other hand were not having it, but they respected my decision to move on from Zion. It was for the best. While I hadn't spoken to Zion much since he'd gotten locked up, I checked on him through Mama Jackie. Out of respect for my newfound relationship, we discussed more about what was happening in our own lives and kept the Zion discussions to a bare minimum.

Unique walked up and joined us as we embraced again. We met with Lonnie before the processional began, and he joined in on the hugs.

"Man, things won't be the same after this. I won't see my boys. And Ima miss y'all whiny asses too," Lonnie joked as we each pushed him.

"That's what summer break is for," I said smartly.

"Yeah, but ain't no telling when I'll be home though," Terica added, quietness stealing the moment and replacing our thoughts with sadness.

"Girl, give Uncle Sam those four years and bounce," Unique joked to try to lighten the mood. "And you," she said, pointing at Lonnie, "can come home some weekends and holidays." She walked up to him and pulled him to her. "I'll have something special waiting on you." She tilted her head and he bent down. They enveloped each other in a kiss.

"Keep kissing me like that and Ima bring you with me," Lonnie said.

Terica and I hid giggles. Who would have thought that senior year would bring Unique and Lonnie together as a couple? They were too cute and inseparable. Despite their banter, they both were miserable about their separation. They promised to keep the relationship going until they could be together again.

"You two are going to be all right," I offered up as encouragement.

"Says the one who is moving in with her lover boy," Unique added.

And there it was. My new reality.

Quincy had quit Kmart and moved onward and upward on his career path. Although he was still a part-time trainer on the weekends at the gym, he'd landed a lucrative paying job at Bainstone Tires as a manager. So, he rented a one-bedroom condo in one of the poshest suburbs on the outskirts of Dallas. Soon after, he'd asked me to move in with him, and I agreed.

Lonnie sucked his teeth at Unique's comment.

"Stop Lonnie. Zion and I will always have love for each other, but I'm with Quincy now.

"I know, I know. But it just ain't *right*," Lonnie threw out. He fanned it off. "But live your life. Zion crapped out and fumbled your heart." He pulled Unique close to him. "But see, I'm no fool. I learned from his mistake, which is why I ain't fumbling this one."

"Preach!" Terica and I hollered as Unique blushed.

"I'm happy for all y'all for real," Terica added. "All this love in the air. Maybe I'll catch me some."

"Well, we'll let y'all have your time," I said, motioning for Terica to come with me. As we walked away, I put my arm on her shoulder. "You all right?"

She shrugged. "I'm gonna miss y'all asses so much. Especially you. I wish you would've enlisted with me or something. We could've gone in on the buddy pass."

I cringed at the thought. "Girl me? And do what? Get kicked

out the first time they ask me to run five miles in two minutes?"
I joked.

Terica nodded. "Yeah, you right about that. You are not about
that life."

"At all. Heck and you know I can't stand for someone to yell at
me. Eugene's ass did enough of that. His PTSD was contagious."

"Yeah, I know," Terica relented.

"But we'll stay in contact, and I promise to meet up with you
whenever you're at home."

"Thank you, bestie. I love you mayne." She spread her arms apart.

"I love you right back," I said, leaning in to hug my friend.
She tried to hide the tears forming in her eyes. I looked away for a
beat before bringing my attention back to her.

"I never straight up said this but Zion stayed on that bullshit
and we all witnessed how that affected you. I can see that Quincy
is a good dude. He'll treat you right."

"Aww, thank you. Sometimes I felt like the crew hated me for
choosing him."

"Nah, we were a little salty because we're loyal to Zion. But
all of us knew you made the right choice, even Pac-Man and
Lonnie. They won't ever admit that, but they know you did." Her
eyes squinted. "Even if a *tiny* part of us still wishes you and Zion
were together," she said, smiling. "After all, y'all are married."

I scoffed at the reminder.

"Seriously though. What if y'all have like a soul tie or some
shit. You know they say that twin flame thing is real. What if this
is like some real urban legend shit and we find out that y'all share
the same soul and are the yin and yang—"

"Okay, stop." I laughed. "You sound crazy!" She laughed along
with me.

"No seriously though. I love seeing you happy."

"And I love being happy."

"Even though I really think you and Zion are twin—"

"Bye, *Felicia*!" I joked, walking off and leaving her behind.

———————

After graduation, we all met up outside the auditorium to meet our families. The time was filled with well wishes, sentimental hugs, and plenty of pictures to mark the momentous occasion. Once we'd all taken time to gather with our families, we reconvened with each other. In our usual fashion, we were passing time and cracking jokes when Pac-Man walked up to us.

"Pac!" we yelled in unison. Each of us ecstatic to see him. He hugged each one of us.

"Congratulations fam! Y'all did it!"

Lonnie tapped his chest. "Wish you could've done it with us." We all agreed.

"Nah, it ain't my scene. As long as I got to see y'all walk, I'm good." He reached in his pocket and pulled out a wad, then blessed each of us with a hundred-dollar bill as a graduation gift.

Pac-Man turned to me. "Zion sends his love. He's keeping his head up in there. I'm looking out for him. He ain't wanting for nothing."

Giving him a lighthearted smile, I nodded. "I know. I talk to Mama Jackie often."

"Good to know."

He seemed happy to hear that I hadn't completely abandoned Zion.

Suddenly Mama, Justice, and Quincy approached us. Pac-Man turned to him, and Quincy steeled. To all of our surprise, Pac-Man extended his hand to Quincy and they dapped each other. A collective release rang out among us all at the full-circle moment.

"Take care of her, man. If you don't, you'll have to see me. Real talk," Pac-Man said.

"I will," Quincy assured him.

Pac-Man nodded his approval and stepped out of the way. With Pac-Man all clear, Quincy came up to me and hugged me so tightly that he lifted me off the ground. "I'm so proud of you."

"Thank you." I reached out and took the flowers he held in his hand for me. "These are beautiful, babe."

"Just like you." He kissed my lips, and everyone relished in the moment.

"Congratulations, sweetie!" Mama yelled, rushing over with Justice by her side. She wrapped me in her arms before embracing each of my friends.

"And these are for you," Justice said with a mile long smile on his face.

"Thank you, Lil' Bro," I said, accepting the flowers and reaching in for a hug.

"Y'all gather together now so I can take a group picture. You too, Pac!" Mama said. Quincy stepped back and Mama pushed him forward. "Get back in there, Quincy. I want you all to cherish this very moment for a lifetime."

I pulled Justice in closer and positioned him directly in front of me as we all stood together, and Mama yelled, "On the count of three, shout… 'For Zion and Shaneria!'"

We all took in the moment and then smiled about our two lost friends, one to the grave, the other to the system.

"For Zion and Shaneria!" we shouted as she snapped.

―――――――

### October 10, 2014

As I sat with my fingers hovering over Terica's number in my phone and holding our old graduation day photo, those memories seemed so distant now. We'd lost contact, only hearing about each other in passing through old classmates and relatives. Lonnie lived in North Carolina with Unique, Terica was home and out of the military—living with her wife, Pac-Man and Shaneria were both gone to glory, Zion was in the wind, and I was happily married to Quincy with our beautiful baby girl, Queenie. In the hinterland of my mind, I reflected on what life would have been like had Mama not covered for me. My mind shifted back to Zion. What if I had to walk in his shoes and be behind those bars? What if I had stains on my record that prevented me from getting a decent job? I grew chills at the thought.

# CHAPTER 29

*December 24, 2016*

"GIRL, WE ARE gonna tear this Bundt cake up! Do you hear me?" Terica howled as she and her wife, Vanessa, stood from my living room sofa. "Lawd knows you can bake just like your mama."

"Aww, thanks, T! You know I try."

"Nah, you did that shit," Terica bellowed. "Our Christmas dinner is gonna be on point tomorrow."

Vanessa pointed at her. "If it makes it to dinner tomorrow," she teased, holding the wrapped cake pan in her hands and soliciting giggles from Terica and me.

"See how she do me, Liberty?" Terica feigned a pained expression, and Vanessa walked over and pecked her lips as an apology. "I guess I can forgive her this time." Terica moved closer to me and gave me a sideways hug. "Thank you for real for taking the time to do this for me and letting us hang out with you and this adorable bouncing boy today." She lifted King's little hand and kissed it as he offered her a toothless giggle.

"Girl, you already know you're welcome here anytime. You and Vanessa." I tilted my head toward her.

Vanessa placed a hand over her heart and cooed. "Thank you, Liberty, and likewise for you. It was so nice to finally be able to hang out with you and T today instead of phone calls and flyby visits."

Vanessa's assessment was spot on. We'd been trying to set up an all-girls day for forever, but between Vanessa's schedule and mine, it rarely panned out and usually wound up being solely Terica and me. During and after my pregnancy, even those times became scarce. The holidays seemed like the perfect time to Hallmark and wine—my friends' version of Netflix and chill. Vanessa was a huge romance fan like me, so we planned a light lunch with our favorite wines and the torture of Terica, who absolutely loathed those sappy love stories. Though Terica protested, our tag team duo was victorious, and Terica powered through because between her wife and me, it was a losing battle. Terica happily accepted her Bundt cake as the consolation prize.

I extended my arms, pulling Vanessa into me briefly before she turned and played with King. Once she was able to pull herself away from King, she turned to Terica. "Babe, I'll give y'all a minute. I'll be in the car." Terica handed her the car keys, and Vanessa and I said our goodbyes before she headed out of my house.

"She's beautiful and so sweet," I said to Terica once Vanessa was out of the door.

"Hell, that's 'cause you don't know her. I mean, yeah, she's gorgeous and sweet, but that woman is a Jamaican pit bull in heels. You know how y'all short women do."

My face turned red from trying not to keel over. "Well, us vertically challenged women aren't beat for the games y'all taller folks always play."

Terica and I shared in a bonded moment over our banter before I placed King in his bouncer. That's when she bear-hugged me, squeezing me with a locked grip. "I don't know how I made it through without you all those years, man. I'm glad we reconnected."

As we pulled away, we shared a solemn gaze between us of nostalgia and regret over our lost time together. "But we're back now. This time this shit is forever, girl." We locked pinky fingers as our promise to always keep our friendship tight.

"Listen, Ima call you on tomorrow and tell you how I destroyed this cake… probably before dinner like V said." She grinned. "But Ima let you get ready to go over to Ms. Jackie's. I can't believe y'all still close even though, you know… you and Zion…"

No one could have predicted that at the end of all of this, Zion and I wouldn't end up with each other. For a brief moment, Terica and I both got lost in the old memories of our crew and my past relationship with Zion. It seemed like our destiny had been usurped by a wrinkle in time that warped us into this alternate reality. It seemed surreal, but I couldn't be more grateful for life's twist and the blessing of Quincy and our family. I composed my thoughts.

"Yeah, Mama Jackie and I's relationship was always built on our bond aside from Zion. I honestly love her like a second mom."

Terica put her hands up in surrender. "Aye, you ain't gotta explain it to me. I remember how close you two were. Hell, closer than him and her back in the day, which was crazy as that was." She paused before continuing. "I know I've said it before, but seeing where you are now in life and what you've built…" She peered around my home, her gaze landing on King before she re-centered her attention on me. "You made the right choice. You and your little tribe here, it's a blessing. And I'm so proud of you, Liberty. Real talk."

Her words brought tears to my eyes, and I dabbed them hurriedly. "Ugh. Get outta here, T! You're going to make me ruin my makeup."

"Fine! Still overemotional, I see." She smirked. "Bye Baby King. Your mommy is kicking me out. Be easy and tell Ms. Jackie I said hello."

"I will."

She smiled down at my toothless and grinning son before chucking her deuces and heading out.

"Y'all be safe."

When she left, I quickly got myself and the kids together for

Mama Jackie's Christmas dinner. Every year, she hosted the small affair for her family. This year she insisted that we come because she missed us, and she wanted to see our newest bundle of joy.

When Quincy arrived home, the kids were ready, and I was putting the finishing touches on my makeup. With a lip pop, I examined myself in the full-length mirror. I'd worked hard to get rid of my baby weight gain and was thrilled at the results. My long-sleeved, sheer-patterned top complimented my red leather pants and black pumps. The outfit contoured to my slim, thick body, accentuating my curves and assets in all the right places.

"Looking good, Mrs. Bridges," Quincy said, swatting my behind before stepping into the shower.

"But don't I always?" I fluffed my hair with a shoulder shrug.

He pulled back the shower curtain and winked at me with a lip bite. "Sure do. Don't make me climb out of this shower and show you just how good you look to me."

A blush covered my face. "There's always later tonight, Mr. Bridges."

"Tonight it is!" His words filtered through as a shout above the loud streams of water.

I allowed him to finish up as I went to load the car with the Bundt cake I'd made for the party and pack up all King's necessities for a night out.

# CHAPTER 30

"THANK YOU FOR agreeing to come to Mama Jackie's dinner. She really wanted us there," I told Quincy as we approached her house.

Quincy pointed at me. "You're lucky she can cook." We laughed as we exited our Mercedes with Queenie and King in tow.

The night felt very intimate because it was only Mama Jackie and us. Her daughter had a new man, and she and her kids were visiting his people out of town. Mama Jackie's divorce from Calvin had been a little over a year ago, so she was feeling lonely, hence the reason she really wanted the extra company. I understood that she didn't want to spend the holiday alone.

We'd feasted on a meal fit for a whole kingdom. Mama Jackie put her foot in some collard greens, skillet macaroni and cheese, cornbread dressing, ham, turkey, potato salad, yams, broccoli casserole, chicken wings, black-eyed peas, white rice, flapjack, buttermilk pie, and sweet iced tea. Between the food and drinks, conversation flowed effortlessly. Jackie got acquainted with King while Queenie enjoyed playing all the games upstairs that she could stand.

"Whew, Ms. Jackie, you outdid yourself. I'm about to pop!" Quincy bellowed, patting his stomach as he and I sat down on the living room sofa to prepare to watch a Christmas comedy with her.

"I'm so glad you enjoyed it," she said with a smile as she sat in her favorite lounge chair, holding our sleeping son in her arms.

231

Queenie had clocked out about thirty minutes before King and was asleep in the guest bedroom. We hoped we could make it through the movie without King waking up. Those days of carefree quality time were already few and far between for Quincy and me.

Just as we settled into the movie, the front door opened, scaring the life out of all of us.

"Hey, Mama! We made it."

My eyes widened, and I stopped breathing momentarily at the familiarity of the voice filtering from the foyer to the living room. All three of us gawked at the man and woman entering the living room hand in hand, in coordinated designer fashions. And if our expressions resembled even an ounce of theirs, they were just as shocked and clueless as we were about our presence as we were about theirs.

"Zion?" Mama Jackie's voice floated out, breaking the deafening silence.

Rather than answer, Zion's bafflement could not be mistaken as his eyes darted back and forth between Mama Jackie and me.

"What are you doing here?" Mama Jackie quizzed. "I thought you said you were spending the holidays with Tonya's parents?"

"Oh, my sister surprised them with a cruise for Christmas. So rather than spend the holidays alone, just the two of us, I wanted to come visit my future mother-in-law," Tonya answered for Zion, smiling.

I felt ambushed. Mama Jackie never mentioned that Zion was out of jail. Let alone joining us for dinner. I peered over at Quincy. His energy matched mine. We were both ready to go.

"Well, Zion, I'm sure you remember… Liberty."

Zion cleared his throat. "Of course I do, Mama. Don't be funny." His eyes rolled over at me, but he was speaking to Tonya. "Bae, this is Liberty Banks—"

"Bridges," Quincy corrected, his tone filled with a sternness I had never witnessed before.

I felt lightheaded, and a knot immediately formed in my stomach.

A smirk graced Zion's face before he flicked the tip of his nose and nodded. He patted his chest with his hand. "My bad." Using that same hand, he extended it back in my direction. "This is Liberty Banks-*Bridges*." He stressed my name with all the smart-aleck arrogance he could muster. "And this her man—"

"*Husband*," Quincy interrupted again, standing from the sofa and extending his hand for a handshake to Tonya. "I'm Quincy. Liberty's husband."

Tonya shook his hand. I extended the same gesture, offering a handshake. "Pleased to meet you," I said.

"Beautiful family," she complimented, looking at King in Mama Jackie's lap.

"Yeah, this my newest grandbaby right here. Ain't he handsome?"

Tonya nodded. "He is."

"My Queenie pot is right upstairs sleeping," Mama Jackie said. "You'll get to meet her, too."

Tonya's smile was interminable until curiosity washed over her. "And how exactly do you two know each other again?" Her eyes were trained on me, but she was speaking to Zion.

Had to be.

I diverted my attention.

"We've known each other since what… fourth and fifth grade," Zion answered.

I cut my eyes up at him. "Sounds about right."

"That's cute… childhood friends. So y'all are basically like brother and sister."

"Humph. Sounds about right," Zion replied, this time cutting his eyes down at me. "Which reminds me, *sis*… happy belated birthday."

I looked up. I could feel Quincy's pounding pulse the instant he grabbed my hand.

"Oh wow. You just had a birthday, too?" Tonya asked me.

"I did. On the fifteenth."

Tonya looked from me to Zion. "Friends *and* twins? Interesting."

I pressed my lips tightly together.

Mama Jackie shifted in her seat and adjusted King. "Tonya, Zion, we have a lot of food in the kitchen. Go help yourselves to some dinner."

"Don't mind if we do. Come on, bae. I'll make your plate," Tonya said.

Zion snatched his eyes from me, and he and Tonya headed toward the kitchen. As soon as they were out of sight, my gaze landed on Mama Jackie. "I think it's time we head out."

"Nonsense." She waved off my comment. "I want you guys to stay with me and watch the movie. Don't worry about them. They probably only came to eat and leave anyhow," she scoffed.

My eyes darted to Quincy, who was wedged between irritation and obedience. His home training never allowed him to disrespect or refuse his elders, but I could sense that tonight would be the one time he'd reconsider that.

Turning back to face Mama Jackie, I started to decline when Quincy touched my arm to stop me. I turned my attention to him, and he shook his head. "Let's watch the movie, then we can leave," he said.

My eyes narrowed with the are-you-sure question embedded in my gaze, and he reassured me that it was fine. Giving him my silent agreement, I turned to Mama Jackie. "Okay, we'll stay for the movie."

With everyone comfortable, we settled in for the movie. It

wasn't long before the comedy filtered out the awkward energy and tension that had invaded the room.

Once the movie ended, Zion sat back on the sofa with his arms outstretched across the back with his long legs sprawled out in front of him. He and Quincy were a stark contrast. Zion now wore shoulder-length dreads, and his caramel-toned body was adorned by a fitted, royal blue Gucci jersey sweatshirt paired with black denim jeans and matching Air Jordans. He wore a diamond-encrusted, big-faced watch and pinky ring. His diamond-cut Cuban link chain hung low around his neck, and his custom grill had diamonds across the top row, signifying that he'd gotten his bankroll well above our poverty-stricken days. The tattoos on his hands were the only visible ink. Still, it gave the impression that an entire inkwell was underneath the barrier of his clothing.

On the other hand, Quincy's navy blue three-quarter-sleeved sweater, black tapered casual slacks, and blue and black chukkas complimented his cinnamon-colored skin. And I could appreciate his attire more because it was hand-picked by me. The only jewelry and fashion accessories he owned were his wedding band, a gold watch his grandfather gave him, and three belts. Both men had come from the hood and were acquainted with the struggle but resembled two sides of the same neighborhood coin. Yet, I saw the strength and worth in both men. They were kings and had the heart of a lion.

Before Quincy and I could get up to leave, Zion decided to engage us in conversation. I had a sinking feeling that the pleasant terms we'd managed to embrace were quickly coming to a halt.

"So, Libby B.… anymore babies in the cards?" Zion's question gave everyone pause.

I pulled my hair behind my ears.

Shifted in my seat.

"I don't know. Maybe. What about you?"

He cleared his throat. Sat up a little more and looked over at Tonya.

Tonya looked at me.

"Unfortunately, I'm told I can't have children. So…"

Zion rubbed her back.

Touched her leg.

Offered her a kiss.

Suddenly I felt nauseous. "I'm sorry to hear that," I managed. My sympathetic eyes held her. Then I looked up at Zion.

We were having a conversation, only our lips weren't moving.

"So, when did you get out?" Quincy asked.

Zion broke his connection with me and eyed my husband. The glare in his eyes reeked of deliberation. He was trying to get a sense of Quincy's angle. "I've been out a lil' minute. And I plan on staying out this time. Don't wanna let life pass me by."

"Good for you," Quincy said.

"Speaking of life passing by…" Tonya chimed in, nudging Zion. "It's time you took a few notes. Beautiful ring by the way," she complimented, staring at my hand.

Zion looked over at my left hand and pretended to strain his neck and his eyes.

"Thank you," I said to Tonya, refusing to give Zion the satisfaction. "It's actually quite sentimental to us because it was Quincy's great grandmother's wedding ring. She blessed our marriage before she transitioned."

"Oh my God, that's so sweet," Tonya said.

"And at the time, I couldn't afford the ring I really wanted her to have. So, I proposed with this one," Quincy shared, smiling the entire time.

"Thank you, honey. But a ring is only a piece of jewelry. I believe that when you find love, and you can share that special connection with someone, every second spent on the journey together, cherishing each other and all the memories made in between, is the ultimate gift and symbolism—of not only marriage—but eternal love."

"That's so deep. Now I'm curious to know how you two lovebirds met?"

"Humph, *Kmart*. Oh, my bad. It's y'all's story."

"He's right. We met at Kmart. I worked there part-time, and so did Liberty, back when she was in high school. When the opportunity arose, I shot my shot," Quincy said, smiling over at me.

Sitting forward, Zion raked his fingers through his locs. "Opportunity, huh?"

Licking his lips and zoning his eyes on Zion, Quincy nodded slowly. "Yep, opportunity."

Zion leaned forward, scoffing. "Funny thing is opportunity knocks. We all have seized opportunity. It's *inopportunity* that causes desperation."

"True, but when opportunity knocks, someone else has to *open* the door. Inopportunity is stalled at the door. But once that door is opened, it's fair game."

Tonya's face was now twisted. "I think I'm lost. What was the opportunity?"

I cleared my throat and placed my hand on Quincy's forearm, patting it. "Ultimately, things work out as they are destined to. That's all I'm sure Quincy is saying." I smiled, trying to ease the tension that Tonya was oblivious to. I looked over at Mama Jackie. She had dozed off. "Baby, pass me King," I told Quincy. He stood up and walked over to Mama Jackie, tapping her on the knee to not startle her.

"I'll take King off your hands, Ms. Jackie."

Mama Jackie stirred from her slumber and opened her eyes fully. She looked around at us as Quincy loaded King into his arms. "Y'all doing all right?"

"Yes. We're going to get going," I said, scooping King's bags.

"Okay. Now, don't you leave out of here, Liberty, before signing my magazine," Mama Jackie reminded.

"You got it. Let me do that right now."

"So, Libby B is still out here making moves in the entertainment world, huh?"

"And she has a featured story in *Essence!*" Mama Jackie bragged with a hand clap. "My baby!" she said proudly.

"*Essence?*" Tonya questioned. "How'd you manage to swing that?"

"Because she's a great writer, that's how," Mama Jackie enlightened.

I reached for the latest *Essence* magazine on her coffee table and went straight to my article. I had entitled it "Beautiful Scars." My picture graced the left page, and right underneath it, the opening of my personal story and experience on love, marriage, loss, and the power of self-healing—well, the cliff-notes version.

I reached inside my purse and fished for my special pen. Afterward, I begin to sign right underneath my picture. While I embraced my married name, I still adored my maiden name and the connection to my mother and grandmother. So all of my columns, articles, and creative works had Liberty Banks in the byline, but having it appear on the pages of *Essence*, was truly special.

"Congratulations. I knew you'd go far. Just thought it'd be more in the direction of music," Zion said. "Man, I remember how you used to battle rap in school and take those dudes' lunch money every time you fired off those bars," he chuckled. "You were cold, Libby. You could've been a star."

"She is a star! You better recognize," Mama Jackie retorted.

"Here you go, Mama Jackie. All signed." I passed the magazine to her, and she looked it over before pulling it close to her chest.

"Thanks, baby."

One of the reasons I had ventured away from spoken word and songwriting was because it reminded me of Zion. He never knew it, but he inspired all my poetry. He had been my muse. Once my muse faded, so had my desire to write poetry and music.

"I'm going to go ahead and knock out the last bit of dishes," Tonya volunteered. "Again, it was a pleasure to meet you both," she said, shaking my hand and then Quincy's. She stood and disappeared to the back of the house.

"Guess I'll go wake Queenie," I said. Tonya's exit was irrefutably my cue to leave.

> *"From the first day I met you,*
> *I knew our souls were tied.*
> *Lovers of hide and seek,*
> *Wishing wells won't tell...*
> *So if you run, I'll ride.*
> *Can't be the Bonnie to your Clyde...*
> *But I'll be the beach to your sand,*
> *That key to Forever Land...*
> *Crown my heart and my spirit,*
> *You already had my hand."*

The words Zion spoke serenaded my soul. I turned around and stared at him as the realization of what he'd spoken seeped through the crevices of my mind. He sat forward, holding my gaze.

"You heard it?" I managed through my surprise. He nodded, holding my attention hostage.

"I did."

My heartbeat quickened and I felt flushed.

"He heard what?" I heard Quincy ask.

"But how? I didn't think you..." My words trailed off, and Zion filled in the gaps.

"Every time you performed, I had the DJ at JC's put it on wax. That particular piece is committed to memory, but all the others, I have on CD. Mama been holding them in safekeeping for me."

I looked at Mama Jackie incredulously. Boy was that woman full of surprises.

"Y'all keep me out of it."

Before Zion could speak another word, Quincy broke our connection with his stance.

"I think it's best we go ahead and leave now," Quincy said tightly, passing King to me. "I'll go get Queenie." His expression was void of emotion, but I knew my husband. Inside, he was stewing. I nodded my agreement. His attention went to Mama Jackie as she stood. "Ms. Jackie, as always, thank you for the food and the hospitality."

Stepping in line with Quincy, she replied, "No problem, son. And I'll help you with baby girl."

That left Zion and me alone, King in my arms. For a few seconds, we stood deadlocked in a stare-down, and it was the first time that I had no clue what he could have been thinking. It was as if we both wanted to speak but couldn't find the words.

"I've always..." he started, then stopped. He blinked and looked away, but his eyes found me again. "You took away my oxygen, Liberty."

Our breathing fell in rhythm.

Our hearts cried out.

Our souls danced.

"I love you... still," Zion professed. "And I wish..."

His lips stopped moving.

I felt another presence in the room, so I fretfully looked over my shoulder. I exhaled when I saw that it was Mama Jackie.

"I better go." No sooner than the words left my mouth did

Quincy appear with our daughter in his hands. I followed his lead out of the door and to the car. Once inside, there was radio silence. I knew then that a storm had brewed, and all I could do was brace for impact as it made landfall.

# CHAPTER 31

ON CHRISTMAS DAY, Quincy and I enjoyed the day between our children and parents, however, there was still tension between us. He kept up pretenses, going along to get along, but I knew my husband. He was piping hot. Still, we carried on as if we had no care in the world.

The day after Christmas, Quincy still barely spoke two words to me. All of his attention went to Queenie and King. After he ate, he excused himself from the table and went to his man cave to watch television. I took the time to prepare my mind as I cleaned the kitchen and settled the kids.

While King was asleep for his nap, and with Queenie busy playing with the gazillion toys she'd gotten for Christmas, I made my way to Quincy's mantuary. I wanted to turn away the instant I got to the door, but we had to settle this matter between us. I hesitated for the briefest of moments before I lightly rapped on the door. His voice bellowed, "Come in."

Easing into the room, I stopped near the door. I observed my husband sitting in his recliner, his eyes fixed on the massive television screen mounted against the wall. After about five minutes of going between him and the television, I realized that if this conversation were going to happen, I would have to initiate it. When the game went to commercial, I made my move.

"So, you want to tell me what's eating at you? I know you're upset, but we need to address the elephant in the room. *This*," I said, waving my finger between him and me, "isn't us."

His face turned toward mine, and he scoffed. "Address the elephant in the room, huh?"

"Yes," I answered, pleading.

"Well I really don't want to talk about it."

"Quincy, don't do that. You're on vacation—"

"Exactly! I'm resting. I don't want to get into this conversation with you, Liberty."

"Ignoring the elephant in the room isn't going to solve anything either. Just… rip the bandage off."

His face scrunched before he slowly stood. "Okay, let's 'rip this bandage off' as you suggest." He tossed the remote and then walked until he stood face-to-face with me. "I have tolerated a lot of crap behind Zion, but what I won't do is let you continue to disrespect me. Furthermore, I won't allow him to disrespect me while you stand by all googly-eyed."

"Okay. I get it made you uncomfortable, but I don't think you were being disrespected. You're taking it too far."

"And that's exactly where the hell it went. Too far."

"Quincy, I think you're being unfair. Sure, the three of us have history—"

"You say that like I signed up for this damn unspoken love triangle you've pulled me into."

"*Love triangle*? How dare you."

"Well, that's sure as hell what it feels like. You have my ring on your finger, but Zion has his ring over your heart. You guys got married as kids for crying out loud. I can't compete with that. And no matter how hard I try, I can't unsee how you still look at him." He paused. Emotion rattling his words. "You think I can't see that Zion still has feelings for you?"

I said nothing.

"And you know it, too. That man is still in love with *my* wife, and judging the other night, you might be feeling the same way."

He turned around, pacing the floor, his frustration boiling over.

I remained silent. Allowed him this moment to speak his mind.

He turned back to me. How do you think it makes me feel knowing that you have a better relationship with his mother than mine? Ever consider that I may not want to hang out at my wife's ex-boyfriend's mother's house? Then I have to sit there and listen to his ass discount my role as your husband while taking you for a stroll down memory fucking lane!"

"Please," I sniffed. "Don't do that! And we've discussed my relationship with Mama Jackie. It's complicated, unconventional maybe, but you've always said that you were cool with it and that there was no threat. So you have no right to throw this shit in my face right now."

"Like hell I don't!"

The boom of Quincy's voice caused me to recoil. My heartbeat accelerated and Eugene's voice echoed in my mind. I threw my hands up. "We don't need to discuss this right now. Tempers are high and I'm afraid one of us is going to say something we will regret later."

"No. You wanted to talk about it, so let's talk."

I backed away toward the door. "Not like this."

"You want to skirt away now that the topic is too hot. When it's on you, you can't handle it, but when it's me, it's fire, hell, and brimstone."

That drew me back in. "What the hell are you talking about?"

"I'm talking about the fact that when my old friend, and ex, Eva, reached out to me, you felt disrespected and wanted me to walk away from the situation. I respected that. I did that for *you*. Hell, I even put up with this ridiculous and obsessive need for you to maintain a relationship with his mother for you, but the one time I needed you to stand firm on my team, you leave me hanging."

"Oh, I get it. That's what this is all about? You're feeling slighted because you missed out on an *opportunity*."

He waved me off and paced. "See, there you go. It's not even like that. You're taking what I said way out of context…" As Quincy was about to continue, the door crept open and Queenie ran inside. The concern and worry plastered on her face halted both of us as our attention turned to her.

"Daddy, Mommy, are you two fighting?"

Without an ounce of hesitation, Quincy rushed and picked up our daughter. He held her closely. "No, baby girl. We were just having a discussion, and we got a little excited. That's all." He kissed her cheek as a tear slid down. He wiped her face and leaned her head on his shoulder.

"It sounded like you and Mommy were yelling at each other. It sounded really scary," she whimpered through muffled cries.

"Oh no, baby. We were only having one of those serious adult debates, and like Daddy said, we got a little too excited. But we're okay." I placed my hand on her back and rubbed soft circles against it as Quincy eyed me, letting me know that at this point our conversation was dead in the water. Queenie lifted her head and wiped her wet eyes. I hugged her tightly, and while in the embrace, Quincy kissed her on the forehead and then turned and kissed my lips. Queenie smiled at the gesture, calming down even more.

"I'll tell you what, why don't I take you back upstairs, and we can play any game you want? How does that sound?" Quincy asked.

"Even tea party?"

Quincy jokingly groaned and nodded ardently. "Even tea party!"

"Yayyyyy!" Queenie screamed. "Mommy, can you come and play, too," she asked as Quincy placed her down on her feet.

My eyes glided over to Quincy, and he gripped my hand into his. "Of course she can!"

I winked at Queenie and agreed. "I sure can!"

She yelled excitedly and ran out the door full steam ahead, her pigtails flopping and her barrettes knocking. As soon as she turned the corner, Quincy released my hand. One look into his eyes and I knew that we still had an unsettled issue.

"Next time, trust me when I say it's not the right time to discuss something." His words were tight as he began to walk away to head upstairs with Queenie.

"Quincy..." He turned back, and the scathing expression on his face halted my words.

"*Later*. We have a child to tend to, and she comes before this blast-from-the-past bullshit."

With that, he retreated. All I could see was his masculine body moving down the hallway toward our daughter's bedroom. Although my heart was aching, I put on my mommy hat and plodded a few steps behind. He was right. Regardless of what we went through, Queenie and King came first. Still, at that moment, it had never been more apparent that I needed my husband back.

# CHAPTER 32

THE STILLNESS OF the night was something that I could finally appreciate. At first, it was a struggle. Chaos was a twenty-four-hour constant in the cage. During the day, the hustle between duty detail, the common area, COs and officials scurrying about, and the constant arguments and fights. At night, there were the moans and cries of inmates who had succumbed to their fate, and then the singing, banging, beating, and everything in between that helped the rest get through the night. Peace was something you were never afforded on the inside. Peace was a delicacy I appreciated in a way I never had before. Even when I'd obtained it, it took a moment for me to get used to it. Now, I was thriving in it.

As I lay against the bed, I was thankful for my newfound peace—Tonya's absence. Since the Christmas Eve dinner at my mother's, Tonya had been acting brand new. She had a trillion and one questions about my history with Liberty and then told me her intuition was telling her Liberty and I had been more than friends. She went as far as following Liberty on social media to see what she could uncover. Sadly, I knew she would only be spinning in circles because, with all that history, Liberty and I didn't have any physical evidence of what we shared. We didn't even have one single photograph. All we had were memories, poetry, and music.

Nonetheless, Tonya's insecurities were starting to have an undesired effect on me. I knew it was only a matter of time before we went our separate ways. Besides, she had given me an ultimatum. I cared for Tonya, but there was no way in hell I would marry her.

And rather than take her through the motions and finesse her with empty promises just to keep her around, I suggested we take a break. It forced me to think about the path I took in life. Despite the promises I had made while I was incarcerated, I eventually reverted to the street life. Hustling was second nature, and I already had the muscle and grind for it, which made it easier to bounce back after my bid. Otherwise, it would have been hard to survive with my rap sheet. My OCG family held me down when I was at my worst, and the second I hit the free world they were right there to put me back on my feet.

I took another pull of the blunt and allowed the 90s R&B throwbacks playing on my surround to settle the score with my misery. "On Bended Knee" by Boyz II Men fused in. At that moment, I knew the universe was fucking with me. My eyes started sweating. I couldn't hide from myself or the sadness rising inside of me. As the lyrics poured out, I found myself shedding a few tears. I wanted to press the replay on life. The replay on love. I thought about what I had gained and all that I had lost. Thought about my past hardships, transgressions, and my shortcomings. I questioned where I fit in with the rest of the world. In the midst of my weakness, I contemplated calling Tonya, then immediately decided against it. It would never work out. I couldn't love her the way she deserved to be loved. That much I knew for sure.

I took another pull of the blunt, shaking my head. There was a pang of achiness in the clefts of my heart as thoughts of Liberty consumed me. She had been the missing piece in my life—the rose that grew from the concrete. Seeing her thriving in her writing career and enjoying life with her family only added to my regrets. I didn't see much of a future for myself when we were kids, but I was in my rolling thirties now, and I knew more than anything that I wanted more out of life before it passed me by. It was about that time, and I knew exactly what I had to do.

I waltzed inside the haze-filled bando. A concoction that I was all too familiar with wafted right under my nose. To the front, Abel had his rooks—as he called them—running the count. When I swagged inside the room, everyone greeted me with respect.

"Pull up a chair, youngblood," Abel called out to me as he balanced a cigar at the tip of his lips. He and a few other members were playing dominoes.

I picked up one of the metal chairs on my path to the table where Abel and a few OGs were seated. "What up, folk?" I greeted the pack before shifting my attention to Abel. "Mind if I holler at you solo?"

Abel put his hand up to halt the game, peering at me through squinted eyes. When he saw the seriousness in my face, he nodded. "Aye yo! Everybody file out for a minute."

The OGs at the table wasted no time sliding back, but Jace, the main rook on the count, grumbled, then voiced his irritation.

"Come on, Abel. Shit gon' fuck up the count!"

All noise ceased as the focus of every man turned to Jace. Abel's face was scrunched as he eyed the rook. His hand instinctively moved to his waist making his position known. "I'on think I heard you. Say it again."

Jace went to open his mouth, but one of the rooks with sense put a hand on his arm.

"Seems like somebody got smarts," Abel said to the other rook. He pointed at Jace. "Your problem is you got more heart than smarts. You need both in this business. You damn sure need less mouth, too. Who money is it, Jace?"

He shook his head with disdain. "Yours." He flicked the tip of his nose.

"Right Mine. My money. My count. My order. My time. If

the count fucked up, you start over. Now, get your ass up and exit the *muthafuckin' premises*."

Jace and the other two rooks stood up and swaggered toward the door behind the OGs, who were also ready to put down whatever play that Abel called. When Jace walked past me, he gave me a shitty look. He moved along outside, and once the door was shut, Abel and I glanced at each other, and he shook his head.

"These young cats getting bolder by the generation. They don't breed them like you and Trei no more."

The mention of Trei shot a pang of guilt through my heart. I hadn't heard that name in years. As a unit, we still looked out for his mother, but I avoided her at all costs. Still, the mention of Trei reinforced my reason for being there. Get out before it was lights out.

"Speaking of Trei…" I said to Abel, "I'm gonna cut straight to it. I want out the game, Abel."

Abel leaned back in his seat and blew out a sharp breath. "So, you wanna bait me today, too?"

"Nah, fam. That's why I'm coming to you direct. Man to man."

"You know there ain't but two ways out."

"I know. But I also know it's your call. And no offense, big homie, but I ain't asking."

Abel pulled on his blunt and slowly released the stream of smoke in the air. His contemplation was evident, but so was his concession. "This shit was never you in the first place. You made it you. I made it you. But it wasn't. I knew that, so I protected you more." He huffed and stood up, then patted my shoulder. "But even baby birds gotta learn to fly."

I stood, and Abel pulled me into a one-armed hug. "I 'preciate the love and release, folk."

"Where you at with that last load?" Abel delved right back into business.

"Not much left to move. A couple of weeks tops." I patted his chest with the back of my hand. "You can pass it down to the next soldier."

He stood back and stroked his chin as his wheels seemingly turned. He nodded. "Good. Good. We straight then."

As we sealed it with our handshake, Abel lingered there momentarily. "Your presence will be missed."

"I'm retiring, OG, not leaving the damn country." A lighthearted chuckle bounced between us.

"Real talk, fam. We both know this retirement plan way different."

He was right. Some old heads still hung around, giving wisdom and keeping their eye on the block. They only removed themselves from a position that could land them in prison. He knew without me saying so that my departure was a clean break. No turning back. Still, this had been my life since I was young knucklehead, and Abel, what he'd done for me over the years wasn't something that I would easily forget.

"Yeah, but OCG is internal," I said.

"For the rest of us, it's eternal. Once the eternal is gone, the internal will follow, and for you, that's a good thing. Accept it," Abel offered as his final words of wisdom.

We left the conversation there. Our unspoken goodbye.

As my hand touched the doorknob, Abel said, "I know that county bid ain't make you change your tune." I turned slightly to face him as he blew out more smoke. "Ain't but one little red robin that makes you sing a new song. Liberty. Am I right?"

I didn't respond, but the goofy smile plastered said it all. "Nah, this decision was all me. Besides, she's married now."

"Being married doesn't make her bad people, or bad for you. Shit, she's just *married*. Truth be told, a lot of us would be better if we had a "Liberty" on our side."

"I hear ya. Y'all be easy, fam." I eased out of the door feeling freer than I ever had in my entire life. It seemed like everything good started with Liberty, and hopefully, ended with her, too.

I pulled away from the spot with a Nipsey Hussle banger in rotation, headed for my brand-new lease on life. Just two weeks away.

# CHAPTER 33

*January 10, 2017*

T-MINUS EIGHT HOURS. That's how long I had left as an official OCG member. It'd been thirteen days, sixteen hours, two minutes, and thirty-six seconds—but who was counting? As I cruised my hood, I swear I couldn't stop smiling. I had a few more hours to freedom. My obligation to my work with Abel had been fulfilled. Now, all I had left to do was move the new work he'd given me for safekeeping to the new stash house for my replacement. After that, I was done. For good.

The ring of freedom coursed through my veins. The banging, the dealing, and the jacking from back in the day—all of it had been cast into the sea of obliteration, and I'd survived it all and emerged transformed. It was as if the entire universe had aligned to welcome my rebirth. And I was ready.

The wheels of my souped-up Chevy Caprice turned the corner toward the old bando. I'd run these blocks for years, and it was the first time I ever really took in the scenery. As a young cat back then, I had been happy... proud even... that Abel had trusted me with the territory. The power I felt at the time was nothing more now than embarrassment. My steering wheel glided back to the left as I straightened the car into the street, headed to the last house on the block. My burner buzzed on my hip, and I lifted it to my ear.

"Speak on it."

"We at the spot."

"I'm pulling up in a few seconds. Shit locked up? We good?" I asked, pulling up in front of the bando to see my mans standing outside to the side of the house. The troubled look on his face said it all.

"Nah, fam. We ain't good," his voice came through the receiver before I slammed the phone down, threw the gearshift in park, and jumped out of the car.

My fluid steps matched my heartbeat as I approached Dru. "What the fuck happened?"

"Follow me."

I followed suit as we jogged the three steps to the trap house. "Nah, man… Fuck!" I shouted, laying eyes on the nightmare in front of me. On the floor, in a bloody mess, were the lookout, Stone, and one of my youngsters, Maintain, who was on watch. Their cold eyes stared back at me. I looked over at Tone, who stood beside them.

He lifted his hands. "When we got here to pack up the load, me and Dru found them stretched out like this."

My eyes shifted to Dru to gauge whether or not the truth was being spoken. Dru didn't even flinch. "Soon after I saw the shit, I called you. Whoever did this planned it. No product. No witnesses."

"We couldn't have been gone twenty, thirty minutes top," Tone added. He snapped his fingers. "Then poof, shit gone."

Silence gripped me before I let out a bloodcurdling scream and kicked over the few chairs in the makeshift living room. A gamut of emotions erupted in my body, but none more than rage. Rage over the young lives that had been snuffed out. Rage over the product that was now gone. Rage over the fact that I was so close to freedom.

I faced Dru. "Put the word out on every fucking corner. I

want every hustler from here to PG with their fucking eyes peeled. 'Cause somebody knows something. Whoever can put that information in my hands gets five bands. I need this shit resolved today. Not tomorrow. Today! Tone, call the cleaners."

"Got you," they said in unison.

"What about Abel?" Dru asked.

"I got him."

I hurried out of the spot and back to my Caprice. Taking a deep breath, I grabbed my burner.

"Yo, Zion. We wrapped?" Abel answered.

"Nah, fam. We robbed."

"The fuck you mean?"

<hr/>

For the next thirty minutes, Tone, Dru, and I put in calls and plays to find out who'd robbed me and where the product was located. Abel had arrived so fast I was sure he'd burned all the rubber off his brand-new Pirellis. Soon after his arrival, I dismissed Dru and Tone to beat the block for information while I explained the situation to Abel. The cleaners had wrapped up, but that didn't stop me from pacing the floor.

"You making me fucking dizzy. Calm down," Abel said once it was just us in the house.

"I can't!" I roared, my pent-up emotions spilling over.

He stood. "Calm down!" His order came out with finality. "We gon' get to the bottom of this, and when we do, we will handle that shit accordingly. Believe that."

My shoulders fell as my mind continued to mull over this major setback. Rubbing my neck, I propped one foot on the wall and leaned my head back. I knew this shit was too smooth. Nothing in my life had ever been smooth. Why had I expected this to be?

"Ain't nothing changed on my end. My word is my word." Abel's statement caused my eyebrows to arch in question as I opened my eyes, lifted my head, and stared at him to be sure I had heard him correctly. "You heard me. Somebody's gotta make it outta this hellhole to tell the story."

It was the first sense of relief that I'd felt since I rolled up to the bando. I walked over and slapped hands with him. Instead of our usual handshake, we pulled each other into a brotherly hug. No matter what, Abel was family.

"Let's get outta here. You need to clear your mind, and I do, too. 'Cause the way I'm set up, I'm merking the first thing moving," Abel said, as we headed out of the door.

———

The hours left passed by so slowly that I swore I heard each second tick in my mind. A different level of rage had set in by 9 p.m. when we made it back to the trap without any updates. Soon after we'd returned, our attention was snatched by a commotion at the front door. Dru had snatched some unknown youngblood through the doors, bumping him against the doorframe as he brought him into the room where Abel and I were posted.

"Aye, man!" the youngster protested. "You ain't gotta handle me like that."

"Shut up," Dru boomed, then snatched him by his arm and slung him in front of us. "Talk."

His fearful eyes met my and Abel's fearless ones. He didn't speak, but he had enough sense to lower his eyes. When Dru pushed him and ordered him to talk again, he kept his lips sealed.

The Glock was off my hip, cocked, and trained on his dome before he had the chance to plead for his life. "Trust me, your loyalty is hitched to the wrong muthafuckas. He asked twice. I ain't asking at all."

Shaking his head in frustration, he looked back up at me. "It was Jace, and two other rooks from y'all set. He said something about 'you ain't deserve no easy outs 'cause you already had it easy.'"

"How you know this?" Abel chimed in.

"My mama owes him. She on that shit heavy. Payback was to use our place as a stash spot," he admitted.

"Take me to them. I know you know where they are."

Abel put his hand up and patted my shoulder before addressing the youngster. "Nah, you take *me* to them. Give my man here your address." He pointed at Dru.

"Just don't hurt my moms. Please."

"Long as this info gucci, she gucci."

Abel pulled me to the side. I was seething. Retrieving the product was a must, but my personal vendetta overpowered the business obligations.

"I know you wanna get at them lil' niggas, but that's my problem. Get that work back in place, so you can be out."

"But Abel—"

"What you do this shit for?" he interrupted abruptly.

"Huh?"

"Why did you set all of this in motion?" he repeated. "If you still want to be about that life, I ain't got no issues with it. This is your first step. Let OCG deal with OCG matters. You retrieve the work and be out. Dru and Tone can stock once you put it in their hands. If you come with me on this other end, you ain't gon' never get out." Gripping my shoulders with his hands, he stared sternly into my eyes. "Ain't nothing worse than a man who wants to stay in bondage. You free."

As angry as I was, Abel was right. This was my parting test. If I couldn't make it out of this situation without resorting to street justice, then I couldn't trust myself to make it without OCG. Therefore, I took the high road. I left Jace to Abel and followed his directives.

Taking the address of the youngster, I headed over to his place and gave Dru and Tone the order to meet me at the new spot. When I arrived, a woman answered. Her hair was matted on her head, and her ashen lips told the tale of her addiction. All I felt for her was pity.

"Who you?" she asked defensively.

"I'm here to cop that work that Jace stashed here."

She pulled her arms around her waist tightly and eyed me skeptically. She shook her head. "Nah. Jace said only he touch it."

Lifting my shirt to show my piece holstered in my waistband, I eyed her again. "It's how you wanna play this 'cause I ain't asking. I'll give you grace because you need all you can get, but not your son. So, either I'm copping this work, or your son is copping this lead. Your call."

Good thing she wasn't high at the moment, and her motherly instincts kicked in. She slid out of the way.

"Jace is gonna kill me," she mumbled as tears trickled down her face.

"Trust. Jace ain't never gonna be yo' problem again."

A look of understanding passed between us, and she sat on a broken stool at the table. "Back bedroom closet."

I made my way to the bedroom, and as she'd directed, the product was there. All of it. I had to admit Jace had a little juice in these streets to trust his product with a fiend. That meant she knew better than to cross him. He would've made one hell of a soldier if he hadn't been a snake.

"Say, can you cop me just a little before you go? I ain't holding nothing right now. But I'm good for it. I promise."

The look on her son's face as he had to admit to us that his mother was a junkie skirted through my mind, and it was the first time since I started that I felt messed up on the inside about what

I did. At the time, it was only a means to an end for me, and I couldn't see above my own necessities to understand the bigger picture. Families were being destroyed, all for the sake of our greed and desire for a fast dollar. I had spent years pushing the poison, but now, I was ready to walk away. I couldn't live this lifestyle another day.

Spotting a picture of her son, I walked to the table, picked it up, and walked back over to her. I placed the photo in her hands. "Be good about quitting this for him. Instead of saving his own life, he was more concerned about yours."

Without another word, I left her house and packed my trunk with the product. Last stop was to meet Dru and Tone at the stash house, then my hands would be clean. I would officially be done. I couldn't wait to start my life anew.

I was lost in my plans for a new life when a block away from the new stash house, blue lights lit up behind me.

"What the fuck!" I instantly panicked. While I wanted to chance it, I knew better than to keep driving, so I pulled over. I forced myself to remain calm as the officer approached my vehicle. "Good evening, Officer."

"Good evening. Where are you headed tonight?"

"To visit a friend, sir. Is there something wrong?"

"Broken taillight," he answered. "License and registration, please."

"Yes, sir." I handed everything over to him and watched him return to his police car to run my license and plates. That's when it dawned on me. I was riding dirty! My head fell back, hoping and praying he would write me a citation and keep it pushing. I began to pray like I'd never prayed before. A sinking feeling came over me when I looked up in the rearview mirror. My prayers had gone unanswered because as the officer stepped back from his patrol car, he placed his hand on his gun.

"Zion Mitchell, please step out of the vehicle."

One of the problems with being an ex-convict is that you were always a convict in their eyes. Worse, my last stint was for possession, and with the amount I had on me, I knew two things: he was going to search my vehicle, and two, I was heading to prison.

"Place your hands on the hood of the car, Mr. Mitchell."

I cooperated and followed the officer's orders.

"Got any weapons on you?"

"No, sir."

"Anything in your pockets?"

"No, sir."

He began to pat me down.

"All this for a broken taillight, sir."

Out of the blue, a black unmarked SUV pulled up to the scene, and two more officers exited the vehicle. My heart raced. I started sweating bullets. Once I saw that the two men approaching looked more like FBI agents, I knew immediately it was lights out.

"Zion Mitchell, you have a federal warrant for your arrest. I need you to place your hands behind your back."

*A warrant.*

I damn near lost my equilibrium. The officer who was already searching me slapped the handcuffs on my wrists as one of the federal agents began reading me my rights. The other agent slipped on his gloves and went straight to my car.

God had a funny way of showing you lessons. This had to be his and Karma's get-back plan for everything I had done throughout the years. All the things I had put my mother through. All the things I had put Liberty through. My sister. Everyone.

"We have a gun!" the agent called out. He pulled out my Glock and placed it on the hood. After he discovered the weapon, he popped my trunk.

I couldn't think.

I couldn't breathe.

This was it.

I had met my fate. And there wasn't a damn thing I could do about it.

# CHAPTER 34

NINETY DAYS. I had been locked in the cage for ninety days. Shit was driving me insane. Walking down a three-year sentence was different from the fifteen-year stint that I was facing. My previous bid wasn't a cakewalk either, but at least there was a possibility to get out and pick up the pieces without so much time lost.

I hadn't contacted my mother or anyone since I'd been down. I was sure family and friends thought it was selfish of me. It wasn't my intent to be selfish. I just wanted the time to myself. I didn't want them to see me broken by the system, and I was embarrassed that I'd allowed myself to get caught up—again. Therefore, I'd resolved in my mind to do the time alone.

However, there was only so much I could take. The solitude had begun to mess with my mental, as did the constant fights and jail house drama amongst the inmates. There was uproar and chaos at every turn. Not to mention, I was still reeling from the fact that I'd been only an hour away from freedom.

With all those thoughts swirling, I decided to call my mother. I knew she was worried, and I needed to hear from someone who could support me through this, at least enough to get the monkey off my back. If not, I was going to lose my mind, my temper, or my life. It was that serious.

"Zion!" my mother yelled once the call connected.

"Hey, Mama."

"Thank God you called, son. I've been so worried about you." Her relief could be felt through the phone.

"I've been worried about you too, Mama."

"What took you so long to call? Did they have y'all on lockdown? Were you in the hole? Were the payphones not working?"

"No, Mama. It wasn't any of that. I needed time to myself to process everything. That's all."

Silence passed between us. I sensed that she understood what I meant but didn't know how to respond. There were no words to ease my pain or my situation. Not this time.

"Well, I'm glad you decided to call. At least I know that you're alive."

"Alive but not living." I looked around to see how many inmates were standing in my line to use the phone.

"Zion…" Mama sounded defeated. "It seems bleak right now—"

"Mama, please don't start with that 'everything is going to be all right' speech. It's BS, and we both know that."

"It's not. But I ain't gonna spend our first phone call arguing."

"I ain't got much longer anyway. Plus, these lines are longer than Loop 12 right now."

"Well, hopefully, I can brighten the rest of your day."

"How so? You see something on the news saying they're freeing all the hustlers? 'Cause shit, that would definitely brighten my day, my week—"

"Liberty came to visit me a couple of months ago. She brought me the scrapbook her and Queenie had been working on. It's really nice, too. Lots of pictures and memories. I'm gonna put it in keepsakes with all of her CDs."

Tears clogged my throat and that's exactly where they were going to stay. I couldn't dare let anyone see me vulnerable.

"That's good, Mama. Yeah, keep 'em with the CDs. Sounds like you're both of our beloved human treasure chest."

Mama laughed. At least I could put a smile on her beautiful face for a change.

"I told her about what happened with you."

"For real? Damn," I managed. Those tears clogged in my throat rushed me so fast I had to squeeze my eyes shut.

"She was pretty worried. Especially when I told her what you had on you when they pulled you over, on top of an indictment."

"The last thing I want is for her to be worried about me, Mama. She has a husband, kids... work."

"She does. But that doesn't mean she doesn't care or that you could ever stop her from being concerned. You already know how Liberty is." My mama exhaled. "You two really need to hash things out."

My mother's words struck a chord with me. More than anything, Liberty and I had always been friends. I missed her friendship and wisdom. Right now, I needed all of that.

"How about you call her, son?"

"Hell nah. For Mr. Kmart to start flippin' out. Pssst. That's a negative." A chuckle passed between me and my mother. That's when it struck me. "She could write me, though. Do you mind asking Liberty to do that?"

I could feel the uneasiness oozing from my mother, and in that moment the operator was informing us that we had two minutes before the call would disconnect.

"I'll ask her, Zion. No promises, though."

"I understand." The CO yelled out that it was count time in five. "I gotta go, Mama. They're about to do count."

"Okay. Take care of yourself, and I'll give Liberty a call."

"Okay, Mama. Love you."

"I love you, too, Zion. And we'll get through—"

The call automatically disconnected. I hung up the phone and jogged over to my cell for count.

# CHAPTER 35

*April 18, 2017*

ALL DAY I'D glanced at the text message from Mama Jackie asking me to call her. It came in at 7 a.m., and I still hadn't responded. While I had no clue what it was about, I could make an educated guess. For one, Mama Jackie never texted me. Never. She was old school. She believed in picking up the phone and having a conversation. Secondly, I hadn't talked to her in at least three months. My last time speaking with her was after the Christmas Eve dinner party. I had taken her one of the scrapbooks Queenie and I created. It had a slew of family photos, even a few precious memories that the kids and I had with her. She had attended birthday parties, doctor's appointments, Queenie's ballet classes, and even Sunday dinners. We had history, but our history was attached to her son. A son I had once managed to forget—but had resurrected. So after that visit, I consciously decided to distance myself. For the sake of my marriage. For the sake of my peace.

The decision was one of several shifts I'd committed to after Quincy and I had our heart-to-heart regarding the situation with Zion at Mama Jackie's. We had never allowed our past relationships to affect or threaten our fifteen years of marriage, and we agreed we wouldn't start now. When Quincy poured out his heart about how the event and interactions made him feel, it forced me to step into his shoes. His transparency, coupled with my own quiet introspection, further opened my tunnel-visioned eyes to the remarkable man that my husband was. Not that I hadn't always known Quincy was the crème de la crème of men, but his love and honesty revealed how unselfish he'd been during our years together.

After vowing to press forward with the newfound understanding, we sealed the deal in February with a private recommitment ceremony. It wasn't anything elaborate, just a simple getaway to Hawaii, where two best friends stood hand-in-hand, committing to forever—a second time.

During our romantic dinner, Quincy surprised me with a stunning 3.00 carat emerald-cut diamond ring. I was surprised and blown away. I had always loved and appreciated my first ring, but this beauty was all mine. He said it was an upgrade for *our* upgrade and I could not agree more.

It was beautiful.

Just like him.

Just like us.

With the dust of the Christmas Eve dinner settled and the renewing of our vows, we were back on track with what had made our marriage work all the years before, but most importantly, we were back to what kept our connection intact as lifelong lovers and best friends. Trust, honesty, and communication. Those were the top three pillars of our marriage and would always be the hallmark of our love.

My phone buzzed again. I picked it up, and it was another text from Mama Jackie with the message to call her. Two text messages in one day. It had to be serious. I looked down at my sleeping young king in my arms. I could only smile as I admired every feature, including the cute little birthmark underneath his chin. It was identical to the birthmark on Quincy's left arm. With King asleep, I figured it was the perfect time to knock out a few domestic duties, check my emails, and start on dinner. I laid him in the bed, connected my playlist to the speaker, and rocked out to Sade. I passed Queenie's room to see what she had been up to since the last check-in. Quite the fashionista, she had swapped the princess dress for her Doc McStuffins dress-up clothing. Our adventurous seven-year-old was seated at her round table, flanked by her favorite two dolls. Each had a pretend drink and a small pink plate in front of them.

"Dinner will be ready in a few, stinkbug, okay?"

"Okay, Mommy."

After the cleaning was handled, I tossed in a load of laundry and started on dinner. The pitter-patter of rain against the windows, laced with Sade's vocals over the "Your Love is King" track, created the perfect harmony. I sang along, slowly rocking my hips as I seasoned the meat for the spaghetti and simmered a combination of sauces. *"Gotta crown me with your heart…"* I crooned. I paused midsentence when my cell phone alerted me to a text notification. This time I picked up the phone and called the number.

"Liberty!" Mama Jackie squealed into the phone. "Thank you for calling me, baby."

"Is everything okay? Are *you* okay?" I inquired, uncertainty milking my voice.

"Well, no. I mean, well, yes. Kind of," she rambled. "I'm sorry, I don't want to cause trouble, and I feel like I may be overstepping my boundaries, but I promised Zion."

I listened intently.

"Liberty, I spoke to Zion yesterday. He's going through it right now and could really use a friend. Someone that he trusts. He asked if you could write him."

Dead silence.

I couldn't think.

I couldn't breathe.

Was this really happening to me?

"Are you still there, Liberty?" Mama Jackie's voice brought me entirely out of my reverie.

"Yes, ma'am. I'm here."

"I know it may be a lot to ask. But if you could do this one thing for him. For me."

"Okay." My answer slipped out before I could even consider the request fully.

"I'll text you the mailing address as soon as I get my hands back on my glasses."

"Okay."

Mama Jackie and I hung up on that note because I couldn't bring myself to say more, and she probably couldn't bring herself to press more. About an hour later, a text message came through with the address. Before it landed, I had already cross-examined myself and had several reasons why I shouldn't contact Zion. Whether I wanted to be there for Zion or not didn't matter. I couldn't. Out of respect for my marriage, it was time to cut that cord.

Biting back my emotions for him and our past, I closed my eyes, inhaled deeply, and released.

"Go wash up for dinner, Queenie!"

"Coming, Mommy!"

I pulled the garlic and cheese bread from the oven. Like clockwork, I heard the jiggling of keys five minutes later. My husband was home. Queenie hopped down from the table and took off running to greet her father.

"Daddy!"

I slipped off the oven mitts and placed them on the island.

"Look who the wind blew in?" Quincy smiled as he walked over to grab his kiss and feel.

I turned around, and my hands flew to my mouth once the six-foot figure rounded the corner and entered the kitchen.

"Justice!" I shouted. I rushed over to hug my baby brother

who I hadn't seen in years. I looked him over in his Navy uniform.

"What's up, sis," Justice said in his baritone voice.

"When did you? How did you—"

"Grandma asked me to come visit her."

"Oh," I said, pressing my lips tightly.

He studied my face.

A stillness fell over the room. I looked to Quincy and then back to Justice. I inhaled deeply, agony etched on my face. Cancer was taking our grandmother from us.

"How long?" Justice asked, cutting straight to it.

Before I knew it, tears trickled down my face. Quincy rubbed my back.

"Six months," I said.

# CHAPTER 36

*August 5, 2020*

THE SHRILL SOUND of my cell phone ringing at 3 a.m. startled Quincy and me. Kicking the covers around, I finally became untangled enough to find my way out of the comforter contraption to locate my cell on the nightstand beside me. My heart thundered as I picked up the phone, only to realize I didn't recognize the number. Unknown numbers in the middle of the night were never a good sign. My mind immediately went to Mama, who'd been taking more trips to the hospital lately due to her diabetes and congestive heart failure. To make matters worse, the coronavirus pandemic was wreaking havoc on the world. I was terrified for my family. I sat back against the headboard, trying to steady the phone in my trembling hand.

Quincy slowly sat up, and our worried eyes connected. "Who is it?" he mouthed.

With a shrug, I shook my head. "Unknown."

Quincy found my left hand and held it in his. "Answer it, baby."

It was all the encouragement I needed. I pressed the green button and placed the phone to my ear. When I was met with sniffles on the other end, panic set in.

"Hello?"

"*Liberty*?" a female's voice asked with unsureness.

"This is she. May I ask who's calling?"

"Thank goodness. Liberty, this is Janet," she answered.

I gasped. "What is it, Janet? What's happened?" I instantly braced myself for whatever news she was about to deliver.

"It's Mama. She had a heart attack."

"Dear God!" I blurted as some semblance of reality entered my body. Tears streamed down my face. "Where is she?"

"She's in surgery right now, but the doctors say it's critical."

Looking over at Quincy, my worried eyes turned apologetic. "I'm sorry, baby. I have to go be with Mama Jackie. I have to go."

Quincy nodded his understanding, and that was all the signal I needed.

"Which hospital? I'm on my way."

Janet rattled off the information, and I dressed and gathered my purse quickly. I kissed my husband on the lips, snatched up my keys, and made a mad dash from the bedroom to the garage, headed for Hilltown Hospital.

I called Janet while I was on my way and prayed that Mama Jackie would be all right. Once I arrived and finally made it through the stressful visitation check-in process, due to social distancing protocol, I ran to the hospital's chapel to find Janet. She was alone in the room, praying. She finally looked up, and we rushed toward each other. She embraced me in a tight bear hug that seemed to last for hours.

"It's so good to see you," she said through her tears and the mandatory face mask they made us put on once we entered the hospital.

"You too. It's been so long. Too long," I managed. I adjusted my mask slightly.

Janet pulled back but still held me about my arms. "And I apologize that circumstances like this had to bring us together. Mama has about an hour left in surgery, and I knew she'd want to see both of our faces once she got out."

"Thanks for calling me."

"You're family, Liberty. And like a sister to me."

I smiled.

"Unfortunately, I haven't gotten the word out to Zion. I don't even know where they're holding him now. With this pandemic, everything has been so messed up. I don't know where my brother is," she wept. "Our mama is back there fighting for her dear life, and he's behind bars. It's not fair," she said, more tears careening down her cheeks.

An uneasiness swept over me as I hugged her. "I have the information," I said.

"You have it?"

I nodded.

She exhaled.

"Liberty, could you please try to make contact? He needs to know what's going on."

Suddenly, I felt like I'd been transported to three years prior when Mama Jackie had asked me to write Zion.

"Please, Liberty," Janet said again, her voice breaking into my silent thoughts.

"I'll try," I promised. "And I'll call you as soon as I make contact."

"Thank you," she said.

I contacted the hospital clergy on duty as Janet conversed with Mama Jackie's doctors. Hours passed, and I sat in my thoughts, worried, praying, and hoping Mama Jackie made it through.

Around 9 a.m. I called Mama to explain everything going on with Mama Jackie and my predicament. As always, Mama offered her advice, but then she left me with comforting words that Grandma Sadie Pearle had instilled in her long before she transitioned. It was the confirmation and encouragement that I needed. *It's okay to lend yourself, as long as you don't give yourself.*

"Are you Liberty Bridges?" an older Black man with black slacks, a black shirt, and a white collar asked as he entered the chapel wearing gloves and a mask.

"Yes," I answered and stood to greet him.

He shook my hand before offering the pew so we could sit down. "I'm Chaplain Bennett. How can I help you?"

"Chaplain Bennett, I find myself in a unique situation. My friend's mother is here in surgery after having had a heart attack, and the thing is, he hasn't been informed."

"Well, where is he?"

"He's incarcerated. And I really want to help, but I'm unfamiliar with how it works. I reached out because I assume prisons have chaplains, and I was hoping you could reach out to the facility on the family's behalf."

He nodded. "Come with me to my office. I can do that for you. I'll look up the on-duty clergy for the facility and put in a call. He'll be able to get the message to your friend."

"Thank you for your help. I was worried I wouldn't be able to make contact."

"Help is never out of reach. You just have to know who to ask."

I followed Chaplain Bennett to his office. We made small talk along the way. Once at his desk, he powered up his computer and searched the internet. I rattled off the name of the federal holding facility that Mama Jackie had provided. I was praying that he was still there.

"Do you happen to know the inmate's number?"

I pulled out my phone and called off the eight digits. He jotted them down. Looking at his computer and then down at the notes, he picked up his office phone and dialed. I waited patiently.

"Yes, this is Chaplain Bennett calling from Hilltown Hospital with an urgent message for an inmate regarding his mother." Chaplain Bennett began to call out Zion's inmate number. "Yes, sir. Thanks for the transfer." Chaplain Bennett looked over at me and smiled. "They're transferring me to the chaplain now."

# CHAPTER 37

THE ENTIRE RIDE home from the hospital, I could only think about my dilemma. As I pulled into our driveway, I hit the button on the remote and waited for the garage door to open. After going through the motions of sanitizing everything, I tossed my gloves and mask in a bag, slipped off my shoes, then entered our house through the kitchen door.

"Hey, honey," I said to Quincy, who was making himself a protein shake.

"Hey, baby." Quincy walked over and kissed my lips before rubbing my shoulders. "You look exhausted. How is everything with Ms. Jackie?"

I placed my purse and keys onto the island, then turned and leaned against it. "She's stable. Not quite out of the woods, though."

"I understand. Mom and Dad called this morning. We prayed for her. And you know how Mom is. She's gonna add Ms. Jackie to the church's prayer list."

"It's certainly needed right now. I'll have to call your mom and thank her." I looked around. "Where are the kids? And did you call off work?"

Quincy nodded as he took a swig of his shake.

"I called off, and I dropped the kids off at Lucille's so that you can get some rest."

I outstretched my arms, and he walked toward me. I nestled into him. "Thank you, baby. You always know what I need and when I need it."

"I'm your man. I'm supposed to know these things." His hands lovingly stroked my back in a tender caress. "Now, you can get some rest for a while."

I peered up at him. My messy hair bun and tired eyes spoke volumes. However, I hadn't revealed the source of my consternation. Quincy pulled out of our embrace and cupped my chin.

"What's on your mind?" he asked.

I reached for his hand and led the way to the breakfast nook. I sat and motioned for him to take a seat beside me. Apprehension masked Quincy's face, heightening my anxiety.

"Babe," I spoke softly, picking up his hand and cradling it inside mine. "I know that you've expressed your concern over my relationship with Mama Jackie in the past, and I want you to know that I heard you loud and clear. I did. But Janet asked me for a favor."

Quincy shifted.

I scooted closer to him.

His eyes eventually met back up with mine. And when they did, I held him.

Held him close.

Held him tight.

"What type of favor?"

"She asked me to contact Zion to inform him about Mama Jackie. I didn't do it, but… I had the chaplain at the hospital call the prison."

"Okay. Sounds like it's handled. He'll likely get word right away."

"Yeah, but…"

Quincy studied me long and hard.

"You want to be there for him, don't you?"

I shifted.

"Quincy, I never want to experience anything like our last argument. We made a vow, and I am honoring that. I just know that Zion needs a friend right now."

A moment of silence grew between us.

"Okay," he said.

"Okay?" I asked.

"I trust my wife. So… be there for Zion. I'm sure he could use the moral and emotional support." I blinked and the droplets welling in my eyes spilled over the hills of my cheeks. I hugged my husband, and he lovingly slid his hand down the right side of my face. "You mean the world to me, Liberty Mae Banks-Bridges. And I love you. Beyond forever."

"And I love you more, Quincy Myking Bridges."

He chuckled. "So, you're just gonna *create* me a middle name, I see."

"Well, if Mama Bridges had given you one, you wouldn't be out here middle-nameless," I teased.

We fell into hearty laughter.

"Ugh-huh. I'm gonna tell her what you said."

"You wouldn't dare," I said, calling his bluff.

He leaned in and wrapped his lips around mine. Before I knew it, we began shedding every article of clothing. We christened the kitchen and the living room before slowly making our way upstairs and to the shower. The throes of our passion lasted for hours as we fulfilled every fantasy and stroked every inch of curiosity.

And then we came.

Together.

As one.

# CHAPTER 38

*August 6, 2020*

QUEENIE WALKED THROUGH the house in her favorite sea green narwhal onesie pajamas, headphones draped around her neck. Her wild kinky-curly mane was a dreaded reminder of tonight's to-do list. She rested those darling eyes and that infectious smile on me. I couldn't believe my little stinkbug was turning the big ten in two weeks. She was blossoming into an incredibly talented young woman right before my eyes.

"Morning, Mommy?"

"Good morning, daughter."

"Are the beignets ready?"

Queenie loved my homemade beignets. When Grandma Sadie Pearle passed, she left me with the family heirloom recipes that had been handed down for generations. I had typed each recipe to save them electronically so that I could pass them down to Queenie and King someday. When I came across the beignet recipe, I knew it was a special gift from my ancestors.

"Yes, they're in the kitchen waiting on you." I smiled.

"Sweet!"

I had been tucked away in my home office since 5 a.m. and decided to change the scenery, landing in our breakfast nook. The golden shafts of sunlight wafted through and lit up the entire room. I took one final bite of the pastry as I sipped on a golden milk latte and checked my emails. My eyes lifted in excitement, and I flirted with the possibility of partnering with one of the leading digital platforms for millennials and people of color. I couldn't reply to the virtual meeting invitation fast enough. I sent it and said a quick prayer. I reflected on Mama Bridges' words when I first shared how the company had expressed interest in having me crossover my #SoldiersOfLove followers to their platform. I had gone over for brunch and to catch up. To my surprise, Mama Bridges was not only a loyal supporter and fan of my work, but she had been waiting on the opportunity—and the perfect timing—for *us* to bond since we had never attempted to do so before. It turned out that we had a lot in common. We even shared the same love affair with beignets and lattes. It was an eye-opening moment.

Mama Bridges reminded me that most people only have a fixed idea of love based on childhood experiences, starting at home. Until we grow and experience relationships with other people, only then do we start to learn and compare what feels good to us versus what hurts us. She believed my column was inspiring and empowering because it explored not just one side—but every version of love. So without a doubt, I knew that this partnership would garner more exposure and reach. I didn't just want this. I needed this.

I closed my laptop and walked into the living room, listening intently to the CNN reporter's troubling report. I raised the volume on the television. The global pandemic had caused the nation's death toll to rise, and the nation's top infectious doctor was warning America that an attempt at herd immunity would result in a lot of people dying. It was depressing. I switched the channel to cartoons, expecting King's grand entrance at any given moment. As I mentally combed through a list of items that I needed Quincy to grab from the store, my cell phone rang. I grabbed it off the counter to see it was my colleague, slash sister-in-pen over at *Love & Lifestyle*. I muted the television.

"Hey, Brandie!" I greeted.

"Ex-cep-tion-al!" she exclaimed in her New York accent. I could hear the excitement swelling in her voice. "Woman, you had me on the edge of my seat! My gawd!"

"Awww, seriously. You liked it?" I lit up inside.

"I LOVED it! You have to expand this. Twenty thousand words aren't enough, Liberty. And you can't leave the audience hanging like this. Stretch that imagination and send me more words!"

"Oh wow. Okay, I'll get right on it."

"You'll need a literary agent for this one, and I already have the perfect person in mind."

"Agent?"

"YES!"

Brandie was taking me fast, sending my thoughts into overdrive. The short piece had been pages from my childhood diary, creatively interwoven and embellished to serve as a cautionary tale. There had been way more to my story, but I wasn't sure if I was ready to reach inside myself and wake up that part of my past.

"Okay, I'll think about the agent part, but I will revisit the story and see what I can conjure up," I tittered.

"You've got this!"

"Thank you for always… Brandie, let me catch this other line. I don't recognize this number and it might be our new intern. He started yesterday and I told Leiann to have him call me."

"No problem. Call me later," she said quickly.

I clicked over and a voice recording started to play.

"This is a prepaid call from—"

"Zion."

"An inmate at the…"

# CHAPTER 39

M Y HEART RACED, but I tried my best to keep my composure. We only had thirty minutes to talk, which was nowhere near enough time, but I had to make the best of it. I pulled the mask down from my face and began to speak.

"Liberty," I said once I heard her sweet voice merge into the line. It had been years since I'd heard it, and despite the gloom of the reason behind it, it still did my heart well.

"Zion Malik Mitchell." A heavy pause hung between us. "How are you holding up?" she asked finally.

"Humph, as well as to be expected, I guess. How about you?"

"I'm okay… just wish this didn't have to be under the current circumstances."

"I appreciate you being there and looking out for Mama. I hate to put that on you. If I wasn't in here, I swear I'd be right there with her."

"I know."

"How is she doing?" I dreaded the answer.

"Much better. She's on the path of recovery but not quite out of the woods. She'll need to implement some lifestyle changes. But you know your mom. She's a tough cookie."

"You're right about that. Tough as nails. Humph, but I need her to chill out and do better with her health 'cause you already know it scared the shit out of me when I got the message that our chaplain called for me."

"Yeah, I bet that was scary. I'm sorry I had to be the messenger of that news."

"It's okay. Don't apologize. It might've been meant for you to be the one to tell me. You already know Janet would've straight-up blamed a nigga. Mama's heart attack would've somehow been because of something I did or didn't do. No matter what, I'd be the blame." I inhaled deeply. I didn't have to say another word. Liberty knew the deal. She'd always known.

"Well, if it's all right with you, I'd like to support you through this."

My heart pounded in my chest. "I would love that. And I know Mama will be back up and rocking in no time…"

I took a deep breath, working up the nerve to pop the question. This was my final shot while I had her back in my grasp.

"Liberty…"

"Yes, Zion?"

"Will you…" I couldn't do it. It felt like my tongue was cemented to the roof of my mouth, blocking my speaking ability.

"Just say it," she encouraged.

That was all the motivation I needed.

"Okay. Will you help me with my case as well?"

Silence.

Even with the distance between us, I could hear her heart racing through the phone. I grew anxious and desperate. "I mean, if you can't, I would understand. I know you're a busy woman."

"Wait, you haven't been sentenced yet?"

"No."

"But haven't you been gone three years?"

"Yeah. It's twenty-seven of us wrapped up in this mess, and COVID has slowed everything down. The court keeps resetting the dates, and on top of all that, I don't have the financial reach anymore… so I'm in here stuck with a public defender. And you already know how I feel about that."

"I do. And you don't have the luxury of complaining. I'm sure they do their best, but be mindful of how they're already overworked and underpaid."

"You have a point. More of the reason why I need your support as well."

Silence.

"Zion, I don't even know what this would look like... how heavy this might get..."

"They tryna give me fifteen years, Liberty. Fifteen. If I don't get the *right* lawyer to step in and review my case more closely, then I won't have a fighting chance."

Silence.

"Say something. Please." I sighed in frustration. I was starting to feel like a charity case.

"Fifteen years?"

"Yes," I said gravely. "I can't do this without you, Liberty. I need you more than ever—"

"Zion, before I can consider helping you with your situation, we must establish a few things. I know you and I have history, but I'm married to Quincy now."

My chest nearly caved. Here I was begging, hell, pleading for her help in the midst of everything that was going on with me, and yet again, she throws her "marriage" in my face. I knew I needed her help but fuck that.

"Listen, I know you're married. You made that point very clear to me. But since we're establishing a few things, let's establish this. Tell me how you just gone up and ride off with this dude and expect everything to be copacetic with me. I'm talking, no explanation. You just straight ghosted me."

"I ghosted *you*? Wow, so now you have selective memory. You cheated on me. And you're the one who stayed in and out of jail. What was I supposed to do? Wait for you to get your shit together?"

"Those girls never meant a thing to me. You are the love of my life and the woman I wanted to marry and have children with. Everything you have with Quincy was supposed to be *us*, Liberty."

I paused to get a handle on my emotions. I clenched my fists and bit down on my bottom lip. I checked my watch to catch the time we had left before the call disconnected. There was so much more to say. So little time. Time was supposed to have healed this, instead, it had robbed me of a future with my wife—and the only woman who has ever completed me.

This was killing me.

"I'm sorry I messed up," I began. "But Liberty, you knew what it was between us. Yeah, I was young and wildin', but nobody came before you. Nobody. And even though I'd always feared that you would move on, I never imagined moving on would mean ghosting me to get under some new cat. Then to witness the betrayal with my own eyes... yeah, my energy was different after that."

"What are we even talking about right now, Zion?"

"You and Kmart. I saw you kissing him that night in his truck. And yeah, I know it's the past, so I won't sweat it now. But Liberty, you knew my truths. You knew my secrets. And you knew my dirt. So, ask me how *I* felt when I pulled up on that shit?"

Silence.

"Ask me?"

"How did you feel, Zion?"

"Like my life was coming to an end." I paused. Stabilized my breathing. The operator recording chimed in to warn that we had five minutes remaining.

"I'm sorry," she said.

"Sorry that it happened, or sorry that I saw y'all?"

"Both, Zion. I... I was in a tough place and struggled with that even after it happened. And you're right. I shouldn't have kept that from you. I should've been forthcoming about my decision to move on. Humph. Looking back, how can we even call what we had love?"

"Don't do that. Please."

"I'm serious. You never beat on me like Eugene did Mama and me, but Zion, you beat me emotionally. I had believed for years that it was my responsibility to protect you. But how do you protect someone who *beats* you? That's not love. That's hurt. That's pain. That's toxic and unhealthy to the mind, body, and soul. When I met Quincy, he showed me *real* love. And for the first time in my life, I realized that my vision of love was way different from yours."

Silence.

"So what are you saying to me, Liberty?"

"I'm saying that we had our chance. But we didn't share the same vision. And that's okay. No one's to blame."

After finally releasing that pain off my shoulders and hearing how my actions impacted her, I was able to breathe and reset. "I'm... I'm very sorry. And I swear on everything I love that my heart has always belonged to you. I didn't know how to love you the way you needed me to. I never had that. You taught me love. You! I guess time just ran out on me."

Silence.

"*You have two minutes,*" the operator warned.

"We're going to take baby steps back into this."

"Okay. That works for me. I'll do anything to have my best friend back."

"Zion, I'll always be here for you as long as the boundaries are respected."

"That's fair."

"And... I have to speak with Quincy more about everything, so give me time to think over everything and get his go-ahead."

"I respect it... does Quincy know we're speaking now?"

"Yes."

Her answer told me that Quincy not only trusted his wife, but he did not see me as a threat to their marriage.

"Well, you know how to find me," I said. "Can I check back in on Mama next week?"

"That'll be fine."

"Okay. Well, you stay safe out there, Liberty."

"And you stay well and safe in there. I'll be praying for you."

*Click.*

Our time was up. I might not have had my Mrs. Forever the way I'd envisioned, but I had her in all the ways that mattered. This cage wasn't the end for me. Liberty was on my side, and together, we were a combination that always won. Liberty and my faith would set me free.

# EPILOGUE

"LADIES, WE'LL BE back on in thirty," the producer, Kris, said through the intercom speaker inside the glass booth attached to the studio.

The host gave her a thumbs up as she and the co-hosts began shuffling papers around, preparing for the show's second segment. Nervous energy settled in the pit of my belly as I sat back in the plush leather chair and crossed my leg at the knee, my stiletto heel swinging slowly. As the countdown began, I slid my chair closer to the roundtable and pulled the microphone closer to my mouth as if it were the key to calming my fears. As the producer cued the host to speak, I picked up the custom GCU mug filled with piping hot tea prepared by the show's production assistant. I sipped the brew with my eyes trained on the intricate logo brightly layered in gold, green, pink, and purple in the center of the table.

"Hello, hello, hello! Welcome back to the *Get Caught Up* podcast. I am your host, Crystal, and I'm here with our guest co-hosts, your favorite sisters, Nikki and Syretta. If you are just tuning in, we are here tonight with the multi-talented, one and only Liberty Banks—wife, mother, and journalist."

I smiled at the acknowledgments. I was humbled and grateful for my gifts and every waking moment to walk in my purpose and do what I love. This was my first interview since hitting the *New York Times* bestseller list. The *Get Caught Up* podcast was an international show that catered to minority storytellers. Known for their playful banter and love of BIPOC stories, it had become the crave for many literary creatives and a mass of supportive readers. Listeners tuned in from around the globe to hear their candid conversations with literary giants in the industry. And I was now one of them.

I'd always known that my life story was one for the ages, but I never imagined it being the impetus for my creativity. More importantly, the impact it would have on other women—young and seasoned who, like me, were navigating through the tests, trials, and triumphs of life and love.

"And now, we can add *author* to the resume," Syretta added anxiously.

"That's right!" Crystal and I chimed in unison, agreeing with Syretta's declaration—our guffaws filling the posh studio.

"Before the break, we spoke with Liberty about her groundbreaking "Soldiers of Love" column that garnered a monthly viewership of over a million subscribers, and the *Essence* article, "Beautiful Scars," that became the catalysts for the launch of her debut novel *Soldiers of Love: Beautiful Scars*. Now, Liberty, we've covered much of the book, which follows the coming-of-age and tacit *entanglement*, if you will, of Liberty, Quincy, and Zion... but sis, you know we have to discuss this ending."

"I knew that was coming," I admitted, behind a chuckle. "Absolutely. Up until now, mum has been the word, but today, I will give you and the listeners what you want."

Cheers rang out amongst the three ladies in the room.

"That's what I'm talking about," Nikki quipped. "I do have a question about the alleged unspoken love triangle... as Quincy referred to it... but I know Crystal wants to dive into the one tidbit that's been on all of our minds first."

"Indeed, I do," Crystal agreed. "So, I'm going to rip the bandage off," she sneered. "Y'all see what I did there?"

"Love it!" I yelped in delight. "When readers quote my

work, it lets me know they connected with it and that I left an impression. So yes, let's rip it off!"

"All right, here we go," Crystal said, warming me up. "Did you really help Zion with his case, and was he released?"

Leaning forward, I picked up my mug and took another sip of the steeping brew before I answered. "With the blessing and the assistance of my husband, we were able to help Zion. He has been released from prison and thriving successfully with a second chance at life."

A roar of applause erupted in the studio as the ladies hummed their sweet sentiments before each giving Zion their on-air words of encouragement and well wishes.

"Now, that leads me to my question," Nikki piped up.

"Yes, because she has been itching to ask before the show began," Syretta volunteered.

"I honestly think *my* question is the one everyone is buzzing to know," Nikki said, eyeing me closely.

Holding her gaze, I dared ask, "And what's that?"

"Because the love between you and Zion was so potent, was there ever an attempt to rekindle the flame between you two?"

A hush fell over the studio, and I had a hunch that it also extended to the listeners over the airwaves. Each of them hung on with bated breaths. I prepared to answer their most anticipated question and provide the closure they desired.

"Well, Nikki, as you and all the readers know, Zion and I shared many years together. We were mere babies when we embarked on our journey together, and we've seen each other through a mountain of exuberant times and a valley of tumultuous times, too. With the kind of history that Zion and I hold, there will always be a special place in both of our hearts for each other. That goes without question. But when it comes to the relationship, I will always be his forever… *friend*."

A light sigh fell across the room at the realization of my words, and as I cast a glance at each lady in the room, their faces revealed an air of contentment and acceptance that soothed my wary soul.

"Forever Friends," Crystal reiterated airily. "That is simply a beautiful message of healing and resolution. A wonderful note to end our episode for tonight. Just know that we here at *Get Caught Up* wish you guys the absolute best."

I bowed my head and hands in appreciation of her well-wishes.

"So, before we get out of here, you have to tell us what's next for Liberty Banks?"

"Well, after the *Soldiers of Love* tour, I plan on vacationing. Because soon after, we go into pre-production."

"Wait… a book-to-film… on Soldiers?" Nikki blurted.

"Not yet, but that's definitely a goal. Actually, my first screenplay, *The Surrogate Wife*, is being co-produced with a major network."

"And now we're adding *screenwriter* to her resume!" Syretta boasted.

"And *producer*!" I added for good measure, with a wink.

"Now, that's the Black-girl-boss-magnet-energy we love to see. And you heard it here first. That is all the time we have for the evening. Please be sure to follow Liberty Banks and stay updated on her upcoming projects, and if you haven't already, go pick up, or download, your copy of *Soldiers of Love: Beautiful Scars*. Now, before we get out of here…"

As I listened to Crystal, Syretta, and Nikki close out the episode with the show particulars, a sensation washed over me, renewing my spirit and solidifying my reason for baring my soul to the world.

Peace.

Despite all that had transpired, I was healed, stronger, and at peace. There was no greater feeling. It was the perfect ending to my beautifully scarred story, yet the genesis for my next chapter.

# FOREVER

*From the first day I met you,*
*I knew our souls were tied.*
*Lovers of hide and seek,*
*Wishing wells won't tell...*
*So if you run, I'll ride.*
*Can't be the Bonnie to your Clyde...*
*But I'll be the beach to your sand,*
*That key to Forever Land...*
*Crown my heart and my spirit,*
*You already had my hand.*
*~ LIBBY B*

*"Love makes your soul crawl out from its hiding place."*
**—ZORA NEALE HURSTON**

# ABOUT THE AUTHORS

**N'TYSE:** A wife and mother of two, Dallas, Texas native, N'Tyse, currently juggles her creative endeavors as a novelist, screenwriter, and film producer. A former personal banker for over 12 years, the multihyphenate enlaces her visceral storytelling between American female-centric dramas and crime thrillers. Her literary works have been highlighted in *Library Journal, Black Expressions, USA Today,* and *Dallas Morning News.* N'Tyse received her B.A. from Arizona State University with a multicultural, interdisciplinary concentration in Creative Writing and Film & Media Studies. Her first independently produced book-to-film feature *Gutta Mamis* streams on Tubi, Peacock, etc.— while her co-written romantic drama *Bid for Love* is an original television film on the BET network. *"Soldiers of Love: Beautiful Scars"* is the author's most intimate and liberating novel to date. She can be found on IG @ntysethecreator.

**UNTAMED:** Literary phenom, Untamed, brings enlightenment and amusement through real-life, everyday stories with resonating characters. As a Cum Laude graduate with a B.A. from UMUC and a certification from eCornell University in Women's Entrepreneurship, she attributes her passion for the literary arts to her extensive educational background. Her creative talents afforded her opportunities with *SWAG Magazine* and *Intellectual Ink Magazine* as a columnist and with Boss Magnet Media as a screenwriter and producer. She's an expert movie quoter with a hankering for all things 90s. Untamed resides in Georgia and relishes family time with her husband of over twenty years and their children. She continues to push the creative envelope, delivering content that is unapologetically real and candidly untamed. Please visit her online at www.authoruntamed.com.

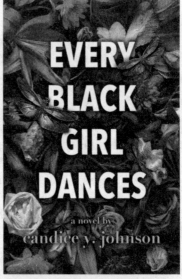
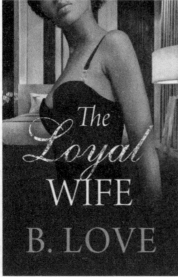
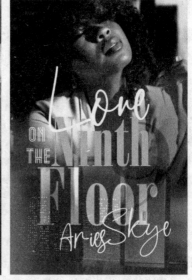